THE SEDUCTION

BY THE SAME AUTHOR

Mothers and Other Lovers
Skin
Sleep with Me
You
Touched

THE SEDUCTION

JOANNA BRISCOE

BLOOMSBURY PUBLISHING
LONDON • OXFORD • NEW YORK • NEW DELHI • SYDNEY

BLOOMSBURY PUBLISHING
Bloomsbury Publishing Plc
50 Bedford Square, London, WC1B 3DP, UK

BLOOMSBURY, BLOOMSBURY PUBLISHING and the Diana
logo are trademarks of Bloomsbury Publishing Plc

First published in Great Britain 2020

A catalogue record for this book is available from the British Library

ISBN: HB: 978-1-4088-7349-6 TPB: 978-1-4088-7350-2
eBook: 978-1-4088-7352-6

2 4 6 8 10 9 7 5 3 1

Typeset by Integra Software Services Pvt. Ltd.
Printed and bound in Great Britain by CPI Group (UK) Ltd, Croydon
CR0 4YY

To find out more about our authors and books visit www.bloomsbury.com.
and sign up for our newsletters.

For Clem, with all my love

You have the face that suits a woman
For her soul's screen –
The sort of beauty that's called human
In hell, Faustine.

> Algernon Charles Swinburne, 'Faustine'

She had always had a fear of something wild
in her own nature which she kept tightly
controlled.

> Margaret Forster, *Daphne du Maurier*

I have drunk the wine of life at last, I have
known the best thing worth knowing.

> Edith Wharton, diary

ONE

Danger wore a sweet face.

That was why she had travelled through the night to be there. There in someone else's home, lying like a fool on a hard couch and staring through the first grains of dawn, while those she really loved were quite elsewhere. She waited on that make-shift bed, willing the house's inhabitants to wake as she tracked tentacles of sound up the stairs and through rooms. Disbelief at what she had done drove into her.

Everything in this house was different from Beth's own home: the screaming of birdsong, the loitering of taxis instead of the canal traffic that had lined her existence for so long. She rolled on to her front, attempting to decipher a human presence beneath the scents of the bed linen. The fabric conditioner itself seemed exciting: comforting, ineffably alien.

She would text her family soon. She didn't know what. She had no idea. Nothing about this act of self-sabotage could be explained. Yet she knew it was an undertow of wildness that had hooked her and brought her to this room; it was that promise of life as life was meant to be led, at its rawest and most frightening and most beautiful.

Two

The previous summer, before the chaos had begun, there were too many visitors at Beth and Sol's house on Little Canal Street. There were, as always, artists who turned up, Beth's childhood best friend who lived nearby, and now a group of twelve-year-old girls, the chemical shock of their deodorant overlaying new hormones raining down the stairs. It was hard to keep the house tidy, to have enough milk for tea, to hear the doorbell. The rackety appeal, the candles, paintings, giggling, arguments, charged their home with life, the only half-dead thing out there on the canal that backed the house, because water brought up the ghost.

'Can you get them all to fuck off so I can fuck you?' Sol said in the kitchen.

Beth paused, smiled. 'I might not want to.'

'Let's see.'

'It might be that I want to do a few things to you,' she said in a self-conscious tone, making an effort to manufacture lust. She turned as she left the room and laughed at the sight of him watching her. 'That got you, didn't it?'

He hesitated. 'Praise be the Lord,' he muttered.

Their daughter Fern skedaddled through the sitting room trailed by other girls, and bulleted into her mother, flung her arms around her, kissed her, causing Beth's childless best friend to throw a smile touched with yearning that made Beth's throat tighten in empathy. Was it meant to be as good as this? The candles flattened, and the house's rooms melted into one another, its levels and terraces water-suspended. This home was precious, but it was theirs, Beth's and Sol's and Fern's, after so much longing and working. A poster for Beth's last show hung in a corner; an increasingly famous artist she had known since school held court by the fire; Sol winked at her and rubbed Fern's shoulder as he passed, and Beth swallowed and felt a flicker of fear, of guilt.

The changes were coming, though, with Fern; Beth could see them more clearly later. The beginning was there: the slight lateness from school, the distraction, the tension with Sol, even if it could barely yet be defined. It was the very end of summer then, August drying and dying, a glare of duckweed still on the canal. Fern would be thirteen in a few weeks' time.

***

'Your phone just rang,' said Sol, coming into the bedroom that night and sending Beth's mobile spinning into the air. She caught it neatly with one hand.

'*Impressive* ...? Who was it?'

The promise of sex hovered over them. The sounds of the owners of the houseboat on the other side of the canal arriving home drunk floated through the open windows.

'*No Caller ID*,' he said. '*No Caller ID* was calling you. I couldn't get it in time.'

The phone rang again. *No Caller ID.*

'Hello?' she said.

There was a silence.

'Hello?' said Beth again.

A pause was followed by a whisper of throat clearing. 'Hello. I—'

A moment of paralysis, of panic, delayed Beth, and then her finger moved reflexively and jabbed the Off button. She looked again at the phone, then pushed it away.

'Hon,' said Sol. 'Who was it?'

She shook her head.

'Nothing,' she said.

He raised one eyebrow. He touched her shoulder, his stubble brushing her temple, and went to the bathroom.

She began to sort her clothes for the morning, and the ghost was at large again, but this time creased in an underwear drawer. Beth made a slight mewling sound out loud. She thought she had cleared the house of the last possessions of her mother's that she had treasured as a girl; but here, as she searched for some thin tights, was an object that faintly smelled of Lizzie Penn in its creases: a flimsy camisole, laddered, a suggestion of perfume and human life in the grain of the fabric. How had it got into the back of this drawer? Beth dragged items from where they were jammed. She breathed in her mother's DNA again, close to her nose, hesitated over the wastepaper bin, then slammed the pile in the washing basket.

And yet what was this ghost? A tumour of past regrets. Absence. Guilt. Beth had not seen her mother for many years.

She brushed away some crumbs on the sheet in case Sol commented on her oatcakes-in-bed habit. Lizzie Penn. The thought of her mother made Beth go and see Fern, to say goodnight again. Fern's bedroom was a tongue-and-groove-clad sloping square that led straight into a box room used for storing Sol's photography equipment, with no space for a corridor between. There were Fern's objects crammed into papier mâché bowls, into wasabi dishes, Ikea and Tiger containers: the scented erasers, highlighters, tiny monkeys, Barbapapas. Fern lay in a rumpled spread of limbs.

Beth felt a ferocious desire to protect that stalky girl in a T-shirt with her fair colouring and mousy hair, one leg scissored over her duvet. The skin between her nose freckles was pinpricked with pimples, and her scents familiar: her cheap lip balms and her teddy, flattened and faintly urinous after a lifetime of love.

Her fetishistic hoarding of tissues was in evidence, a pile stuffed between the mattress and the end of the bed. Beth leaned towards her, skimmed her lips over her hair, so she stirred. Her own love felt, at times, cannibalistic. A barely perceptible odour of scented smoke, or something fragrant, like eucalyptus, hung about Fern's body, and Beth breathed in again, more deeply, but lost track of it. Fern opened her eyes very suddenly, looked straight at Beth with a glazed expression, broke into a smile. 'Love you, Mum,' she murmured. 'I …' she said, tailing off.

'I love you,' whispered Beth, and left.

* * *

Back in her bedroom, the expectation of sex still lingered in the air: that slightly unpleasant, primitive hunger, and Beth knew that Sol was guiding her to keep her on track, and in that moment, there was something defenceless and irritating about his male needs.

Her phone vibrated once on the pillow, then stopped. Beth picked it up, her hand shaking. *No Caller ID* again.

'Hon,' said Sol, turning to her with an abrupt sloping of the mattress. 'I can see you're agitated. Did *No ID* call back?'

Beth pressed her nails into her arm superstitiously. She said nothing.

'Put whatever it is – put it aside till the morning, or you won't sleep. I know you. You're going to be angsting. Listen to you,' said Sol.

'What?'

'Your breathing. I think you suffer sometimes. But you don't let on.'

Beth sighed, and let out her breath. 'I'm really OK. Just a bit of a worrier.'

'Look at you. Your pulse is crazy. What is it?'

'Sorry,' she said. She was pressing so hard into the sheets that a nail broke. 'My breathing just feels a bit funny.'

'Bet. Who was it?'

She shook her head slowly. She took a deep breath. 'I'm pretty sure it was Lizzie.'

'What?' He slapped the bedhead. 'Jesus H. *Christ*. You certain?' He pulled her into his arms.

'No,' she muttered. 'I think so.'

'That woman is not permitted back into your life. If she contacts you again in any way, you put her straight on to me.'

She nodded. 'My fierce protector.'

'Always. But Jesus, Bet. Look at you. You're all in a panic. You are going to that fucking appointment.'

'What appointment?'

Sol was silent. His mouth twitched behind his beard.

'Uh?' said Beth. 'Oh, you're banging on about that shrink referral again? I don't know if I want one.'

'Psychologist,' he said.

'We don't even know when I'll get one. I only kind of asked the doctor because *you* told me to.'

'It's not really your way, is it, Bet?' he said. 'To do something because I've "told" you to.'

He put his arm round her and bear-hugged her, easing her spine, and she leaned against his shoulder. He stroked his beard, as was his habit. It echoed his hair, its former curls close-cropped so that they undulated like wave-ridged sand, his brows darker. As his beard's edges became grey-frosted, he reminded Beth of some taloned yet benign bird of prey, his nose lightly curved. His eyes had an alertness to their black-brownness. His body was strong in his determination to stay fit and defeat family heart problems.

'Even though you bloody annoy me, I love you,' she said into his shoulder. 'E*xtremely* dearly.'

'I think I heard that, but whatever you said, I love you very much.'

She stretched out on the bed.

'Take advantage,' she said suddenly into his ear, laughing.

He turned and propped himself on his elbow, his eyes' charcoal impenetrability without glasses lending him a nakedness.

'Really?' he said eventually.

'Yes!'

'Music to my ears.'

9

'Unusual music,' she said in an attempt to diffuse tension with acknowledgement.

He reached over to kiss her, and an old fantasy bobbed through the reality, turning, as it occasionally did, to the boyfriend before Sol, Jack Dorian, who had since married and divorced. She barely saw him, but they had had sex whose salient details still played through her mind, and from time to time in bed with Sol, she summoned figures for speed and arousal, saving Jack Dorian for the end.

He kissed her further, but he was clearly uncertain of her desire. She lifted her hips, pressed her nails into his back, and suddenly they were fucking, fast and urgent, and it was all she wanted, to grab at life and block out the darkness: that moment of mating, that mobile knot of flesh.

THREE

The morning was a thin blaze, a scrawl of light through trees on the walls; sex was done and out of the way for the week, and made them closer, and they touched in passing, that bond a secret from the world, from Fern.

Beth looked at the canal, smelling its sluggish plant drift and overfed duck excrement from Camden Lock, and at the towpath opposite, where she had recently noticed a boy or young man standing. She was now uncertain of what she'd seen, the late August sun with its show of high summer flaring over such worries. Anemones, purple in a yellow French jug, held the same papery transience as the dying summer. The voice from the night was there in her ear, a revolting worm, but bleached by the day.

They drank tea, chatted over the Saturday paper, pottered, Sol clearing some of his piles of paperwork, picking out chords with his left hand as he passed the piano. Fern's music vibrated through the ceiling. The scent of the eggs and pancakes he cooked at weekends greased and sugared the air, and he had already laid in logs for the wood burner, bought from one of the longboat travellers who cut them illegally on their cross-country journeys.

'You think you're in the backwoods still,' said Beth, and inaccurate banter about lumberjacks and beatniks in Vermont, where he had never lived, followed.

'You doofus, missus,' he said.

She reached for him before Fern emerged from the shower, and pulled at her cotton nightie that was sour with chilling night sweat. Why was chest sweat always different? She wrinkled her nose in disgusted fascination.

'Want to smell me?' she said, leaning over Sol.

'Mmm, I like it,' he said, as she had known he would.

She laughed. 'I stink. Your doing.'

Soon he might take out the rubbish before she would have done it, listening to his Nu Country as he worked in the kitchen. He would pick out tunes on the piano familiar from his earlier listening. He might heat the Folgers coffee she teased him about, gargle with warm water.

Here, then, was her husband, this one she made her life partner. How odd; how grown up; how prosaic; how astonishing. She told him the thought, laughing, and he understood.

'I think your habits are almost like *breathing* to me now,' she said.

She looked at her phone as a text arrived. She tried to brush the call from the previous night away: that cracked in-breath, self-righteousness in half a word.

Fern's voice rose with her music from upstairs. Beth made more tea and handed a mug to Sol. There was the usual weekend chaos, the appeal of laziness over paperwork, of nesting over outdoor activity. Sol had been someone else's, a young husband and father in an unhappy marriage; Fern had been hard to conceive; their existence seemed halfway inexplicable, the comparison with Beth's own childhood making her strained and superstitious with appreciation. At other times, she took it all for granted.

'Has the mortgage gone through yet?' said Sol.

'I dread to think. Can you check? The weekend might throw the date.' She made a shuddering sound. 'Just the mention of that is going to make me get on with *Mice* in ... precisely five minutes.'

Fern was coming down, her speaker booming on the stairs. She stood there, dripping water from strands of hair like ink marks over her shoulders, her curves more apparent beneath her towel. This was what Beth called her Amish look, hair a headscarf of modesty over pale skin.

'Hey, oldies,' she said, carrying a notebook in her mouth. She dipped her head to let it drop on the table, and bared her teeth into a silly grin at Beth.

'Hello, darling,' said Beth. Her phone was beside her and she glanced at it.

She adjusted a board on her easel, the wobbles of canal light making mobile surfaces of plaster there. From that corner, their jigsaw of a home with its low ceilings and narrowness, its added spiral staircase and mezzanine, appeared as a doll's house that reached to the sky. Sounds of discord floated up from outside. Change was clearly imminent: King's Cross money would come creeping even further along, regenerating the masonry, ousting the hippies' canal boats and the drug dealers. But it was still as it had always been in this ratty tree-shaded section beyond the Lock. She stretched, to try to clear her neck and shoulder pain. The post clattered through the door and she went downstairs to fetch it, to delay working a few seconds longer.

It was an image that flickered through her mind later. How accurately? She couldn't be certain. She looked back at that post on a mat, Fern's name in writing that appeared uneducated, pizza flyers and airport taxi cards pushed to the corner with a leaf stuck to a rolled-up cobweb, and one of Fern's hairbands caught in the mat's bristles. But there were other events around that time that could have signified the start of the trouble, blurring what was later seen as a clear trajectory.

'Look at this,' said Beth, showing Sol the envelope addressed to Fern.

'Huh,' he said.

'I bet it's from a boy. Look at that inarticulate writing.'

'She's going to be into boys,' he said in his steady voice. 'Any minute.'

'Yes. But she's twelve.'

'Almost thirteen. And, hon ... I'm aware you're going to find that difficult.'

'What?'

'Thirteen. The age.'

'Why? Oh—'

'Likely.'

'God, you're perceptive. For a man.'

She ripped open a letter from St Peter's Hospital offering her an initial therapy assessment. 'Oh no, they had a cancellation.' Her shoulders dropped.

'Good,' said Sol, not looking up.

'I've only got this at all because you bamboozled – harassed – me, you beardy sadist – to get referred.'

His mouth twitched. 'No exaggeration or anything,' he said, studying the letter. 'OK, Bet. You'll do this, right? Think how you were last night ...'

She marched to her easel.

'I suppose—' She shrugged.

She turned to her sketch for the children's books she illustrated on the side as E. E. Brierley, the deadline approaching. The *Metropolitan Mice* series was popular in Japan.

She began to paint in the style of the tourist tat sold along the banks of the Seine, working with loose gestures. She twisted her hair and attempted to pin it with a chopstick from the pen jar, but it

15

flopped back into place. She was still in her nightie, under a moth-holed cashmere cardigan. First thing in the morning, she looked washed out, as though lacking in sunlight's benefits, her eyes large and dark in contrast with hair that mixed dishwater with muted golden-reds. Despite Sol's easily expressed admiration, she had not felt attractive for a long time.

She sketched the disposable-cups boats in which the mice would sail. She added beams from the Thames-side attractions as explosions of light: a Dufy imitation veering into Lautrec, St Paul's and the London Eye crowded together, recognisable in a parody. The mice would appear in pen and ink later.

'I just don't know how you do that, honey.'

She stood back.

'Nor do I. If only I could do my real work a tenth this quickly.'

He paused. 'So – to continue the discussion,' he said in the near-monotone he always used when saying anything of significance.

'Er, yes, *Dad.*'

'Your anxiety is— Honey, *anyone* with a mother like yours needs help, from the get-go. David has always said this, and he only knows the basic facts. Doesn't the letter say you're getting to see a consultant?'

'Yes, yes, but – I'm not going to go masturbating on a couch about my childhood,' she said. 'Leave that kind of thing to your friend.'

16

'I mean a professional psychologist,' Sol said patiently.

She shuddered. 'I—' She shook her head. She swallowed. An image came to her: a faceless practitioner probing her to expose all her failings. In the most extreme corner of her mind, she was naked, spewing the truth as he pinned back her insides until her psyche was revealed.

'They'll make me talk about Lizzie,' she said rapidly.

Sol opened his mouth. 'You're scared?'

She paused. 'Yes,' she said in a small voice. She turned to one side, and couldn't catch his eye.

'I know.' He held out his hands. 'Well, view this as a challenge,' he said. 'Then there's a chance you'll rise to it. Come on. Stubborn creature. You are brave. That's what you are.'

She buried her head in the comfort – wool, air scent – of his shoulder.

'I can't help you with this on my own,' he said. 'And if that was really her calling—'

'I do not want to talk about that woman.'

He raised an eyebrow.

She wanted to laugh, reflexively, and tease him, but his expression stopped her.

'Your paintings are becoming darker as well,' he said.

She hesitated. 'I didn't even know that. Really? Look ... oh, hello Fern!'

Suddenly, Fern was standing between them, just as she had done as a young child, headbutting her way into a hug, so they had called her their Oedipus, their little Foedipus. Now she was there in T-shirt and leggings, and they were all clamped together; Beth kissed Fern's head; Sol eased Beth's shoulder.

Freeze this moment, she thought.

It froze. A picture in her mind she summoned later, treasuring it and hating herself.

* * *

'That is so goddamn amazing, Mum?' said Fern, gazing at Beth's completed illustration. She reached up and whispered one of their ongoing jokes in her ear then gurgled laughter that Beth echoed until her hand wobbled.

'Oh, the mice are legitimately cute,' said Fern, resting her head against her mother's shoulder so that Beth lifted her left hand and stroked her hair as she worked. 'Massively. I want to live with them. They're the nicest mice in the world.'

'Oh, Fern,' said Beth. 'Thank you. Don't feel the need to …' *please people*, she was going to add, but stopped herself, because there was a genuine generosity to Fern, as well as politeness. And yet it seemed to her that it was a decision Fern had made early in her life to be positive, and that beneath the determined buoyancy lay a vulnerability that Beth could not even explain to Sol.

'Who's it from?' she said, passing Fern's letter to her.

'*I* don't know.' A shrug, envelope stuffed away. Then a smile. 'I challenge you to Monopoly after lunch, Mama, but only if I can be the *dawg*,' she called as she left the room.

Beth's phone rang. Sol wheeled round, snatched it, answered it.

'*Who?*' said Beth, and her voice was shaking.

'Oh, baby,' said Sol. 'Look at you. Come here.'

'It was the same, wasn't it?'

'Yes, but hung up. You're all white. Jeez, I hate it that she does anything – anything at all. You don't need that therapy appointment, then?'

'I do.'

'You do.'

'I just said I do.'

* * *

While Fern shut herself in her bedroom with music, Beth went around the corner to her studio, to seal the day with real work. But the studio, though so close, was too small, and once there, instead of painting, she began some of the immense task of sorting and packing materials in preparation for a move in autumn to a better space in a warehouse used by some artist friends.

She looked at the cityscapes she was working on, waiting for the disturbing element to emerge from the hyperreal. It didn't. She had called the series *City Lies*. Why? She didn't know. It sounded vaguely modish. But in fact, the answer was there: lies. Lies of omission. There was technical accomplishment, the layering and brushwork critics wrote about, but a lack of real meaning. Subconsciously, she had been playing with the tropes of earlier success, and therefore at some level she lied.

She put her head in her hands. Fern's face slotted in front of the paintings, and the canvases receded in all their emptiness. What did lurk there, in Fern, in that shuttered Pollyanna? The daughter Beth had spent so many years spooning as she fell asleep, hair rubbing; sewing her Sylvanian Family clothes; chatting together, Fern fast-talking on the loo lid as Beth brushed her teeth. And what was she doing away from her child on a Saturday? She glanced at the almost complete series again as she closed the door. She would have to delay her gallerist's studio visit. It wasn't right. Many things, after all, were not quite right.

* * *

By the time she came back, the house was, as so often, filling: her childhood artist friend Aranxto, who lived nearby, on a flying visit with some of his retinue, and clearly irritating Sol; a neighbour there ranting about illegal canal moorings; and Fern's best friend Maia practising make-up and back bends on the sofa.

'When's the studio relocation?' asked Sol in the kitchen, as they fetched more tea.

'There's *never* enough milk. In the freezer? Oct ... fourteenth.'

'Aranxto sounds like a goddamn trumpet. A studio upgrade. But the same price? In what world does that happen?'

'It's so much less central. Back end of Finsbury Park. And cold water only. So probably freezes in winter. But who cares? I'm so excited! The space is big, good for client visits, and I can see the friends working there for the odd lunch.'

She bit her lip.

'Which ones are there?' he said, as she had feared he would.

'Oh you know, the usual. Anna, Killian, Lars, Chris, blah ...'

'Cool,' he said.

She opened her mouth. 'Oh and Jac—' she began, but he was turning round and opening his computer.

'I need to prep for Leeds tomorrow,' he said, checking emails.

Later, she went up to Fern's room and kissed her head as she lay in bed.

'Mmm, rub,' said Fern, and Beth pressed her fingers into her scalp, their age-old ritual, while gazing round the room in case the letter Fern had been sent was visible.

'I love you,' said Beth.

'Love you more.'

'Fern, what *is* that weird smell on you?'

'Bath stuff? Like, nothing?'

Fern's phone buzzed. She reached out and snatched it.

'I don't think it is,' said Beth. 'Hang on, *Aranxto* just texted you? What? He—'

'Mum, do not look at my phone!'

'What's he saying?' said Beth. 'He's here, for a start! Why does he even have your number?'

'Duh, Mum,' said Fern. 'He's my godfather?'

'Yes. Aranxto the crappest godfather in the world! Who forgets your birthday.'

'I think basically he's got a bit better,' said Fern, in flat tones.

Beth waited. Fern fiddled with her phone. 'Night, Mum,' she said eventually. 'I love you.'

'I love you more times infinity.'

'I love you infinity times infinity times a million billion times infinity.'

'All that, times infinity, forever,' said Beth, planting a row of final kisses on Fern. 'Goodnight, beloved.'

'Times infinity,' shouted Fern through the bedroom door.

'That times infinity,' shouted Beth from the bottom of the stairs.

And more and more and more, she thought.

FOUR

'The thing is, there's basically stuff I can't – I'm *not* – going to blabber on about,' said Beth as she was led from the waiting room into the overheated guts of the hospital. The late September morning was cold outside.

There was a silence. The therapist who had been assigned to her after her assessment held the door open and guided her down further corridors.

After several weeks of insomnia, Beth was wearing make-up that functioned as protection, her eyes enhanced with dark shadow so that they were almost too large.

'That I can't blurt out to *anyone*,' she added.

The therapist nodded slightly.

'And so.' Beth hesitated. 'This may be a shocking waste of your time.'

'We'll talk in my office.'

'Just *where* are we going?' Beth asked jokily, as corridors led into others.

'Now that would be telling,' said the therapist with a single moment of flippancy, but she didn't look at Beth, and carried on walking, straight-backed, into the strip-lit gloom.

They approached a room whose clinical aspect, in what appeared to be a deranged Victorian castle of a hospital, made Beth hesitate at the door. She swallowed. The blinds were lowered; a fan heater blew in the corner of the room, creating a hush of privacy above the activity of the river shifting four floors below.

Beth sat and attempted, for some minutes, to sketch out her life history as requested. She stumbled, unusually lacking in fluency, and blushed.

'So what sent you here?' asked the therapist eventually, her tone gentle.

'My "increasing overprotectiveness and excessive anxiety", in the words of the man who originally urged me to come. Oh, and my "disproportionate reactions",' said Beth, having already formulated the answer in the hope of forestalling probing; but its delivery sounded rehearsed, and not quite accurate, and she made a couple of gestures to denote spontaneity that only betrayed self-consciousness. She took a breath. 'I knew I needed to come, really. There were – reasons.'

The therapist gave a suggestion of a smile, and nodded.

'So,' she said, and she drew out some worksheets. 'Practicalities. With this number of sessions, we're meant to be doing fairly straightforward CBT.'

Beth looked blank.

'Cognitive Behavioural Therapy.'

'Of course.'

'But if I can, I go beyond, into more eclectic therapy. I have a psychotherapy training as well. I suspect you'd shoot too many simplistic worksheets down in flames ...'

'I suspect you're right.' Beth smiled.

She moved in her seat. She was thankful for her work clothes, yet still she felt inadequate: an escapee from her part-time teaching job. There had been too long a gap since her last show. A clump of eyelashes was twitching with tiredness; her face seemed exposed, the contrast of dark brown eyes with the muted reds of her hair a little uneasy. She unhooked the hair where it had caught behind one ear. She could veer into rabbity flaring, she realised, her skin reactive. Shame washed over her.

This Dr Tamara Bywater, Consultant Chartered Clinical Psychologist, didn't resemble her idea of a female therapist: a moulting hen, or an upholstered termagant in strict glasses. She was neat, faintly dull-looking, without descending into full-blown dowdiness. She wore a grey skirt and appeared older than Beth.

'Anything else brought you here?' asked Dr Bywater, who then waited, no judgement visible, only the smallest head tilt of encouragement. She waited more.

'Um. Sometimes I fear I'll just fuck everything up,' said Beth in a rush.

Dr Bywater nodded.

'That things are just – well, they're good at the moment. Better than I deserve. Things'll go wrong if I ...' she said, waiting for the therapist to contradict her, to reassure her. 'I fear – what if I sabotage everything? Accidentally.'

'Why would you do that?' said Dr Bywater eventually.

'I just – I just fear it. I kind of want you to just tell me to stop being neurotic.' Beth laughed. 'I did before,' she said, when there was silence once again.

'When?'

'As a child.'

'It's one of the great tragedies of childhood that children imagine they are to blame for adults' actions. Or simply for chance events,' said Dr Bywater.

'I kind of was, though – or later,' said Beth in a stutter. 'To blame. And –' she looked around the room '– a – a phone call disturbed me.' She swallowed. 'A lot. And my daughter Fern going adolescent. Turning? Turning thirteen, I mean. She has been changing.'

* * *

The memory of Fern unwrapping birthday presents formed the next snapshot later in Beth's mind, to follow the post on the mat. She could trace more changes back to that day, and yet, when she really searched her memories, they had been there before: the brief absences, glimmers of evasion.

Fern was a joy, a pleasure to buy for; a girl awash with passions. There was the anticipation of her receiving gifts – the usual puppies calendar, a monkey top, stationery, animal-based objects, oversized fluffy slippers, the token products from Sephora and lip gloss – but a flicker of uncertainty made Beth pause, and Fern's over-bright politeness as she opened her presents, face buried in a big hug, confirmed that they were wrong, too young, and the clothes were only ever worn in bed, with strange excuses. Later, she had her party, pubescent girls huddled together and hysterical, easily bored. They sat in a row and held their phones to their faces, photographing the set, semi-seductive smiles that accompanied Snapchat messages.

'*Visit?*' one of them said to Fern, leaning towards her and glancing at her phone.

Fern nodded stiffly and looked at her lap.

'*Who?*' Beth wanted to say.

Aranxto gave Fern an iPad. She looked embarrassed, then grinned self-consciously.

'What?' Beth said to him later. 'You neglect her for thirteen years, and then you suddenly give her a massive present? Of course, I'm grateful. She's thrilled. Thank you. But—'

'They're boring when they're rug rats,' said Aranxto lazily. 'They get more interesting when they can talk.'

'Ha ha.'

'She's quite cool, your kid.'

'And her godfather has just discovered that?'

* * *

'It doesn't sound much now, does it?' said Beth. '*My daughter's become a teenager* – ooh dear!'

'It's likely to be a trigger,' said Dr Bywater. 'Perhaps it links to a similar occurrence in the past. Is there anything you can think of?'

Beth gazed at her, her jaw slack. To her horror, tears were needling her eyes. 'Yes.'

'So you were challenged.'

'Yes.' Beth glanced at the clock. The walls seemed to expand. Then came an image of the back of her mother's head, details of her hair magnified into rustling shining ropes.

'Well. Perhaps you experienced something yourself at the same age. Past events can be powerful triggers. We'll see if we can help you.'

Beth closed her eyes.

'Do you have other issues you want to explore?' asked Dr Bywater.

Her enunciation was notably old-fashioned: a soothing therapeutic tone overlaying an accent that resembled an actress's from an earlier era, and Beth followed its swoops and clambers even as the content of the speech made her stiffen. The heater blanketed tatters of river traffic below.

'"Issues"? I'm allergic to some of this therapy language. At least you don't say "issues around",' said Beth. She winced, hearing her own tones. 'OK. I'm sorry. I seem to be going into my direct, un-English mode that I've been warned about. So ...' She blushed a little. 'My anxiety. But I'm not sure this is the route ...' She looked around the room. 'It's funny. I thought I'd be getting a man. I think I *assumed*. That is very prejudiced of me.'

'Perhaps it makes you uncomfortable, seeing a woman.'

'No. No, of course not.'

There was silence.

'Well,' Beth blurted, 'I think actually I kind of pictured myself sparring with a trained-up male in a cheap suit while bristling at his sexism.'

Dr Bywater's mouth twitched minutely.

'You see, you might penetrate some of my attempts at concealment more easily than a man,' said Beth.

Dr Bywater nodded. 'Stay with your feelings about this,' she said. 'You don't need to use defences such as humour here.' She continued to gaze at Beth with an understanding smile, clearly aware that there was prevarication occurring; and a longer silence followed.

A picture of Fern as a toddler flashed in front of Beth, the skin scent, the milky need. A click of her throat was audible.

'I worry that something is happening with Fern that's perhaps beyond all the changes of adolescence,' said Beth. 'But my – what does one say? Partner. Yuk. Sol. He is not worried at all. So it leaves me feeling paranoid.'

'Can you describe him? What does he do?'

The therapist's voice dulled her like a tranquilliser. Despite her resistance, Beth found herself breathing more slowly.

'Oh, Sol. Reportage. News photography. He's always busy. He's good, kind, all integrity. Benignly impatient, I think of him as ... um ... quite grumpy. Eccentric even. But romantic. He buys flowers, arranges dates ... He also irritates me stupid sometimes, but he's ... well, he's lovely.'

Beth took a breath, shrugged. 'I find him interesting, still. American. He's lived here for years. Um ... he had to fight a big custody case to keep access to his son by a previous marriage, but he was completely determined to see him. I love it he's such a good father. To both of them.'

The therapist nodded.

'He's infuriatingly self-contained.' Beth paused, and smiled. 'I want to shake him to get a reaction, sometimes. Determined underneath it all. Otherwise I think I'd get bored. But it does mean we argue. Quite often.'

Dr Bywater said nothing.

'So I don't get it,' said Beth suddenly. 'Why aren't I more of an obvious mess? Everyone except Sol thinks I'm fine.'

'You're high-functioning.'

'*Oh* ...' said Beth. 'That's a thing?'

'It is perfectly possible, while suffering very real pain inside. But outsiders will largely just see the woman, mother, the acclaimed artist you are.'

Beth paused. 'How do you know that? The last bit.'

Dr Bywater hesitated. 'I do. If you're acclaimed, then I and others would know about it.'

'Have you been googling me?'

'I don't spy on my patients,' she said somewhat stiffly.

'Sorry.' Beth paused again. 'I never *feel* successful. Anyway,' she said rapidly, 'so, Fern. She's been coming home a bit late from school. She's evasive. Almost hiding from me. She needs to grow up, I know that, to separate.' She swallowed. 'But my instincts tell me that something else is going on. Sol disagrees. He's impatient about it, unusually ...' She shrugged, pulled a tolerant face. 'So here I am.'

'And you're not taking this seriously?'

'Fern, very. Sol?'

'Yes. Does it make you worried about your relationship?'

'Oh,' said Beth, feeling her cheek. 'I actually rarely worry about him, weirdly. About the only thing I don't. And he'd never, ever even consider leaving Fern. The opposite! We've been together a decade and a half. Almost. He wouldn't really *leave* or anything.'

Tugboats were hooting in the distance.

'You sound certain.'

'He's just gone all strict and uptight because he's worried about me. I know him.'

Dr Bywater nodded, handed Beth some worksheets with explanations, then they talked more generally until the hour was up.

'Do you think I should worry?' said Beth suddenly, frowning and poking her head back round the door before she closed it.

Dr Bywater smiled. 'We can talk next time,' she said.

* * *

Beth walked through the waiting room on her way out, the pair of psychologists she glimpsed in the department's corridors pale as moles who never saw the light of day. As she headed towards the lifts, instantly lost in a labyrinth of passages and double doors, the daubs on the walls – the sugary pointillism, the Impressionism and mask-like portraits – stimulated the only flicker of professional confidence she had experienced in weeks.

The morning was torpid as she emerged on to the walkway beside the hospital. St Peter's cast a shadow even in the sluggish light. It was an eerie hulk of a building: a Victorian anachronism that appeared to have worked its way down into the bank of the

Thames, sinking beside that slow-seeming, rapid brown river with its currents of diesel and tar, its albatross apparitions in the mists. There in the shadows was her mother Lizzie. Just as an image of her had been on the Dingle shore in Liverpool, or later on Gower Street when Beth had studied at the Slade. And since the voice on a phone in August, a more accurate version had returned in fleshy detail: a high-smelling ghost, human crevices and veins, pores and throat clearings, unwashed hair and sudden words. 'I love you, I love you, Bethy,' she said into her ear.

Unexpectedly shaken by the therapy session, Beth sent Fern a funny photo, then walked to Blackfriars tube, towards her bread-and-butter job goading rich kids through their art exams. The river was choppily metallic, a raw air stirring it, and as she had so often done over the years, she pictured herself riding it: jumping on a raft to sail the restless flow, race over waves to a far horizon. The sense of something missing, of a wilder existence, was there in fragments between real life. Jack Dorian was there, seducing her. She was storming the rapids to infinity, flung through a waterfall, flying, soaring, fucking.

She laughed at Fern's answering meme then hurried to the school where she taught. A colleague had put herself out to accommodate the appointments, disguised as physiotherapy for her neck, but she already dreaded returning to the hospital, could not picture herself walking back into that department and being made to talk about her mother.

* * *

How Beth had loved Lizzie Penn – the feel of her, the smell of her – dressing gown and slept-in staleness, shampoo and scalp, the strange adult sourness of coffee. Her mother had loved her, Beth knew. At ten, almost eleven, Beth was beginning to shrug away some of her mother's embraces; to dismiss her with a wave outside school; to spurn offers of reading, preferring to have friends over to snigger-whisper at tea. Had those stirrings of independence caused Lizzie to spot a glimmer of a different life?

A blind now seemed to come down over Beth's mind, unrolling with a clattering rush. She couldn't think about her. She wouldn't, until the next therapy appointment.

FIVE

'Mum! What the hell?' Fern burst out the moment Beth returned from work, struggled over to the table with some equipment and glanced at her daughter's phone, which lit up with a message. Heat hit her neck.

'Hello, Fern!' Beth said brightly, and kissed her. She put her bags down, wriggled out of her coat and scarf. 'Can you just give me *two* minutes? I'm bursting for the loo.'

She locked herself in the bathroom and took a breath, savouring the moment of silence before trouble. She pictured the Snapchat message she had glimpsed. *Baby when am I see you again?*

She hadn't caught a name.

'*Why* are you looking at my phone?' demanded Fern, the moment Beth emerged.

'What? Darling?'

'Don't de*ny* it!' said Fern, a repressed trembling tightening her voice. 'I've told you and Dad, like, about a million times not to.'

'I did—' began Beth. 'I only glanced down as a message came up. Not intentionally.'

'You saw it, right?'

Beth paused.

'Holy crap!'

You're seeing a boy? Beth so nearly said.

Beth looked at Fern. She was like a drawing in a novel last seen in childhood. *Marianne Dreams.* Precise lines, pencil hair strands, faintly tilted large eyes.

She caught her breath. 'Who sent it to you?'

'What?'

'You know what.'

'Do I have to ask you basically a trillion times not to ask questions?'

Beth waited. 'But still ... who is calling you "baby"?'

Fern reddened. She bit her lip and looked mutinous.

'Well?'

'Someone I know. Like, a friend. *Ob*viously.'

Fern gazed at her then gave a small shrug. Beth pushed through her resistance and hugged her, and in so doing, she detected that same trace of a smell, of eucalyptus or lavender or some other essential oil. 'What is that?' she was about to ask, but it was so faint, she swallowed another question that Fern was likely to rebuff.

Fern looked at the floor. 'Sorry, Mum,' she said suddenly, and her face was flushed. 'I just lost it a bit. *Read*ing my Snapchat was a dick move. But ...' She shrugged.

Then she giggled and put her arms round her mother's neck, and Beth called her names, and somewhat awkwardly, they ran through the house trying to tickle each other, as they had when Fern was much younger, with self-conscious screams.

* * *

'So what was the therapy like?' said Sol in the morning.

'Oh,' said Beth, hanging up washing. 'Hard to say.'

'What's Dr Whatshername like?'

Beth shrugged. 'She's quite nice, ordinary-seeming. Very focused, though. I'm not *sure* what the point of it all is entirely.'

'Ha! You want immediate brilliance and fireworks? Some – virtuoso performance? So like you, Bet …'

'Of course I don't.'

'Right,' said Sol, glancing at her.

'You know me – and my faults – too well.'

'Please,' said Beth to Fern, who stood in the kitchen spooning cereal with one hand, milk wobbling, while brushing her hair with the other. 'Come straight home after school. OK?'

'*Yes, Mum,*' said Fern, then suddenly she reached up and kissed her, and yet she was slightly late home the next day after school, and later the day after, and politely evasive, adopting her innocent face.

'Aren't you worried?' said Beth to Sol on the third day. 'She could have been back twenty minutes ago.'

'She's thirteen.'

'Just. It's becoming darker in the afternoons.'

'She's a teenager, hon.'

Beth bit her lip.

* * *

For Beth, the next weeks of sleep-deprived nights and unsatisfactory work, the first few therapy sessions, seeing her old friends Ellie and Aranxto from Liverpool between work and childcare, Fern's intermittent lateness from school, all merged together in a run of normal stresses and deadlines. The mortgage was too big. They needed Sol's ex-wife to marry someone else; she needed to have another hit show, but it sometimes felt as though *Ghost Walks*, the series that had made her name, would be impossible to better, or even to match, and she was busy sorting the move to her new studio. September became October, and *No Caller ID* didn't ring again. The relief was overlaid with the age-old rejection, which filled her with irritation.

'You know, it's weird, but the Jackass—' she began, assigning her ex-boyfriend and future studio mate Jack Dorian the name Sol used, to please or appease him.

'Yeah, the Jackass,' said Sol, interrupting. 'Fern found an old *Metro* with a picture of him the other day and said, "Who is Jack Dorian?" You been talking about your paramour to her?'

'*Former* less-than-paramour. Er, no,' said Beth. 'But, anyway—'

She reddened, dropped her gaze. He caught it.

'What?'

'What?'

'"But". You were going to say—'

'Oh, I – the people in the studio, he's—'

Her phone began to ring. *No Caller ID*. Her heart bulleted. She hesitated before answering. She cleared her throat. 'Hello?' she said. There was a pause. 'Hello,' she said again, overlapping a marketing recording. She punched at the Off button. 'Fuck off,' she hissed.

She gathered her breath by gazing through the window from behind the big table with its clutter of homework and spilt wax, lens caps and memory cards. Leaves were rocking lazily against a sketched sky, sliding off-course with tugs of wind. She and Fern had collected last flowerings and berries from the canal side and Camley Street, and they stood in a jar whose water surface was greying and contracting. She shook it. The snake-brown wrinkles of the canal disturbed her now and, for the first time, she viewed the houseboats as little capsules of danger. That oily, insistent slow flow that backed their house, trees hunched over its surface, and perhaps a different threat existed now that the illusion of womanhood overlaid the child Fern was. The choke of nettle and branch beyond the bridges, fenced off in clumps of neglect behind the towpath.

It had been her choice; her fault that they had moved from their flat in London Fields to this ill-defined area between Camden, Kentish Town and St Pancras. Had the Regent's Canal somehow reminded her, without her knowing it, of the Mersey? Some slimy echo of the area referred to by her mother as the Cast Iron Shore, where she had once walked?

Her mother had twisted for one wave of her hand, while Beth had watched her from her desk in the unquestioning certainty of her love, that scene with its blithe ignorance always returning to her later. Over time, she learned to call her Lizzie. She refused to refer to her as Mum, Mam, her mother.

She looked towards the towpath opposite, with its occasional jouncing of bicycle light, figures slipping through the shadows.

The therapist was out there, near the bridge. Beth stared. But of course she wasn't.

Traffic was a smudge from the other side of the house, the rumbling of buses a slight vibration. Here was silence, and bats, and shouts of longboat revellers at dusk or after pub hours. She wanted to stay here forever. This house, this life, these people.

'Why's that boy standing still?' said Beth, pointing at a young man in a hoodie. 'I think he's looking up here. Isn't he? What if it's because of—'

'What?'

'Um. You know. Fern?'

'Hon! We cannot *see* where this guy is looking.'

'She gets these Snapchat messages—'

'Of course she does. You'd be anxious if she didn't. Right?' he said. 'Quit this crazy stressing.'

'Yes. Oh,' she said, as her phone rang. 'It's Aranxto. Darl, I need to tell you about Jack Dor—'

'Answer,' said Sol dismissively, and went to the table for more paperwork.

She hesitated. 'Hi, Aranxto.'

'Bethy, hi.'

'Hi! Weirdly, I just said Jack's name,' she said, with deliberate effort.

'Dorian?'

'Yes.' She looked at Sol and smiled.

'Your best-ever shag, right?' he said. Beth pressed the phone hard to her ear, wandering away. "Mr Skilful hands ... thrusting, strong shoulders. You a *leetle* bit hot between the thighs?'

'No. No,' she said lightly.

'You know the ex-wife lives quite near?'

'How are you?'

'I get it. I'll shut up,' he said. 'You got a moment?'

'Yes. Please! Take me from bills and forms.'

'Yeah. But listen, Bethy,' said Aranxto, his voice dropping. 'Just quickly.'

'What? Tell me.'

'I saw Mrs – I don't know what to call ... I saw your mum.'

'*What?*' said Beth. Her heart clattered painfully against her chest. Sol looked up. 'What? Where? How?' She sat down. Her hand was trembling.

'Liverpool. I was back home at the weekend. Bootle.'

'Why didn't you tell me that at the PV?'

'Didn't want to spoil the atmos.'

'Oh. Right. Yes. God. I don't think I want to hear this.'

Sol's eyebrows raised in enquiry. She shook her head slightly. He placed his hand on her back.

Aranxto was momentarily silent. 'OK—'

'What? What? I don't think I can hear this,' she said again. 'But then I'll go mad, wondering. Why did you *see* her?'

'I bumped into her.'

'On the street?'

'Yes. Bethy-Boop. She just said she missed you. That's all.'

Beth tried to steady her breath.

'I kind of pitied the old hag, to be frank,' he said.

'It's not, is it?' said Beth. 'It's never *that's all* with her.'

'Detective-brain as ever. She just said she wished she could see you. That's really all.'

'Well she can't,' Beth snapped.

'Whoah. I know,' said Aranxto. 'I'm putting my hands in the air, babe.'

* * *

'*Talk* to your therapist,' said Sol the next morning.

'Bossy. I bloody do.'

'About—'

'I know. I will. I will. Hi, Fern.'

As Fern arrived in the kitchen, her Snapchat alert sounded, now recognised by Beth, and Fern ignored her phone.

'I'd just like to know – what do you do when you're late home from school?'

Fern looked down. Beth turned swiftly to Sol and widened her eyes.

'Just chat and hang out and shit like that.'

Fern pressed her forehead against Beth's so her eyes were bigger, darker. They maintained the pose until Beth surrendered.

'You always win!' she said.

Her phone rang and she pulled it from her bag. *No Caller ID*.

'Hello?' she said in a small voice, her heartbeat betraying the anticipation she had denied, but there was silence again.

'Piss off,' she said impatiently, but only as she terminated the call did she realise that there was a different quality to the silence, an alive hesitation and not the prefatory blank of a machine. Had there been breath, even? Sefton Park returned to her.

'Mum!' said Fern.

'What's wrong, hon?' said Sol.

43

Beth opened her mouth. She couldn't speak. 'Nothing,' she said, and she stood very still. Dr Bywater, she thought. She needed to talk to her.

Could Dr Bywater be the one to help? There was so much that seemed impossible to unearth. First, she would have to tell her about Sefton Park: her mother's face, entirely unexpectedly, in a first-floor window. And who was Dr Bywater in real life? Beth had started to become curious.

At ten to nine, she took the urban slope of a walk from the Tube down to the river, the dampness of Thames silt creeping up from Blackfriars. Strands of Lizzie were down here now, after years of fading. It was not just the river; it was not just recent events; it was Dr Bywater. Not probing with scalpels to peel her mind, but skilfully drawing Lizzie out: a flash of an expression at the head of her bed in the dawn.

St Peter's was several floors of turreted brick, with no courtyard to light its warrens of round-edged plaster so stained and pitted that it was easy to picture rats scuttling into its cavities from the river, cockroaches clinging to the catering trolleys. It was soon to amalgamate with a similar institution to create some gleaming new complex that might dupe the electorate into not noticing that yet another hospital had closed. Psychology Outpatients was an entirely NHS-run department, the twitching and the high-smelling mingling with the suited and the mildly neurotic.

In her office, Dr Bywater rested her eyes on Beth with a seemingly limitless supply of understanding. Beth's breathing slowed. There was a rare stillness that settled over her in Dr Bywater's presence. She looked at the therapist with her indeterminate-coloured eyes.

Who was she? she wondered again. Why did this culture accept – in fact encourage – this custom of dumping its innermost secrets on a stranger? Beth knew only that she was calm and considerate and that such tranquillity must be natural to her. She was probably, Beth thought, on the dull side in real life: too serene and sensible; even possibly faintly New Age in her interests, immersed as she was in the public-health sector. Then she remembered Sol castigating her for such categorisations.

Dr Bywater sat very slightly forward in her chair and she looked directly at Beth. There was a pale caramel evenness to her skin that enhanced the impression she gave of self-containment, only broken by the tiredness beneath her eyes. Her hair was a dark brown with slight waves, but which was held back on top with a clip that lent her a conventional appearance, flattening it to her scalp while the rest fell just past her shoulders.

Her skin contrasted with both the hair and large, oddly coloured eyes – primarily a smudged grey, or dark blue – so that her colouring was noticeable, almost dissonant, like children's artwork with features drawn boldly on paper: here the spikes of lashes, here the black irises, the upper lip full but not defined. Her nose was authoritative in its size and its faintly imperious angle, her occasional frown drawing wrinkles at its top. Her teeth had a small gap in the middle, her greeting smile incongruously large, her features otherwise self-possessed; and there was an aspect to her look in repose that could verge on sadness.

The therapist looked a few years older than Beth. She wore a gold band on her wedding finger, not plain, but scalloped, and her surname was possibly her married name, as it seemed too English. There was something of old East Europe to her; of sepia photographs at Ellis Island, soul, suffering. Her nails were more decorative than the rest of her: long and oval, catching the light when she touched her neck.

'I'm all right,' said Beth. 'I'm really not bad. I'm coping.'

'And yet,' said Dr Bywater softly, 'you're struggling against tears.'

Beth tried to slow her breathing. The clock ticked.

'You don't think about yourself. You are too busy worrying about everyone else.'

Her voice was the softest confection. Beth absorbed the peace of it, playing back the words themselves with a delay. She wanted to stay there on that NHS chair, and be soothed, and smoothed, and straightened, in the one time during the hectic week that was all for herself.

Lizzie came with the nights. Without doubt, the ghost was risen, the husks of memory animated. Elizabeth Bridget Penn had resembled a boyish dancer at times, with her narrowness and her light strides across a room, that small face with its large mouth that widened at the cheekbones. Sometimes she had looked like Rudolf Nureyev, with a Slavic cast to her face, the cropped trousers in the style of Audrey Hepburn.

'You don't talk about your mother. She will come in good time, but the more we repress troubling memories, the more power we give them.'

What's all this first-person-plural talk? Beth wanted to say, but she stopped herself, suddenly certain that behind the inscrutability and lack of judgement lay kindness.

A double-stalked *Mad Men*-style lamp that was clearly the therapist's own cast its glow on a regulation table. The chairs were low with squeaking surfaces and scuffed blond arms, the resulting informal sitting position encouraging confession, along with the prop-like tissues which seemed to imply that weeping was expected.

'I hope you and your partner are more in agreement about therapy, and about Fern,' said Dr Bywater into the silence. 'How is it?'

'Oh,' said Beth. 'OK. A few ups and downs. He thinks I'm halfway crazy when it comes to Fern and independence, danger, etc., and I'm irritated that he's oblivious, and then there's tension, unspoken, or ex-plosive short rows.'

Dr Bywater seemed to be waiting for something more.

'So everything is OK then?'

Beth laughed. 'Oh God. If I play that back ...'

Dr Bywater was silent.

'With Fern,' said Beth, 'things seem to be changing too quickly. It's natural, I know – but there's some other element to it. I think? And I'm anxious that maybe I can't mother her properly because of my own mother—' She stopped abruptly.

Dr Bywater waited.

Beth allowed the silence.

'Why is that?'

Beth shook her head and swallowed, audibly.

'So I wonder,' said Dr Bywater eventually in her swooping voice, 'if there's something we could explore about your mother.'

'Of course there's something about my mother,' said Beth sharply. 'What would you lot do without mothers? Go out of business. *Bankrupt*. OK, I'm being rude. I apologise. I'm sorry.'

'Then tell me about your father,' said Dr Bywater in the same calm tones, so Beth ran through rudimentary facts about Gordon Penn – his impov-erished childhood, his work as a typesetter, his love for her mother, his quiet morality – until she tailed off.

Dr Bywater handed her some more worksheets. *Automatic Thought. Feeling. Challenge.* Columns in which to note thought processes and add to a data log. Her nails lightly caught the back of Beth's fingers as she passed her the papers. Beth blinked.

'Sorry,' said Dr Bywater. 'Could we make your appointments later in the day, by the way?'

Beth paused. She nodded. Her hand still felt the movement of nails. 'Yes. That would be easier for me too.'

'Was there anything else that brought you here? That you're ready to approach,' said Dr Bywater without looking up.

Beth hesitated. She turned her eyes to the ceiling, and there was a rocking feeling in her head. She tried to take a deeper breath. She gazed at her lap before lifting her head. The urge to confess rose up, flickered, and disappeared.

The therapist gazed impassively at her.

'Your mother—' she said again, softly.

'Yes,' said Beth abruptly. She looked at the wall. Her throat constricted.

'Where is she? She doesn't really appear. In the room—'

'I find it so hard to – talk about her.'

'You don't have to talk,' said Dr Bywater so gently that Beth could think only of water flowing. She sat and let the speech trickle over her, and she tried to breathe normally. 'We could just see what happens.'

Beth nodded. She looked away. She shuddered. 'Look. What can I say? I can't even speak.'

'Beth,' said Dr Bywater. 'It's all right. It's all right. Try to regulate yourself, and we can talk.'

'I'm afraid there's no point,' said Beth into her hands. 'I was always a bit of a fuck-up. Flawed, I mean. What's going to change there? It's hard to explain how much.'

'What proof do you have?' said Dr Bywater, her tones so soothing, they seemed like a voice in a dream.

'My mother left.'

There was a silence.

Dr Bywater looked into Beth's eyes, and in that space Beth bathed for long, stretched seconds. She floated. It was warm there, and it held her.

'Left?' said Dr Bywater, hardly moving her lips.

'Me.'

'Did she—'

'Left home when I was thirteen.'

'And your father brought you up?' she said quietly.

'Yes.'

Dr Bywater nodded, still keeping her eyes on her, her mouth softening into a look of deep sympathy. She smiled at her, and finally, Beth cried, weeping in front of her without stopping, as she hadn't done for years.

SIX

'So how was it today?' said Sol.

'Good,' said Beth. She was googling Dr Tamara Bywater at that moment. 'She said, implied, I should be worried about you. Me and you …'

'Did she?' He paused. 'That is surprising.'

She frowned at her phone. The search returned only a few professional results.

'Should I be?' she said. 'About "us", I mean? Yuk. This all sounds such a cliché. Sol … Well?'

He paused again. He turned to her. 'No,' he said. 'Of course not.'

* * *

Jack Dorian strode towards Beth as she arrived at the vast shared spaces of the new studio, her crates following. 'Bethy-Boop!' he called, Aranxto's nick-name for her sitting uncomfortably with him.

'Jack!' she said. Jackass, she almost said instead.

He wore a smeared sweatshirt which, along with his wide-shouldered boy looks and somewhat spiky hair, seemed to stage an awkward protest against ageing that was not appealing, but when he hugged Beth in greeting, merely the smell of him – oil paint, neck skin – released a twist of pheromones that she was not expecting.

She opened her mouth. She hesitated. 'Oh my God, I love it here,' she said, gesturing too expansively. 'Why did I spend so long working on my own?'

'Wait till it freezes,' said her old college friend Killian.

'We all huddle up,' said Jack.

Beth blushed, then blushed for blushing.

'Over geriatric paraffin heaters,' said Killian.

'I completely love that,' said Beth. 'It reminds me of camping. Of adventures.'

'Adventures. You like those, I believe,' said Jack.

'Ha ha,' said Beth. 'Oh, my man-with-a-van is arriving!' she said, burying her head in a text.

* * *

The weather had tightened into early bruised skies, leaves spiralling to huddle on the towpath, and Fern was later from school as the term progressed. The sound of her Snapchat was ever-present, until she muted it and then constantly glanced at the screen.

'Where's Fern?' said Beth one evening in late October.

Sol's son Laurie came into the room, and she flung her arms around him. He would still permit her expressions of affection, whereas Sol's manly back slaps were restricted. Music blared; milk boiled over. At nearly eighteen, Laurie was towering over his father, and Beth smiled at his new height, stopped herself commenting, and put her hand on his arm.

'Can you stay?' she asked.

'Yes,' he said, his voice lower over the years in increments that seemed to be both natural and acquired.

'Oh brilliant. Let's get some Chinese, then.'

An image of Dr Bywater came to her, approving of her mothering. She suppressed a smile.

'So where's Fern?'

'With her friend,' said Sol, studying images on his camera.

'Which friend? You were having her.'

'Her friend Jemma. Just now. You just missed her.'

'But it's dark! Anyway, I don't understand how she has met this girl.'

'She lives round the corner, doesn't she?'

'I'm not sure. Where round the corner?' Her voice wobbled.

'She'll be fine,' he said, in the tone that flicked tension into the air.

'For God's sake, Sol.'

'I was travelling all over town at her age,' said Laurie, leaning over Sol's camera and shaking his head at an image.

'You're a *boy*,' said Beth.

'Last time I looked.'

Sol snorted.

'I'm going. I'm going to find her.' Beth grabbed her coat again. 'She wasn't going to go out tonight.'

'She just decided now,' said Sol, his glasses on his head, his eyes betraying strain that was normally masked.

'I'm actually really pissed off with you,' said Beth. 'It's – it's disrespectful, as well as dangerous. You know, I'm sick of you implying I'm neurotic about this.' She paused. The therapist's words went through her mind, and she echoed them: 'You're not respecting my instincts. I'm her mother.'

She saw Sol putting his head in his hands as she hurried from the room, feeling his gaze on her back and resisting it, then ran down the stairs to an unseasonal roar of cold behind the door. The street lamp's glow on the alley that led to the small section of canal bank on their side was weak, devolving into darkness, the path empty, only the girl who always hummed on her bike shooting by, her light wobbling as she passed. The owners of the *Mary-Lou*, the houseboat illegally moored almost opposite their house and periodically banished by the police, were smoking in battered donkey jackets on their roof, breath indistinguishable from smoke. The smell on Fern's hair came back to Beth, and then a trace of a memory seemed to spill into the corner of her mind; she chased it, certainty meeting confusion, and it was not what she had expected. It was elusive.

She texted Fern, her thumbs stiff in the cold, but there was no answer. '*Shit*,' she muttered.

Beth stared and, strangely, she had the distinct thought that Dr Tamara Bywater was on the other shore. Then the woman who might have been her lifted her hand, and Beth made a sound, of pleasure, almost of odd relief. There was a half-wave, or was it a rearrangement of hair? The woman turned around, and walked away from the canal, and of course, thought Beth in embarrassment, it could be anyone of a similar slimness and hair length, but she stared, still, through the darkness, longing for her counsel.

She started to ring Fern, then stopped, blocked her own number so Fern would pick up, waited, called again, and Fern answered, hesitantly. She pulled her coat tighter.

'Come here right now,' Beth said, and when Fern arrived, she was indignant and vulnerable in turn.

'Where have you been?'

'Mum. It's fine. Don't flip your shit like this.'

'Where were you?'

'Just – outside,' said Fern. 'With Jemma.'

'I've had enough of the lying,' snapped Beth. She felt a sadistic, uneasy pleasure rise in her as she began, belatedly, to issue rules and threaten punishments.

Fern stared at her, her mouth an obstinate wobbling.

'But Jemma's lonely, she's – it's really really sad, how it is at her school, teased and stuff – and she's nice.'

Beth opened her mouth. 'Fern. You are so kind and thoughtful, but you don't have to take on every waif and stray. Not everyone's your responsibility. What is this smell?'

'Uh?' Fern shook her head slowly, appraising Beth as though she felt sorry for her. 'What the hell?'

'Well?'

'What the hell?'

'Fern, you don't *speak* like this! What, is this new teen talk? Be yourself. I am now coming with you when you go out in the evenings, and accompanying you to Jemma's door.'

'God's sake! Mum! You are – *mad*. Like, legitimately crazy. I just can't believe it! You think I'm a baby. Literally. *Literally* a baby. Oh my God. It's like … you just want to cuddle me and guard me literally all the *time*.'

'I'm just trying to look after you,' said Beth. 'Be – nice to you.'

'Well you're *too* nice.'

'You'd rather I ignored you a bit? Didn't hug you, tuck you in, do … read the bedtime novels?'

'Yes.'

'Right,' said Beth. She took a deep breath. 'OK.' The emptying world tilted. 'OK. You can go home now.'

'On my own?'

'Yes. Text as soon as you're there.'

Fern hesitated, then marched up the bridge steps, and Beth watched her back with its swinging hair. It was as though the love of her life had just left her. But of course, Fern was the love of her life, and she was leaving her, as was natural. Beth lowered her head and pulled at the skin of her temples.

* * *

She waited for Fern's text, slumped against the wall, shivering; she knew that it was ill-advised to allow a thirteen-year-old to walk along the bridge and down two and a half streets to home, but she thought, Go on then. Court danger, and superstition will save you. Twelve years or so. Was that all you had of your child before they didn't want or need you any more?

Had she got it wrong and overdone it, stifling her daughter with childish things: the old-fashioned stand-ards of infancy, the books and kites and canal trips and picnics? An *Orlando* version of a childhood: seaside holidays, tree climbing in London Fields, Woodland Happy Families. Smothering as the oppos-ite of abandonment? But she had taken Fern to films and museums as well, to café breakfasts with friends before school, the girls giggling and cheeky with shyness. 'My friends love you,' Fern had always said, simply. 'I have the kindest mother in the *world*,' she had said at other times.

Fern had always enjoyed accompanying Beth to vintage clothes shops in Islington and Crouch End to find the 1940s dresses and jackets that Beth loved, and which fitted her well. Her 'old Hollywood film clothes', Fern had called them then. Lately she had screwed up her nose. 'They are so *not* in fashion, Mum,' she said. 'And those old gross places smell like *mil*dew.'

Beth now looked across at the canal, could barely detect its ropes of movement, and felt the momentary temptation to curl up, lean forward and roll in. She sat very still. She was suddenly back crouching under the stairs, alone aged thirteen, body taut with a silent scream as what her mother had done sank in for the first time.

Where was her mother? The voice on the phone. *She wished she could see you.* But she didn't, did she? She hadn't tried again.

A helicopter was circling Camden, then another. There was a sound from the water. If she painted now, she would use an umber layer, traces of celadon green beneath washes to capture the undertow, the fish reek in the cold, the towpath a floating trail beside it. But she couldn't paint. Would the new studio help?

The text from Fern came: *Home.*

Beth exhaled the tension that she didn't know was compressing her chest.

She couldn't imagine preparing a canvas. She couldn't imagine ever confidently mothering Fern again. She couldn't imagine a home life without growing marital tension and the neurotic flickerings of fear.

The lights of the *Mary-Lou* came on, and bats flitted over the water in their beam. She wanted to talk to Dr Bywater. She needed the therapy. Quite clearly, and shamefully. She needed to explain to someone. Her mind turned to Aranxto, who lived five minutes away, though his motives would be mixed with *Schadenfreude*. He was at his best when she was down: brotherly, and in control of her. She didn't always trust him.

She rang him.

'Taking a dump,' he said. 'Call me back in five.'

'Classic.'

A longboat travelled almost silently along that stretch of Regent's Canal, and Beth waved to its driver with some vague clasping at humanity. She sank her head, ignored the cigarette beggar Aranxto had nick-named Philter as he crept past, and saw moons against the pressure of her knees, recalling all the unfortunates Aranxto had appropriated to provide him with the same pleasure as his net curtains and claimed taste for Special Brew as he fraternised with them in his kitchen when he wanted to escape the art world. His games when he was bored – ruses and tricks that amounted to meddling in people's lives – were becoming more elaborate the more effortlessly successful he became, a habit that both amused and alarmed Beth, who had once given him a large wooden spoon to represent his stirring. Sol had always disapproved of Aranxto's inconsistent patronage of outcasts. A thought about Fern suddenly occurred to Beth, but Aranxto was jumping down the bridge steps.

'You fruitcake,' he said, leaning over to give Beth a string of kisses on the cheek, their warmth then cooling rapidly on her skin. 'What are you doing in this fucking freeze?'

'I know,' said Beth.

'Having a Bethy crisis?'

'Worse.'

'Are you at—'

'No, not my period, my hormones, my sex life, my – womb,' she said in a drone.

He lowered himself beside her on the earth in his expensive trousers. He pulled her hard towards him, as she wanted him to; she curved into his torso, his body aftershave-spiced and so much taller than Sol's, and they sat shivering in silence, their breaths merged in air-mushrooms.

'What is it, darling?'

'I – I can't sleep for worrying. Fern. She's always late. A boy seems to be messaging her. Or what if he's older? *Some*thing is distracting her. In fact – perhaps you know something?'

'Me?' said Aranxto in the falsetto that had broken into his voice since his teens.

'Well?'

'Why should I know anything about her?'

'I saw that you text – well, message – her.'

He paused. 'You spy on her phone?'

'No. I saw when I was with her.'

'She was my goddaughter last time I was aware,' he said airily. 'I don't know a thing, babe. What do these girls get up to? Do they use tongues yet?'

'Aranxto! God. Please. You'd tell me if she's telling you anything about a boy. Right? Entirely between us.'

'Of course I would,' he said in more serious tones. 'Of course.'

'OK. Thank you. She's really pulling away. From me. Do people always have to leave me? Aranxto?' She blinked, hard. 'No, that sounds self-pitying. But Sol's ... I can't seem to work. You saw my mum. Everything. I seem to hate myself. Ignore me. It's mad.'

'You just have these bouts of self-doubt every now and then. You always have had.'

'Yes. But it's not just *self*-doubt.'

'But it is, babe. You're brilliant. You don't always do the best by yourself, that's all. You need to get the fuck on with it. You're so talented. Come on,' he said, and she let herself be enveloped by his strength. 'What's this about?'

She shook her head, pinned against him. 'I was always. Pretty useless,' she said. 'At heart. Not to be relied upon. You know that more than anyone.'

'You blame yourself for things you shouldn't,' he said. 'None of that was your fault. You're a good person, Bethy-Boop.'

She shook her head again.

61

'I need proper help, I think.'

'Bullshit. Look – loosen up. I'll get you drunk. Get you a boy to shag. Take you to Barcelona. How about a taste of Dorian again? Go on. You know you want it.'

'No,' she said. 'Thank you. I'm seeing a therapist.' She coughed.

'Ha! You. My cynical Bethy. Is he a beardy in terrible shoes? Or a tasty doctor-type and you fancy him already?'

'She's a woman.'

'Oh. Well I hope she's hot shit, to deal with your verbals.'

'I think she is. I'm beginning to think she really is. I wish I could talk to her right now.' She hesitated. 'I really do.'

He glanced at her. 'You a bit intrigued, babe?'

'Well, yes, totally, because they don't give anything away.'

'Hem. Do I sniff a fleeting homoerotic … throb?'

'Er, no. It's impossible to even *know* her, let alone …'

'You getting it from that grumpy American you live with?' He started cracking his knuckles.

'You getting it from every grovelling post-grad you meet?' she said.

'Got a smile out of you! I'm better than that head-shrinker chick.'

'I'm sure you are. OK, you can fuck off now. I hate it when you start to get twitchy about leaving. I've

62

got to get some Chinese anyway. Thank you – thank you – for coming.'

* * *

When Aranxto had gone, Beth looked through the darkness of the canal towards King's Cross, trying to detect the tops of the cranes as the development spread its tendrils ever further, wrapping warehouses in scaffolding covers and throwing down girders. Building work was taking place at the Lock in the other direction as well, so she felt encroached upon in her damp, gnatty run. Again, she wanted to talk to Tamara Bywater. What would she be like, away from the hospital? She would google her more thoroughly later.

She turned to that tumbledown haven across the water, her home on Little Canal Street. House of Cardigans was Sol's current name for it, in reference to the excess of woolly clothing she possessed and their series addictions, often several years behind their broadcast dates. Its roof and higher floors were visible above the trees, the clambering narrow building that defied estate agents' dictates and inspired surveyors' head-shaking, and it brought her comfort. She loved its tiny creaking bedrooms leading into staircases and finally a ladder, its light pipe and miniature conservatory, crammed extensions, its ziggurat of terrace and balcony, and its dance of dazzle and old panel, odd fittings, shelves. Laurie's blue bulb flicked on in the loft room, and she smiled. The ground floor reminded her of Dickens on foggy days; at other times of Disney's dwarves' kitchen; of the Ladybird *Elves and the Shoemaker*. Higher up, its rooms quivered with water and sky, and there you could live in the clouds and the treetops, hear the rain on the roof. She sometimes put her head out of a window there, trying to imbibe the elements, to fly away to a new land, and sex, and extremes: a wilder life.

* * *

As Fern pulled away, her phone silently vibrating, and *No Caller ID* failed to call, Beth was becoming more reliant on the therapist's sessions. She googled her again yet discovered nothing personal at all nestling among the academic papers, the employment histories, the records of conferences attended and occasional quotes given. Only Dr Bywater, she thought, could understand her.

Every night was a land she entered. She approached it knowing she would travel, temporarily eased, through the comfort of darkness before something rocky and acidic slowly surfaced, pressing against her until it woke her in the hours before dawn. The acid seemed to soak into her brain and pump out self-disgust. Bright images rained down on her: her mother turning round to wave at her in her bedroom; her mother's hospital bed; the window by Sefton Park. She had turned thirteen three weeks before her mother left, and it was the not-knowing Beth couldn't bear. The cowish ignorance of what was to come.

Mortgage calculations and Sol's alimony payments scrawled through her mind at night, always on graph paper, in bright blue ink. Sometimes Sol heard her involuntary whimpers and bed-turnings, and rubbed her head until she slid back into sleep. She often slept for an hour or so once the birds had woken, then rose with Fern in the exhausted darkness, as though a caul were over her, picturing the tiredness as the skin of boiled milk.

'This is activating a core schema,' Dr Bywater said. 'It triggers that old fear of abandonment. But look around you. You are loved.'

The session was now the hour of salvation, the soft-voiced cure in which Beth was taken apart and rebuilt, and she emerged upright to face the newly unearthed demons.

'Do you *think*,' Beth asked her old friend Ellie, 'it's possible that my shrink, like – I sound like Fern – kind of *approves* of me?'

'I'm sure,' said Ellie. 'Why wouldn't she?'

'Yes, but she's so strictly professional, it's not as if she ever says anything, indicates anything in any way. It's just this feeling …'

'Well. You always were either a rebel or a bit of a star,' said Ellie.

Beth laughed. 'You mean, either trouble or a teacher's pet?' she said, and they were back to where they

65

had always been, arrested in a version of their teenage alliance with its shorthand and levity.

'I love you, my Ellie P,' said Beth.

'I love you, naughty teacher's pet.'

'Can you be both?'

'I think you are, is the point.'

'Is the point?'

'So perhaps you should watch out.'

'What do you mean?'

'I don't know what I mean. Just that.'

Seven

'I'll bet there's a boy in the frame,' said Sol, at home before setting out on another job. He walked out of the room, his arms swinging from square shoulders.

'Uh?' said Beth, barely hearing what he said. She was looking at the post, which contained some worksheets with printouts about perfectionism and mindfulness from Dr Tamara Bywater that she was meant to use in the week. Beth noted the signature on the hospital comp slip.

'You didn't hear me, did you?' said Sol.

'What?' called Beth.

'It's a boy,' he said, putting his head round the door.

'Well, yes! Duh. This is part of what I've been trying to tell you,' said Beth, her voice uncomfortably shrill.

'When girls entered Laurieworld, he became a lying jerk for a while. Quit the stressing.'

'You go more American when *you're* secretly worried. Where is she, anyway?'

Beth looked out of the window at the shadows on the towpath. Sol went to take a shower.

'Where is she?' she called to him after ten minutes. 'She had Drama, but that's all.'

She rang Fern's mobile, the pause that preceded the voicemail taunting her with frustration, and she stood by the window at the back of the house, willing the sight of that fast-stepped walk in trainers, a rucksack draped with hair, but the water and trees were blurring in darkness.

'It's fine,' he said, as she knew he would; as she wanted him to, and didn't want him to.

'It's five fifteen. Just past. Ten to is the latest she gets here after after-school clubs. Usually.'

'She sometimes talks to her friends.'

'I suppose,' she said. 'Yes.'

'Don't stress yet,' he said, but there was a catch of tension in his voice.

She walked over to the window again, and the sky's grey glare had dulled.

'It'll be dark soon.'

She rang Fern's school, but its voicemail came on after several rings to inform her of office hours.

The trees now crouched shadows over the canal. The pathway was emptying, the *Mary-Lou* unlit, no sirens or bicycle bells rising above the undulating drone of the Camden traffic.

Dr Bywater, she wanted to say.

'She's really late,' she said. She tried Fern's mobile again, and a friend's, then a different one, and their parents, who knew nothing. She sent another text.

'If she's not here in half an hour, we call the police,' said Sol.

'Half an hour!'

'Twenty minutes then.'

'It's dark.'

'Right,' said Sol, and she could hear a hesitation for the first time that tightened her gut.

'You're worried now, aren't you?' said Beth. She opened the window to regulate her breathing. The sweet mould of cannabis hung in the air. Dr Bywater, she thought. Dr Bywater made everything all right. Dr Bywater would save Fern, would save her, would put the worries into perspective.

Only the harmless local alcoholic Philter was out there now, a couple of cyclists speeding through the dusk. She called Fern again, then another friend, who didn't answer. She left a further message.

'I *told* you we should be worried,' said Beth.

Sol said nothing. He put his palms up.

'That is maddening,' she said. 'Don't do that! She keeps getting messages, Sol. That she's all secretive about. I bloody told you that. Say something!'

'Yes. A boy,' he said calmly.

'Exactly! You just think this is some crush. She's *too* distracted, too late, too secretive. Don't you realise? She's thirteen, not fifteen.'

She tried Fern's number again, and again, the only action she could take. She started to pray in haphazard beggings to a god she was hazy about.

'Let's call the police,' he said.

'Yes,' she said, tears beginning to run over her face in silence. 'Hurry.'

He rang as she paced between the two sides of the house, listening. Sol was patiently giving out details. So many stupid details. She nudged him and he looked up. '*Faster*,' she muttered as he repeated their address with his usual clarity.

The doorbell rang. Sol paused. 'Yes. Please. Fern,' Beth yelped uselessly, storming down the stairs, but, oh God, perhaps it was the police, the other police, the ones who didn't know about the ones being called now, and were here reporting an accident. She made a primitive animal sound as she reached the door.

'Mum,' said Fern.

The darkness seemed to bend in front of Beth's eyes.

'Fern, Fern, oh God. Thank you,' she said, clutching her with an urgency that made Fern cry out in protest. 'Sol,' she called up the stairs, burping with a sob as she shouted. 'She's *here*! Don't you have your key?' she said to Fern.

'Uh, yes, sorry,' said Fern.

'Thank you God,' said Beth. She was laughing, and crying, and laughing, and she pulled Fern to her again, ignoring the girl behind her. 'Hello,' she said, beginning to close the door. 'Bye.'

'Mum!' said Fern. 'What are you doing?'

'Where were you?' said Beth. 'Fern, do you realise? My God.'

'Mum! Why are you all red? What's the *matter*?' said Fern, but a wave of self-consciousness passed over her face.

'You are over an *hour* late from school. Nearly an hour and twenty minutes! It's dark. Your phone wasn't on. You – you—' said Beth, her voice rising then cracking.

'God, Mum. Calm! I'm here.'

'*What were you doing?*'

'Jemma's here.'

'Who?'

'Mum! Here. Jemma. You haven't met yet, right?'

She stared through the gloom at the child, a plumper, blonder version of Fern: odd twins, with their denim shorts over thick tights, their trainers and unstructured falls of hair. She could hear Sol terminating his phone call, ever steady and polite.

'Where did she – you – go?' she snapped.

'Cool down, Mum,' said Fern.

'Fern—'

'That's my name. Don't wear it out.'

'Come straight upstairs.'

Fern rolled her eyes and shrugged to her friend, who backed away.

'What were you *doing*?' said Beth, holding Fern again, kissing her. Fern pulled the Tudor mask she was carrying protectively away from her. Sol leaped towards them, two steps at a time.

There was the slightest pause. 'Talking to Jemma.'

'Why would you take that long? Dad's been on the phone to the *police*.'

'Sorry,' Fern muttered, blushing. Awkwardness washed over her face.

'You must have done something else.'

'Talked to my friends,' said Fern, glancing to one side.

'Who?'

There was a pause. 'Jemma. And—'

'And?'

Fern now stared straight at Beth. She started counting off her usual school friends, mock-tolerantly, on her fingers, but Beth interrupted her.

'Tell me where you were,' she said.

'I told you,' Fern said, shook her off and climbed the stairs, her mismatched fluorescent laces shining in the gloom, the Tudor mask blank-eyed.

* * *

'She has a love bite,' said Beth to Dr Bywater that Tuesday. 'I think. I saw it the following morning. She says she doesn't.'

She put her head in her hands. The rows with Sol of the preceding days, the grounding of Fern to volleys of protest, the logistics of supervision, washed over her, the exhaustion only hitting now.

'Our arguments follow an almost identical course,' she said.

'What did he say about the love bite?'

'He didn't believe me. As in, he thought my fevered imagination was seeing things. She was wearing a high neck by the time he saw her, and the next day it had disappeared – she'd used foundation on it, I'm sure.'

'There's a trust issue here.'

'There really is. I wanted to call you,' said Beth. 'I wanted to call you the evening she was so late, I mean. When I was so scared.' She blushed. 'That's strange.'

'Not really,' said Dr Bywater. 'I'm here to look after you. We work well together as therapist and patient.'

'Oh—' Beth's mouth opened.

The changeable pewter of Dr Bywater's irises appeared lighter. After the wincing illumination of the corridors, her consulting room resembled a cinema with its low soupy lighting. She wore a black skirt and a black silk blouse, thin black tights and flat black shoes, the blackness relieved only by small silver earrings. Her nails were long and polished, lightly pink yet transparent, as though she had had a French manicure.

'How are you feeling now?' Dr Bywater said.

'Fine,' said Beth. 'Not fine,' she said, hearing herself, and she laughed with inappropriate volume then cringed. Her eyelashes were twitching. She found herself wanting to please the therapist. 'How are you?'

'I'm well,' said Dr Bywater, and continued to look at her, waiting, as ever professional and reserved.

They discussed Fern's lateness, and Beth's reactions. 'I think a central task here is to look at the effect your mother's absence had on you and your responses and feelings now,' said Dr Bywater, so gently that Beth's breathing seemed to align with her words. 'Start with some facts. Your family in Liverpool. You don't even give me those – you hide them. Her.' She touched the side of her neck, the nails catching the light.

'I can barely bear to think about it.' Beth paused. She took in a breath. 'So … my moth— Lizzie, and my father, lived in a small terraced house in South Liverpool. He was a typesetter. She worked part-time. My brother Bill was five years older. I think I was probably an accident.'

'How would you describe Lizzie?' said Dr Bywater.

'She was – she wasn't your run-of-the-mill working Toxteth – Liverpool – mum. She was … intense, quite highly strung, vivid. She wanted to improve herself, with her reading, theatre-going. The weird thing is, she seemed really *loving*. But when I thought about it later, she was also a bit distracted, as though she had this internal world that none of her family could penetrate.'

Dr Bywater nodded.

'I think my father would have known that, compared with him, she lit up a room,' said Beth. 'Well. I believed that my mother had gone because I'd somehow pushed her away.'

'Children believe this,' said Dr Bywater. 'Which is the tragedy. Even now you're choosing to believe the opinion of someone – your mother – who couldn't fulfil the role she was meant to.'

'It wasn't just her fault,' Beth said, but again she felt heat rising in her. 'I was terrible to her.'

Dr Bywater said nothing.

'Worse.' Beth shook her head. 'Really, I don't want you to think I'm just the victim of—'

'I don't assume anything. Tell me, tell me if you can, about when she left?'

* * *

When Lizzie Penn left her family and home, she didn't say goodbye. Her husband was in the garage and son away at college. She kissed her daughter, seemingly in passing.

'I love you,' she said, as she often did.

Then she turned to wave as Beth, just thirteen – hair a stringy, stained gold, large brown eyes like a bush-baby – watched her unthinkingly from her bedroom window.

Beth followed her narrowing figure with her gaze without really seeing it, speculating about what her mother might buy them for tea. Lizzie carried no suit-case, and she left most of her possessions behind in the house, as though shame or determination to erase her past prevented her from taking her belongings.

* * *

'What did you feel?' Dr Bywater's voice was so even but pliant, it seemed to enclose her listener.

'I … I … felt like shit, to be honest.'

'How did feeling shit feel?'

Beth swallowed.

Dr Bywater waited, sympathy visible in her eyes.

'I – wanted to kill myself, frankly. A junior suicide! Yes, the runty little kid that I was considered it.'

She had wanted to shoot herself. Not on the day of the leaving, when Lizzie didn't come back for supper after all, and Beth's father had knocked on her bedroom door to try to explain what he really couldn't; but just over a week later, when she thought about it as she sat with him in continuing near-silence while he tried, tried so hard to make life normal. Her older brother was away in Brighton, and it was so boring and empty and sad and strange, just her and her father – forever, forever; waiting; no-taste food, clumsiness, kindness, attempts at conversation; the disbelief now stained with realisation – and she thought of the guns at the amusement arcade, and wondered whether she could put a pellet in herself.

* * *

'You've had a life-changing loss at a very young age,' said Dr Bywater. 'It wouldn't be surprising if this affected the way you feel about your daughter.

Overprotective, compensating. All these triggers may make you feel she's abandoning you, when she's not.'

Beth nodded.

'Here, you will never be abandoned,' she said, and Beth instinctively wanted to be held by her, then brushed the thought away.

She glanced at the clock. They had run past the hour. She wanted to stay in this fortress for the rest of the day, floating until morning on the voice's slide from lightness to depth.

EIGHT

Just who *was* the therapist, then, with her consultant status and her unknown life? With her measured but odd lapwing voice that you had to follow up and down, the accent that seemed as glaringly anachronistic as the enunciations of a British film star of the 1930s, incongruous with her occasional use of jargon? Beth didn't know. She had no idea. All that could be ascertained was her gentle nature. A determination to unearth facts took hold. She could tell – though a layer of liberal Londonese coated her – that Dr Tamara Bywater was privileged at some level, probably privately educated. She wasn't the suburban social worker that some of her colleagues appeared to be.

She tried to think of ways to ask Sol to ask David Aarons, the psychoanalyst friend he sometimes met for pre-work breakfast after the gym, but the implausibility of Sol gruffly questioning the manly David about his own feelings for his patients made her want to laugh.

'Ask David if he knows anything about Dr Tamara Bywater?' she blurted.

Sol looked up from the tripod he was collapsing. 'The psychologist? He's an analyst.'

'Married to a psychologist. Dr – Bywater is a trained psychotherapist as well. When do you see him for breakfast?'

'Likely Thursday. Isn't it unethical for you to be told personal information about her?'

'Probably,' said Beth cheerfully.

Fern came into the room, ignored her, and looked through the snacks drawer.

'Hello, girl whom I haven't seen all day,' said Beth, and bent over her. Fern's shoulders tightened perceptibly at Beth's voice.

'Holy shit,' said Fern, lifting only her head for a kiss. 'Do you have to use that proper-proper language all the time? Posh speak.'

Beth snorted.

Fern turned. Beth swallowed. The thoughts crowded in, the catastrophising that Dr Bywater talked about: a repulsive stream of them.

* * *

Beth now often heard the voice of Dr Bywater advising her as she taught at The Dairy. Her classes were relaxed sessions in which pupils played with the astonishingly lavish quantities of materials at their disposal: canvases which they saw fit to slash and smear and literally urinate on for supposedly outrageous experiments that were roughly identical each year, along with manga horrors, videos of body parts and Banksy rip-offs. The school technician would stretch and prime her own canvases for her, however, and she always slipped him some cash.

Beth's studio mate and old college friend Killian messaged and suggested a drink in Covent Garden, where he had a job for the season as a set painter. Sol would meet Fern at school from football club, and so she agreed.

It was unexpectedly pleasant to find herself in a more tourist-filled part of London, a novelty that reminded her of her Slade days when all areas were there to explore before later dismissal. The crowds surged through the convivial chaos around the Piazza, and then Beth jolted as Dr Bywater descended from a taxi with a man. This time, it was her. Beth saw the dark hair, the familiar body, her pulse catching her off-guard at the vision of her therapist out in the world, yet she wore high heels, a tight black dress and a cropped furry jacket that clouded above it. Beth caught just a glimpse of waist, of bottom encased in clinging fabric, before the opera-milling crowds swallowed her with her companion, and of course it couldn't be Dr Bywater. Beth knew that the sensibly attired therapist would never drape herself in a foxy dress over a man. This was what she had done with Lizzie Penn for so many years, strangers transformed by her delusions. She hadn't even seen the woman from the taxi's face. Please, she thought weakly. Please don't start again.

* * *

Beth had always looked for her mother everywhere, all over Dingle, along the Cazzy, and Crosby Beach, on the sandbanks, the park, in case she was there, visiting her half-brother in Liverpool, so often spotting her thin back, her short hair, her ballerina walk. A mirage.

One day, sitting on her school bus in Liverpool, Beth had been so certain she had spotted Lizzie that she had leaped out. There was her mother in her green-blue coat, her hair a little longer, and Beth tore over to her, tripped on the pavement, fell, picked herself up and called out, and it took moments of delay for her to understand that the face was different, a different face on her mother's body, in almost her mother's coat. It was only later that she realised she had cut her knee so deeply it had needed four stitches, her father taking her to the hospital that evening, and she had a faint scar even now.

She started to go to the Metropolitan Cathedral and stared at the Mary to make herself cry, and she felt better afterwards, but she knew her father wouldn't like her to do that, so she bought a postcard of her instead, which reminded her of her mother. She started her periods there, right there in Paddy's Wigwam, searching frantically for a toilet, and she could never tell her father. Ellie's mother, Mrs Playbourne, advised him instead on what to do, and there was always a pile of bulky towels in a high-up cupboard, before Ellie started sharing her tampon supply.

* * *

Beth went to the studio. She had unpacked all her materials in something approaching joy, immediately at home in the new workplace: an affordable, old-style warehouse in a corner of North London that was still resisting gentrification. She loved its camaraderie, its paint-covered dripping taps and concrete floor, its leaky roof with skylights, and even the cold air that made the artists crowd round the heaters moaning companionably. She talked to Jack Dorian less than most of the others in the building, who tended to wander into each other's spaces, borrow materials, work late into the night. She cursed herself for not telling Sol at the beginning that Jack was a member of their group.

* * *

Back at Little Canal Street, the cheek-singeing heat of the wood burner was tunnelled with a draught, its furnace smell overlaying canal scent, and there, on the first floor's balcony, was Sol, with his tripod and camera, the door left open as ever, his body fuzzy in the sodium glare of the street on the other side. Beth paused and watched him. She wanted Dr Bywater to see her house, her husband. It had been a series of miracles that he was here at all, the married American who had had to travel fortnightly to the States to see his son, postponing property purchase and much else.

'Hon, come here, I want to show you something,' he said, turning and breaking into a smile, an expression that somehow combined pleasure with pride in the person he bestowed it upon, a blessing among his poker faces and frowns of concentration. 'Look at the shadows on the moon through the telephoto.' He rested his arm on her as he showed her, cupping her shoulder. 'Let's eat. You get pasta tonight. Penne all'Amatriciana. All'Amatriciana all'Solomone. Steel yourself.'

'Yum,' she said. 'This will be my break. I've got to finish two greetings cards tonight.'

'You're working hard,' said Sol.

'Only at the crap. Oh and you got me flowers! So lovely. Thank you.'

'Welcome. Money-making crap. *Mice* isn't crap.'

'Well ...' Something shadowed the corner of her vision. 'Thank you.' She looked behind her.

'That man. Boy,' she said, dropping her voice and nodding at the towpath with its sepia blur of railings and bushes.

Sol held her and glanced towards the canal. 'Bet ... Let's eat.'

'Are you seeing David in the morning?' she said, in an abrupt change of subject.

'Uh. No? Thursday. Why?'

'Nothing.'

He pushed her into a chair, kissed the top of her head and tossed a tea towel into the air as he picked up the pan with his other hand.

'Pretty deft,' he said.

'You plonker.'

'Ha. You going to the studio tomorrow?'

'Uh. Yes. I have to tell you something,' she said in a rush. She cringed. 'I mean, I don't know why I said it like that.'

'Huh?'

'With a preface. Kind of. I'm talking nonsense. Jack Dorian. The Jackass. He's part of the studio lot. Renters.'

'He is?' said Sol.

'Yes.' Her heart raced.

'So why don't I know that?' Sol was stationary. His expression froze. 'How long ago was it you moved studios?'

'I—'

'He's always been there?'

'Yes. I—'

'That is crazy.' He wrinkled his brow. 'You told me some of them – Killian, Lars, Anna, that lot? Right?'

'Yes, but – it doesn't *mean* anything he's there. I barely speak to him.'

'Well, that is unlikely if you're sharing a space.'

'How many years have I only seen Jack from a distance at PVs?' said Beth. 'Years and years.' She was aware her smile was stiffly wide, her eyes too open, a blush rising up her face.

'I'm well aware you're drawn to crazies.'

'Yes, some of my boyfriends turned out to be on the nutty side. So who did I marry?'

Sol said nothing.

'You. Thank God,' Beth blurted. 'One does usually grow out of an attraction to the wrong sorts of people.'

'I wouldn't really fucking care about this,' said Sol. 'That guy's a schmuck. I'd never be so dumb as to think you'd … But now I do fucking care because you omitted to tell me you're seeing him every day.'

He shook his head slightly, his eyes hidden behind his glasses, shrugged.

'If you'd told me from the get-go, it would have been no big deal.'

'Ah, you'd have made your jibes.'

'Sure. Jackass jokes. The Jackass merits them more than any of your other exes. The Jackass is a major jackass.'

She snorted.

'Sorry,' she said.

'Uh huh.'

He was silent. She bit her lip, pressing her teeth into it to mark off the moments until he stopped.

'There is something,' he said. 'Something going on? I think so. Some kind of distraction?'

'Nothing,' she said. She shook her head. 'Nothing.'

The Tuesday appointment at St Peter's had become the focus of Beth's week, the monsters in her head sedated.

She had begun to look for a thank-you gift for Dr Bywater, scanning various websites until Sol asked her what she was doing.

'A present for Ellie,' she said, clenching at her own lie.

'Did you know?' Fern said, slamming her bag on the table. 'Everyone else is allowed to take literally hours to get home without their slave owners going crazy?' She stared at Beth, maintaining the stare.

'They are not! They're twelve and thirteen.'

'You are straight-up *wrong*!'

'Well, Fern, perhaps they didn't return so late that their parents had to call the police,' said Beth. 'You will be supervised, and basically grounded, until we can trust you again.'

'That's correct,' said Sol.

Fern grabbed a cereal bar. 'My grandma came to me in a dream,' she said.

'Oh,' said Beth. She pressed her nails inside each other, hurting herself. 'You mean—'

Fern waited. 'Yes. She was beautiful, like in those photos of her as a girl. Where is she?'

'You know ... Oma is in Rhode Island.'

'Holy crap,' said Fern, converting her amusement into a sneer.

Beth smiled, and rubbed Fern's shoulder as she passed.

'She's still *alive*, isn't she?'

'Uh? ... Yes,' said Beth, and coughed. She poured water and gargled. 'We'd tell you if not.'

'So where is she?'

'You know, Liverpool. Just outside.'

'So why don't we ever see her?' said Fern. 'When we see Grandad. She might be lonely. Just *because* you don't like her.'

'I didn't say that.'

'Basically, you did. I understand that. People not liking their mothers,' she said, giving a strange bright smile. 'But we literally *never* see Granny Penn!'

'She's not called that!' Beth began to laugh, her eyes suddenly wet. 'I can picture her shuddering at that. Ferny, you know why ... we don't have a relationship.' She took another swig of water. 'Why I don't see her. Oh, my throat's ... I'm really really sorry if that deprives you – you—'

'God, Mum. Don't gulp like that. It's disgusting. Are you OK? You sound like you swallowed a hairbrush.'

'It feels like a bee.' She gargled. 'At least you visit your Oma every year. How many other girls your age get to go to America every year?'

Fern gazed at Beth, then shut her mouth. 'Properly obvious. The toddler distraction technique,' she said.

She narrowed her eyes. 'I think I'll go out with Dad after school. He said we could go for pizza.'

'Oh—' said Beth. 'OK.'

Fern stood and turned. '*Dad*, by the way, understands that I'm not a baby.'

'Fern,' said Beth, taking her shoulder.

'*Oh my God*,' said Fern, and shrugged her off with a violent movement. 'Just leave me alone. You are honestly *crazy*? God. Get a life.'

* * *

My mother is an angel of lipstick and paintbrush cleaner, Fern had written in a school essay only the year before.

* * *

The hospital was on its last legs. Mops in buckets and the odd stepladder stood propped in corridors, taped-off areas appearing with no explanation, and the stains on the sections of paint – rust, parchment, drifts of white – could have been anything: pus; mould spores; infccted blood. Yet, to Beth, St Peter's was becoming a home-from-home. She made her way to the psychology department, jittery with unexpected excitement in all her anxiety. There was a patient in the waiting room who looked up when Dr Bywater arrived, following her with his eyes.

'How have you been this week?' asked Dr Bywater.

'Uh ... Not so good,' Beth said brightly. Her face possessed an unslept wanness. She looked up at Dr Bywater, with her inscrutability.

Beth's breathing slowed. The air seemed more relaxed, the time slower, the atmosphere like a bath or bed before sleep in the restorative tranquillity it afforded. Dr Bywater talked in her level tones about abandonment schemas and contradictory evidence, her measured concern somehow supremely feminine.

'Remember, Fern will have been going through what Freud called the latency stage, an independent age. And your painful early experiences will predispose you to anxiety about this. They set off these automatic negative thoughts.'

'Oh,' said Beth. 'I see.'

'Let's look at the fact that you're a kind, selfless parent. That you have a long-term relationship,' said Dr Bywater after a while.

Beth took this in, then nodded. 'I ... But I feel my roles – artist, mother – are going.'

'How about your role as a wife?'

Beth cringed. 'Oh God. I don't think of that as a role. I don't identify myself by *that*.'

'But it's important. How are things with him?'

Beth paused. 'You keep asking that. OK, maybe you were right that I should focus on this more.'

'Relationships take work.'

'I'm sure that's right, but I hate that notion,' said Beth. 'They should just *be*. Spontaneous, themselves.

Yes, there are compromises, pride swallowing, mine-field dodging, trying to avoid endless irritation – but don't you hate the idea of relationship "*work*"?'

'Secretly, yes,' said Dr Bywater.

Beth heard her with a delay. She laughed. 'You would be my friend, in real life,' she said spontaneously. She blushed.

Dr Bywater nodded slightly, and Beth thought she detected a fleeting expression of recognition in her, but she said nothing. The therapist looked at her lap, and Beth watched her hair falling over her face in slow segments. It was no longer partly held back by the clip, and she looked less demure.

'Do *you* practise all this? This "mindfulness".' Beth smiled. 'Which is not a word.'

'Of course,' Dr Bywater said.

'Always?'

'It informs the way I live. It's almost second nature after a while.'

'It makes you … wise,' said Beth, and felt embarrassed.

'It makes me calmer.' Dr Bywater tilted one eyebrow.

'Do you need calming? I can't imagine that.'

'Perhaps more than you may imagine.'

'Do you ever totally – *lose* it?' said Beth, almost laughing again at the sensation of pushing boundaries.

But Dr Bywater would tell her nothing. It seemed to Beth like a game, such ritual non-disclosure: impolite, power-imbalanced. She imagined herself able to make cracks in the surface of another, less contained therapist, but not this one.

'I suspect Fern may be in an unwise situation, if you say she is,' she said. 'Remember to trust your maternal instincts, which will be the strongest of all.'

'Oh ... you seem to understand,' said Beth, the tears that were now emerging more easily in her appointments prickling her eyelids. 'You're the only one.'

'I understand you.'

Beth breathed deeply. She couldn't catch Dr Bywater's eye.

Dr Bywater looked straight at Beth. 'So,' she said. 'Anyway, so—'

Beth glanced at the clock. 'It's time to go,' she said. 'But how are you? It feels rude not even asking how you are in a session. Or anything. You're married, right? Do *you* have children?'

Dr Bywater continued to look ahead, not changing her expression. 'It's not really relevant,' she said. She touched her neck, lightly, with her fingertips. 'This isn't about me. It's your hour, Beth.'

'I know, I know,' said Beth with an expression of mock-despair.

'Are you uncomfortable with the attention on you? Unaccustomed?'

'Well yes. But ...' Beth saw that they had gone thirteen minutes over the hour. 'I'll trick you into a revelation!' she said.

She glanced down as she stood. In the shadows under Dr Bywater's desk, there seemed to be the very high heel of a shoe lying on its side, but she was uncertain. Beth looked at the other corner of the room as though examining it, then returned her focus to the space beneath the desk until she could make it out. She was still not sure, the possible matching shoe beside it making a less determinate shape. High heels seemed entirely unlikely: she was discomfited in a way she couldn't pin down. Later, she often pictured that shadow under the desk.

No Caller ID was ringing as she approached the main hospital exit. She snatched at the phone, her heart racing. The call stopped. Sefton Park came back to Beth, and then the place she usually succeeded in compartmentalising: the nature reserve in East London.

'Mum,' she said. 'God.'

* * *

'Did you ask David?' Beth asked Sol when he came home. He had been in the House of Commons, shooting a series of political portraits in context, the change it represented from his normal work preoccupying him.

'Ask David what?' said Sol. 'What was I supposed to—'

'You know. Has he – Well, Sofia's a psychologist. So, I—'

'Huh, your therapy. This psychologist of yours.' He cleared his throat. 'David steers away from patients knowing the first thing about him. I guess that's more analysis. He said – I don't know, something anodyne. Like, yeah, she gets high patient approval. Is senior. So I guess you're lucky to have her.'

A smile spread across Beth's face, and she prevented her eyes widening.

'Good. Anything else?'

Sol shook his head. 'He was reluctant to talk about her. I got the feeling he was keeping something back, maybe, but was just being professional. It'd be Sofia who knows her. We're always beat by the time we get to breakfast. Circuit training last week.'

She nodded. She could hear Fern and a friend talking loudly on FaceTime upstairs. Sol was writing something on his phone.

Laurie arrived to stay the night, and Beth wandered over to the canal window, the *Mary-Lou* unlit. One of the neighbours from a narrowboat further towards Battlebridge Basin came past, recognisable in the dark only because of his hair in a bun, and then she saw Tamara Bywater again. Her heart gunned; she was momentarily light-headed. There was a woman out there, on the other side of the canal on the towpath, and her hair seemed, in the night, to be brown and hanging below her shoulders, her slimness and walk Dr Bywater's, and, instinctively, Beth wanted to run to her, to embrace her, because clearly now the longing to meet was mutual; but her clothes, after all, were wrong: a leather jacket over tight trousers. The woman walked up and down on the towpath opposite the house, as if in thought, and Beth began to open the window to call, but she had gone.

Then, as she had known she would sometime soon, her world increasingly seen through Tamara Bywater's imagined vision, she pulled out a pile of cuttings from their drawer in her tiny office extension looking out on to what remained of a balcony with its struggling honeysuckle; tipped them on the desk; and an old *Vogue* flopped on to the chair in all its treasured, several-copies-kept shininess, an obvious tool for masochistic prodding. She found the double-page spread. She longed for Tamara to see it.

'Elizabeth Penn's *Ghost Walks* promise to haunt us through the decades. Her finely wrought evocations of memory and desire have inspired tears and acclaim in equal measure. The Gavron's hot ticket. At the Turin, 3100 Broadway from May 21. Portrait: the artist with daughter Fern in her studio.'

The one small reproduction of an oil from the series jolted her back to a different time, a different place, to the pain of the earliest search for her mother. If it haunted others, it haunted her. She could never look for long at those paintings that had established her name.

Fern laughed straight at the camera, a toddler with a shiny monkey fringe gripping her mother's neck with both arms in a moment of semi-hysteria, the passage of rage and glee always animating her face with a rapidity that made Beth want to laugh. She was only two and a half in that photograph. Beth would have paid for a resurgence of that sweet need.

She herself looked like a slim, blessed mother with a hit show and a promise of a bigger future. She would have assumed at that point that Fern would love her always; that she would have another child; that she would be harmonious with Sol; and that she would manage not to dwell on her own mother again. She had been made up with sculpted cheeks, dark eyelids and lashes so the drama was her eyes, the light golds and browns and muddied reds of her hair that could descend into strands of fawn and mouse, styled to catch the light in a display of youth, hiding the ears, and God, she was once almost beautiful, she thought for the first time with certainty. Again, she summoned Tamara Bywater. What excuse could she manufacture to bring the magazine in? She gazed with pride and pain at herself in her early thirties, as though staring at someone else. She hadn't lost it by then, the girl-woman radiance of one's twenties merely refined by the exchange of flesh for bone, the skin glow still there for a couple more years, the slender exposed arms. She should have been only happy with their lives.

In Beth's childhood, Lizzie had borrowed *Vogue* from a woman she met at her part-time receptionist's job. What if Lizzie had been reading *Vogue* in later years, and stumbled across this glossed vision of her own daughter: mother, artist, London resident? If she had, it hadn't been enough. Even this. Nothing Beth did could impress her, or bring her to her. Nothing. She had to remember that.

She put the magazine back. Her old postcard of the Virgin Mary from the Catholic cathedral was in that drawer, kept safe yet hidden, and she dreaded seeing it, just as a little part of her wanted to glimpse it; just as she dreaded contact from *No Caller ID*, yet its absence wounded anew.

She and Sol argued, bickering before they went to bed. She expected him to cuddle her as they sat propped with the laptop and she tried to ease the clenching of her back against the bed head. He didn't. Resolutely, she talked with a semblance of normality, but the tension took time to subside.

In the eventual calm, she teased him; he rubbed her neck; she accused him of farting and made exaggerated sounds of disgust.

'Shut up now, I want to watch,' he said. 'Stop being silly.'

'Yes, *Dad*,' she said.

'I am six and a half years older than you,' he said in the monotone of a repeated phrase in her ear, then kissed it.

'God, Dad, you're ancient.'

'Watch.'

Sol was staring at the screen. Was this it? Was this now the shape of her life: this domesticity, even normality; a state she had always feared was impossible for her to attain? Recently rattled, she hoped with a superstitious fervour that it would remain this way; and yet, even now, an old drift of fantasy bobbed through the reality, almost every reverie charged with some non-specific glow of romance and desire. Her mind drifted to her next session with the therapist. *'Is there a wildness in me that can't be satisfied by this?'* she asked her.

Sol shifted, and contorted his body to worry at a horn of dry skin on his foot.

She played back conversations from the therapy sessions, her responses rearranged with more wit and wisdom so that their dialogue was poised somewhere between a West End farce and a moving confessional. She devised entertaining phrases she could use the following week, clothes she could combine. The shrink clocked what she wore: of that, she was certain. Somehow, with Jack Dorian and with Dr Bywater, she instantly felt more attractive, although she found her idle fantasies about Jack had abated.

'What are you thinking about?' said Sol.

'Nothing.'

'Nothing again?'

'Yes.'

'Well, honey. Nothing looks pretty interesting.'

NINE

Beth woke early on Tuesday morning. She planned her clothes for the therapist.

'Dad!' said Fern. Sol had hurried back to the house in his gym clothes to see her before she left.

'Just caught you, babycakes,' he said, and he pretended to swing her in the air as he had done when she was smaller, staggering and making her giggle. Beth smiled. Dr Bywater, who was increasingly residing in her head, was somehow watching this endearing family scene.

'You've nearly given yourself a heart attack to get back in time?' said Fern.

'I'd do anything for my favourite daughter in the world,' he said, as he often did.

'Your only daughter, numpty face.'

'And so? You'd still be my favourite if I had a thousand daughters.'

Beth, watching, remembered other moments between them over the years.

'I'll keep them for you,' Sol had once said when Beth was combing head lice caught at school from a six-year-old Fern's hair, and Fern was crying over their wriggling destinies.

'*Where?*' she had sobbed.

'In my beard,' he had said solemnly, and picked one up.

'I would follow you to the ends of the earth to be your daddy,' he said often, and he said it again now, setting her on her feet and miming exhaustion from tossing her into the air.

'And by the way,' he said, 'I will challenge any arse-hole who mistreats you to a duel. I've got to change. I'm schvitzing like a pig.'

'Ew,' said Fern, but she still allowed his parting hug. 'Why are you so dressed?' she asked Beth.

'Am I?'

'Like, yes? For a bunch of snooty kids?'

Beth laughed. 'I've got to go. Bye, darling,' she said, making herself not lean over to kiss Fern, to hug her. She turned from her, as was required, and busied herself by making a call as she put on her coat to leave.

Fern said nothing. There was a hesitation, as though she were reflexively offering her cheek for a kiss. 'Mum …' she said, but Beth was already closing the door and, though she heard Fern, she stood on her tiptoes in the hall in indecision, then forced herself not to return.

* * *

The office at St Peter's was a world down a passage: a house of dreams in the escape from reality it created. Was this what it was like to visit a geisha, a guru? That shivering, heightened calm?

'She your girl crush?' asked Ellie on the phone, after Beth and Dr Bywater had chatted a little at the end of a session, a sense of affinity colouring the formality.

'Ahaha.'

And at the next session, there was no sign at all of anything that could be construed as approval. Dr Bywater closed the session on time; she was gracious, understated, professional.

'Forget what I told you about the shrink,' Beth said to Ellie, cringing. 'I'm just a fuckwit.'

Lizzie's face came to her, uncharmed. The shame of hubris. Again and again. A ball in her throat. The old rejection. She fought it. Where was *No Caller ID*?

* * *

'David!' Beth said, drawing in a sharp breath that made her say his name in a croak when she saw David Aarons with Sol in their gym clothes.

'My patient cancelled,' he said, kissing her and pouring her tea.

'A proper beard!' said Beth. 'Makes you look like a shrink.'

'Oh. Yeah. Honey,' said Sol. 'What was it you wanted to ask David? About Dr whatshername. Darn coffee's two shots. Bowater.'

'Bywater,' said Beth. Blood ran up her neck.

David's face stiffened. 'Sol asked me about this. There's not much I can say.'

'There must be *something* you can tell me! Sofia must mention her? It's maddening to know nothing about the person in front of you. I'm so curious now.'

'Do you know about transference?' said David, then looked up at her with an awkward smile.

'Kind of,' said Beth. The blush returned. She scrabbled for her phone.

'It's about projection,' he said. 'Well handled, it's a useful tool, but—'

'*The redirection of feelings and desires, and especially of those unconsciously retained from childhood, towards a new object ...*' she read out loud.

'Bet, you don't need to be reading a Wiki stub to a senior analyst,' said Sol, and Beth started to laugh.

'Sorry!' she said. 'And what about countertransference?'

David paused.

'So do you get the hots for your patients, Dr Aarons?' Beth swept on in a kamikaze manner, embarrassment fuelling daring. 'One of those actresses I'm suspecting come to you? A stray Hampstead cougar?'

'Bet!' said Sol, but there was laughter in his voice. 'Only you.'

'Countertransference is a response to transference,' said David.

'Yes, but *sometimes* it must not be, right?'

'Yes, and then the therapist must exercise control, consult their supervisor. Or cause great damage. And probably get themselves struck off.' The taciturn David glanced at her.

Beth opened her mouth. 'I— She's nice,' she said in a small voice. 'We seem to get on really well. She's—'

'The therapeutic relationship is vital,' said David in the serious tone he always used when talking about work, 'but she's meant to *challenge* you. Make things uncomfortable for you at times.'

'Oh yes, she does that too,' said Beth, but her voice was light. 'Sofia knows her well?' she blurted.

David hesitated. '"Colleagues' responses are not always the same as patients'," he says enigmatically. And with that,' he said, 'the analyst now maintains a professional silence. Boundaries.'

'You dull person,' said Beth.

'Forgive my outspoken partner in crime,' said Sol.

* * *

Facebook, Twitter, all the normal sources revealed nothing; Dr Tamara Bywater hid in essays which required further Internet searching, the bringing up of PDFs in arcane analytic language, in subscription-only abstracts of academic articles to which Beth found herself fleetingly considering subscribing. She misspelled the name a few ways, even resorting to 'Tammy', with a smile, and still there was nothing more.

Sol began to make Fern her hot chocolate.

He was more attractive as he aged, it dawned on her for the first time, his body dense with regular exercise, his thick eyebrows, the cropped hair, the coal eyes. She looked at his wide hands in the sun, each patch of pigment, knuckle formation, artery so familiar, the wedding ring frank, a statement. And indeed, those hands had been all over her, inside her, cupping themselves to the shape of her breasts, making her come. They looked big, yet could fly over a keyboard, a camera lens, a body. His nails were short, and very clean. She loved his washed smell, his American need for many showers.

Tamara Bywater would smell of face cream, womanliness.

* * *

Beth arrived early from The Dairy at the river with its hooting, gulls circling then swooping on to a spot on the water, and made quick drawings in the November cold to blast through her loss of confidence. She had only sketched, stiffly and badly, since delaying her gallerist's visit, but now some muscle memory took over. She jotted down representations of weed, the fish-tinged depths of mud and diesel, changing her habits while aware of how amateur *plein-air* painting appeared.

She had always favoured angular, menacing landscapes with a history to them, a story: a sense, perhaps, that someone would emerge; she had been drawn east to the smudged geometry of construction, light in puddles, night-blurred buildings. Her work contained some suspicion of a mystery or question, a suggestion of being watched. She so often wondered: had she herself been seen more than she realised in her own childhood? Sefton Park was so close.

It was still early. She worked steadily now through the chill, her hair a brightness against her scarf, her movements swifter as she suspended judgement for croquis drawing. She studied the buildings on the far bank of the Thames, where fingers of darkness padded between walls. A pattern of footfall bled into a corner of her consciousness.

'It's beautiful,' came a voice behind her. 'Profound.'

Beth imagined, moments later, that she had felt the swoop of that voice like the breath of a pigeon, its hot-feathered suddenness pressed against her ear. The reality that Dr Tamara Bywater was out there in a raincoat took a few moments to process.

'I always wanted to see your work up close,' she said. She gave the radiant smile.

'Oh,' said Beth coolly, despite her shaken pulse, 'this is only a preparatory sketch.'

'But you are working again.'

Tamara Bywater gazed, leaning over. There were traces of grey in the sheen of her parting, visible in the growing day. She seemed unreal and shockingly human beside Beth: that creature of artificial light only, who appeared to live in the hospital, forever sitting immutable on a chair, like a Nepalese living goddess.

'It has longing in it. It pulls me in.' She tilted her head.

'Are you allowed to see me out here?' Beth asked playfully, for something to say.

Dr Bywater's expression closed off. 'I have to get back to work,' she said. 'I saw you as I passed.'

'Of course,' Beth said hastily. 'Yes. See you later.'

* * *

Beth took the lift, with its usual drama of wheel-chairs, sighs and exaggerated wall-pinning, and emerged at the fourth floor, St Paul's visible from the north windows before the visitor was swallowed by Psychology Outpatients' inner corridors. The psychologists, almost uniformly drab, came to the waiting room to fetch their patients.

Dr Bywater appeared. Beth saw that a colleague in the waiting room was aware of her, his body language betraying a nervous alertness. He took a few steps back and forth, a pile of papers in his hands and his head stiffly averted, until she finally addressed him, and his Adam's apple bobbed. Beth watched in amusement. What was it about her? Her strange potency was not about her looks. What quality did she possess? What laying of peace, or hope?

Beth rested her head against the squeaking plastic chair in Dr Bywater's office, letting her breath out.

Dr Bywater paused. 'Have you done your worksheets, data diary? This week.'

Beth looked blank. 'No,' she said. 'I'm sorry. Haven't done my homework.'

Dr Bywater gave her sudden smile.

'CBT has its limitations,' she said in formal tones. 'I need to use more psychodynamic therapy to address the source of your cognitive issues. At least we have more than the minimum six sessions.'

Beth caught her eye, a clashing flash of pupils. Her face flared.

'How is the situation with Fern?'

'Fern ... Fern seems almost to hate me sometimes,' said Beth, and the night came to her with its drift of images: Snapchat, hurriedly hidden; and suddenly there had been another message from Aranxto. Aranxto? Had she actually seen that? The picture dripped into sleep, and Beth had woken in the greys and duns that crept in from beneath the blinds to the lone cries of waterbirds, and Sol heard her, and rubbed her back until his hand flopped.

'And Sol?' said Dr Bywater. 'How is the situation with him?'

'Mixed.'

'It often helps to look back at what brought us together. Tell me about meeting Sol. What was it about that early love that still bonds you?'

'Oh ...' said Beth, and she found she was smiling. 'Well, we met because he came into a café I was in. Think of the chance of that. I was working in this artists' colony, the first time I'd been to America, and into this small folksy café in New Hampshire walked Solomon, in the middle of a job, and I had this weird, inexplicable thought: *There he is.* I can't explain that.'

'A sense of recognition.'

'Yes, as though I knew him. He looked at me, and he hesitated slightly – I can still see exactly that look – and I thought, We're trying to find a reason to talk to each other. Anyway, so—' Beth glanced at the clock.

'We have a bit more time. Listen,' said Dr Bywater, her expression serious. 'I didn't know how to remind you ... but ... but you are scheduled only for another two sessions. I'm sorry.'

'*What?*' said Beth abruptly. 'I really can't stop now.'

Dr Bywater hesitated. 'I would be happy to continue seeing you. Let me get back to you on this. How is your work going generally?'

'Better. At least I've started again. But not good. Pretty lacking, really.'

'You are holding back, aren't you? Like here. You're afraid of what you might find. In both places.'

'Oh.'

'Loosen up. You're hiding something from yourself. Paint quickly. See what happens.'

Beth pictured her canvases. She lowered her head. 'You are amazing to me,' she said. 'So brilliant, experienced. I need to continue. But I always want to ask you about *you*.'

'It's generally better if the therapist doesn't talk about their personal life.'

'Yes, Miss.'

'Let's just stay with your feelings,' she said. 'This is all a defence. What are you experiencing? Right now.'

A desire for you to love me, Beth wanted to say, and she was shocked at herself. She bit her lip, then dismissed it. She began to talk instead about her mother, as Dr Bywater seemed to require.

'Children find it unbearable to contemplate that a parent might be that negligent or flawed so they internalise it, and assume there must be something wrong with *them*,' said Dr Bywater. 'But it isn't true. It's all right. It's all right, Beth. You're safe now.'

Beth gazed at the clock. She suddenly remembered being a girl and missing her mother so badly that at a certain point she wanted to curl into a ball and give up.

'And you can comfort the child you were, integrate her with the adult that you are – this impressive adult.'

'Thank you,' said Beth. 'But I'm afraid I'm not impressive. Some of my friends are much more successful than me.'

'Well, that also shows you're successful. It's a matter of perspective. Name one.'

Beth shrugged. 'Aranxto,' she said.

Dr Bywater paused. Her eyes widened, just slightly. 'Aranxto?'

'Yes.' Beth smiled at the thought of the camp and once self-doubting Aranxto she had always known now inspiring this level of recognition as he commanded millions for his self-exposing shock-pieces. 'The mad show-off!'

Dr Bywater regathered her expression. It was the first time Beth had seen her betray her own emotions, and it bothered her for reasons she couldn't fathom.

'Listen. What I was going to say was – you could see someone privately.'

'Can I see you?'

Dr Bywater hesitated. 'Only if you approach me. I can't suggest myself. You'll find plenty of names via the website of the British Psychological—'

Beth interrupted her. 'I'm not going to see anyone else. I'll find you.'

Dr Bywater nodded.

'I can help you. This works,' she said levelly. She paused. 'How I react to you will be an indication of how others respond to you in the outside world.' She held her gaze, calmly. 'Do you find people are responsive to you? You can make a connection with people?'

'I suppose.' Beth shrugged. 'You mean communicate with people? I'm not really Aspergery. I have friends. I, we – relate to each other. If you like.' She shrugged again, like a nervous twitch.

'You bring a lot of charm into these sessions,' Dr Bywater said, the edges of her mouth tilting into a suggestion of a smile.

'Do I?' said Beth hastily.

'Perhaps you had to. It developed in reaction to what happened.'

'Oh. I see … Yes …' said Beth.

'You're blushing, Beth. You bring charm, whatever the reasons.'

Dr Bywater looked directly at her. In that moment, Beth had the uncanny sense she was being flirted with.

Dr Bywater blinked, as though clearing her vision, and tilted her head. 'We must work now,' she said, sounding distracted.

'Look at the time!'

Dr Bywater smiled, a small dimple appearing on one cheek, but she didn't look up. Then she fixed her gaze on Beth, and Beth felt framed by the absolute focus. It dawned on her then, in words: what she had known for some time, and what was the biggest cliché of all: she had a crush on her therapist. And her therapist was female. She wanted to laugh and, somewhat to her surprise, the idea brought her neither shock nor embarrassment, but an odd kind of happiness. She could even picture telling Ellie, mocking the stereotype that she was. Hadn't Ellie herself already realised this?

Dr Bywater stood and fetched her diary. As she moved, her hand knocked against the mouse on her desk at the side of the room, and her computer monitor cleared to reveal her face, the entire screen filled with a cropped monochrome portrait of the NHS clinician. Beth drew in her breath. Dr Tamara Bywater lay on a rug or a fur, hair spread in an abandoned fan around her, her cheekbone moulded in shadow, her mouth a play of curves. She looked glazed, or post-orgasmic, the intimacy of her expression absolute. Beth stared. Dr Bywater glanced at her then turned.

'Oh Lord!' She snatched the mouse, but the screen only brightened. She bent over it, the cursor careering as she tried to make the image disappear. 'Beth, don't look. Please.'

'You look beautiful. I've never seen you like—'

'My husband … It was his birthday request. They were *not* for your eyes.'

'There are more?' Beth said, and laughed.

'Beth! Really, I apologise.'

'No. Absolutely. No need, no need! It's … I like it. You look – you look so beautiful.'

Dr Bywater was flushed as she got rid of the image. 'I'm sorry,' she said eventually.

Footsteps sounded along the passage, the department otherwise silent.

'We have to be quiet or I'll be in trouble. Clinical appointments don't go on this late,' she said. The footsteps came closer. 'The tread of Dr Penrose,' she murmured, raising one eyebrow.

She took in a breath. 'We must end now. I'm going to show you another way out,' she said, hurrying from the room, and they walked together, colluding without speech as they sped effortlessly in a different direction from the waiting room, along other corridors, lights streaming past as though they were on a runway at night, only the two of them, a sole head-bowed cleaner, those heaving double doors, strings of lights, until they reached the staircase and fire escape.

'Thank you,' said Beth. 'So very much.'

She ran, raced down the stairs, so lightly, so smoothly, the stairwell her own white-lit kingdom, and she emerged into almost fallen darkness, took gulps of air and laughed. Inhaling the sharpness of air stained with winter stirred longing somewhere deep and old in her, summoning youth, or the wild excitement of early romance. She talked to Tamara Bywater in her head as she walked along the riverbank, branches thrusting into an inked sky, and they walked as one, huddled, talking, talking. It was always that cold wet scent of early winter, exhilaration tinged with faint unease, that she associated with a sense of having crossed a boundary.

TEN

It was unseasonably cold by the time Beth alighted from the bus where the goths were already gathering, and descended the bridge steps on to the towpath. The sight of the pub-goers was cheering, their presence an assurance that Little Canal Street was still part of a strange no-man's-land, semi-sealed from North London obsessions: schools and tutors, side returns and media careers; yet lacking the financial focus of central London or the City, the incestuous jostling of artists to the east. It was neither known nor popular. She could be herself here, unshackled by expectation.

She felt the greater chill rising from the canal in the greys of the evening, breathing in a choke of diesel as a boat with a faulty engine chugged by. Two bicycles raced past, and geese cried from the water.

She collected Fern from her Year Eight dance rehearsal, and immediately had the instinct that she had just arrived back at school. Fern's cheek was air-cool when she kissed her; she flinched from contact, and the same subtle smell had reappeared.

'Did you—' she said, then stopped herself until later. *Where were you that night?* she wanted to ask, again.

Fern walked ahead, her gait embellished with slight arm-swinging and foot-kicking that denoted a casual, even carefree, attitude, but which only compounded suspicions.

'See you at home,' Beth said to Fern's back, causing a faint break of surprise in her walk.

Later, in Fern's bedroom, Beth began to rub her daughter's scalp with an expectation of resistance, pathetically grateful for servitude. She was so in love with the dirty hair and cappuccino freckles, the smell of her cheeks like a drug to be imbibed in hidden hits. Tentatively, she began to ask questions about Fern's day.

Fern pressed her nose against her Kindle to turn the page. Her shoulders tensed. She answered her mother in icy little shoots of breath between silences. 'Legitimately – enough,' she said.

Beth fell silent.

Fern's phone sounded from her bed with a message. She glanced at it then pushed it quickly under her duvet.

'Why did you stop me?'

Beth paused. 'What?'

'Why?' said Fern. Her face was flooded the scarlet that had always heralded tears when younger.

A rumble of panic vibrated somewhere in Beth's guts.

Your self-punishing introject is very strong, came Dr Bywater's voice. *Are you clinging to guilt because it feels safer?*

'What are you talking about, darling?'

Fern was silent.

'Oh, I don't want this,' said Beth. 'I hate this. What has happened? Let's just *talk* about everything. Please.'

But Fern had clamped down, as untouchable as a junior ice skater in a children's comic. Beth's sweet child was a sharp little knife, her back and shoulders willing her mother away with disgust. Beth wiped a tear, unseen, and left the room quietly. She recalled the moment of Fern's birth, the messy disgorgement followed by the world tilting. The jolt of love when she looked into those blurred eyes, the tiny petal of a mouth.

* * *

How could Lizzie Penn – any mother – have not felt the same? And yet Beth knew with all certainty that she had once been loved by her mother. The mother who had walked with her and read to her and taken her to plays the few times she could afford it. She had met a new man, but was that all of it?

* * *

Dr Bywater was late for their session. Beth sat speculating about where she lived, and who the husband was. He was a tall, somewhat harassed man, an architect in an unstructured linen suit over a T-shirt, she decided. Dr Bywater was still not there. What if she knew through advanced software that her patient had been googling her, and she now viewed her as a stalker?

Dr Bywater sped, straight-backed, from the other direction into the waiting room and then to the receptionists' booth. She was carrying a large black mock-croc bag, and Beth was certain, somehow, that she seen that bag before, but surely never on her. A crowded scene came to her, a street or square. Dr Bywater was in a huddle with the receptionists, and whatever she said was making them twitter with gasps of pretend shock. Her own laugh, different from any Beth had ever heard from her, rang out after them.

'Oh, Beth! Am I that late?' Dr Bywater turned abruptly, put her hand out and touched Beth's shoulder. Beth shivered involuntarily. Dr Bywater gave her a flash of her smile, a glimpse of something more vibrant than the consoling presence Beth was used to.

She walked a little ahead down the corridors, opening the double doors. Her calves were fine and elongated, and she walked as though she were beautiful, with an easy, upright glide.

Beth talked, and Dr Bywater held Beth's gaze and smiled, a trapeze of a smile, suspending her. Beth was certain at that moment that the affinity between them was so overt, she relaxed. It was there to play with. She began to make Dr Bywater laugh.

She tried to focus. She shifted in her seat. 'But let's talk about something other than my boring psyche for a while,' she said.

'Beth, I would *love* to talk to you about other things. You brighten my day – but you are here for therapy.'

Beth suppressed a smile. 'How can a fuck-up like me brighten your day?'

'You do,' she said, looking down with a shake of her head. 'You – you said,' she said swiftly, 'you told me that after all that searching, you did see your mother?'

Beth took a breath. The scene returned to her with sickening lucidity. 'Yes,' she said, and she was back at TJ Hughes' department store, at Christmas, in Liverpool.

* * *

After so many imaginary sightings, there in TJ's, when Beth was almost fourteen, she had seen her mother. There she was, as she appeared to her most weeks, and for Beth there was the fear that, despite the shock of familiarity, this couldn't be her, and she would soon, as ever, reveal herself to be a woman in the crowd with an imagined mother's face.

Beth caught her breath. A tremendous surge of relief rose in her chest, and then she was running, running to her, clawing at her. 'Mummy, Mummy,

Mummy,' she cried, though she had never called her that before. She threw herself at her, butting her, clinging hard so that Lizzie's face twisted in pain before she knew what was happening. Snot, saliva, tears ran down Beth's face; she had to clasp her mother forcibly, keep her. The nightmare fell away, like a torrent of water. She clenched her arm. She clung to the cloth of her coat so abruptly that Lizzie swayed a little.

'Bethy!' shouted her father.

A hand was on her shoulder.

'No!' screamed Beth. People had cleared a circle around them, and were watching, separate bubbles of exclamation rising to her ears. She clung to Lizzie, her mother's tears meeting her own as she kissed Beth's head and said, 'No, Bethy, calmly, Bethy.'

'Come home,' said Gordon to Beth, and he sounded angrier than she had ever heard him. He took her hand.

Lizzie looked shocked, wiping her eyes with her sleeve.

'Mum!' said Beth.

'Let me talk to her,' said Lizzie, and by this time, there was a store guard between them, asking questions and telling them to be quiet.

'Mum!' screamed Beth, with such force that, even in the uproar, people jumped and made sounds of disapproval, and in that moment of confusion, her father dragged her away.

'Bethy! Bethy! Gordon!' called Lizzie, but the guard was beside her, and her voice was weak through the crowd. 'Come back,' she shouted.

'You—' shouted Gordon. 'If you've gone, stay away.'

Lizzie hesitated. She shook her head. Tears were slanting down her cheeks, distorting her features into something Beth had never seen before. She waited for her mother to run to her.

Lizzie stood there, the tears red-pocketing her face, hesitated again on one foot, the people around watching her, and still she stood there.

* * *

'She didn't come after me,' Beth said. 'That was the last time I talked to her during my childhood.'

'Oh, God,' said Dr Bywater, and as Beth looked up, she could see, to her surprise, a shininess to her eyes in the low light.

They were silent. Beth's breathing was shallow. She sat with her head bowed.

'You know, don't you,' said Dr Bywater, 'that whatever profound damage caused this behaviour, she was at fault. Not you. *None of this was your fault.*'

'You don't understand.'

'Don't I? Remember that self-punishing introject of yours. It seems to me, there is nothing terrible that you ever did to her,' she said. 'Is there?'

'Yes,' Beth said. A rush of shame hit her, all these years later.

She waited.

'Do you want to talk about it?'

'No.'

'So,' said Dr Bywater gently. 'Can you describe what it was like without her?'

'Well.' Beth gazed at the ceiling. 'Dad was good to me. He is a kind, lovely man. But we couldn't *talk*. Excruciating near-silence.' The wobble of last river light through the blinds tightened into bright focus. 'It's very very odd, really, being female but brought up without a woman.'

'Poor child,' said Dr Bywater unexpectedly.

Beth fixed her gaze at a spot on the wall. She blinked.

'Beth,' said Dr Bywater. She stretched a hand briefly towards her arm, hovered over it, then pulled back.

Beth put her face into her hands, and cried. She wanted, so much, for the therapist to hold her, but instead she made a sympathetic sound and sat very still.

'You experienced a huge loss of the idealised parent,' said Dr Bywater. 'So you punish yourself.' A hurry of seagulls momentarily drowned her little wartime RADA voice. 'But perhaps punishing yourself feels safer than loss of control. Protects you from the worse pain beneath it, lends a sense of agency. These are more defences you use.'

'What are yours?' said Beth, looking up, her face wet.

'I think it will be a long time before I can tell you that,' she said with a dimpled flash of a smile. She hesitated.

'Oh?'

Dr Bywater looked down; she was silent. 'Listen,' she said. The sounds of professionals speaking passed, muted, behind the consulting-room door. She glanced to one side. 'Sometimes I wish – I think, I wish ...' she said in a rush. She stopped. She opened her hands. 'When you leave the office, I often think – I wish I could be her friend.'

Beth swallowed. 'Well, can't you?' Her voice emerged quietly.

'I shouldn't even be *talking* about this to you,' said Dr Bywater, and a pained expression passed over her face. It made her look older, a touch of ugliness visible in the moment she screwed up her features. 'I have to be wary of an enactment.'

'An enactment? When we finish therapy, then we can be friends!' Beth said brightly, but it sounded simplistic.

Dr Bywater shook her head, smiling slightly. 'My governing body ... There are rules about that. You have to wait at least two years and, even then, it's not advisable. In the meantime, I've answered your email, suggesting an appointment time.'

'Oh! Thank you so much. I'm so grateful. It's – really helping,' said Beth self-consciously. 'It's time,' she said, and rose.

Dr Bywater's hair fell forward on her face as she stood up after her and leaned towards her, reassuringly. Beth suddenly pictured herself kissing her, and jolted; almost hugged her instead, pulled herself back, blushed, expressed heartfelt thanks, barely able to look at her, and left.

* * *

As soon as she was outside, Beth positioned herself where the hospital was hidden, and looked at her phone. Tamara Bywater's email was formal. She had a Kennington postcode. Kennington was interesting and unexpected. It brought the thrill of illicit knowledge; the trophies of the amateur hunter.

The river was tumbling grey with black, with a watchfulness to the air, a stray bird sound pulsing vibrato from the trees on the bank. Beth walked on, then ran over the bridge still smiling, the river and sky anointed for her, the world of others humdrum, knowing as she now did this soaring well-being, this power.

* * *

'She wants to be my *friend* ...' Beth murmured into Ellie's voicemail. 'Call me back.'

'So I seem,' she said, rashly calling Aranxto, 'to have developed a ridiculous schoolgirl crush on my therapist.'

He barked in delight. 'I thought the shrink was a chick?'

'She is.'

He let out a bellow of laughter.

'A chick with a dick?'

'*No.*'

'Since when have you been a muff muncher, babe?'

'I know. I know. I'm supposed to have this thing called transference. But it's a proper fascination. I can barely make a decision without her. God, Aranxto, it's actually a bit like being *in love*! You do *not* fucking tell anyone!'

Aranxto giggled, followed by Beth.

'Don't think you're much of a lezzer, Bethy,' he said.

'Yeah, yeah. I know. And she isn't either. Does it matter, you gay dinosaur? Given we're all meant to be *flexible* now? There's even a LGBT plus whatever club at Fern's school.'

'Imagine that in our time. I could have got it off with Rob Smith in the gym showers after all. Instead of being beaten up as a poof. Happy days.'

'Yes, Aranxto. So we're back on to you, are we?'

'When are we ever not, my dear? When am I to meet your girlfriend?'

'Ha ha. Just imagine. Oh my God.'

***

Fern walked straight out of the room as soon as Beth arrived home. She tried to clear the table.

'Honey.' Sol caught her expression. 'How she's being is really hurtful, right?'

Beth steadied her breathing. 'I try not to let it. But … what am I doing wrong?'

'Nothing, Bet. Come here.' They hugged. She drew in the clean, showered smell of him.

'I always feared maybe I can't mother because of – well, I don't have a role model, do I?'

'For sure. But you could not have been a more loving mother to her.'

She opened her mouth. She swallowed a tightness in her throat. 'I don't know.'

'The most caring, considerate, affectionate mother. You glow with that love for her, Bet. And fun as well. She's lucky to have been born your daughter.'

Beth exhaled, and pressed her eyes against his shoulder. 'Thank you. That is kind of you to say.'

'Just true.'

She nibbled his shirt. She kissed him. 'Then what's changed? Gone wrong?'

He shook his head. 'Her age.'

'She's very young for this. I can suddenly do *nothing* right. Usually fifteen-ish when they reject you. Sixteen.'

Sol was silent.

'Sol? I know you. The way you breathed in through your nose.'

He made a small sound, as though to speak.

'What?' said Beth.

'Detective Penn misses nothing? Presently ... just now ... you are kind of distracted,' he said.

'*Am* I?' she said, and she loosened herself. 'What do you mean?' She turned from him.

'It's as though your mind's elsewhere. You don't sleep, but then you seem ... yes, distracted. But happier, right?'

'I don't know ... I'm really feeling much, much better somehow.'

'More than that, honey. Hyped.'

'Really?' Beth laughed slightly, with a hectic flavour, so she buried her head in his neck.

They hugged for a while, and then he took out his phone and put his glasses on his head as he wrote.

'What are you *writing*?' she said.

He put his phone away.

***

Searing excitement over Dr Bywater was alternated with the familiar nagging question over whether Lizzie would call her again.

Almost two decades after Beth had last seen her mother at the department store in Liverpool, but before she had given birth to Fern, Lizzie had written to her via her gallery, requesting to see her.

'I'm pretty much thinking you should do this,' Sol had said.

'*What?*' said Beth.

Sol, who had lived with her then for three years, lifted her hair and kissed her head. 'Maybe just one chance? I suspect mental health problems ...' he said gently.

Beth took a sharp breath. 'How do you know?'

'It's kind of clear, isn't it? Given her behaviour. Likely deep depression?'

'When do you mean?'

'Oh, from the get-go.'

Beth stood there, and the world began to change. 'Oh, God.' He carried on holding her. 'I never thought about it,' she said.

Three months later, she waited for her mother to arrive at the Gavron gallery.

'She would be so fucking proud,' said Sol, having finally persuaded Beth to respond to Lizzie's request by inviting her to the private view for her first solo exhibition.

'You *think?*' said Beth, raising her eyes.

'I do think. With no proof, I grant. Hey, Bet, we can hide her there. Spike her drink if it comes to that. She'll be one among a whole bunch of people.'

Her first solo exhibition was, at some level, the moment she had worked towards all her life. She barely felt it: it was a scene that came back to her later, as though she stood outside herself as a camera, looking down from the light tracks on the ceiling, or through the window on to a swirl that seemed a luminous blue or ultraviolet to her afterwards, a substance that she swam through, yet the only sensation she remembered was the waiting: an ever-stretching thread of anticipation that grew thin and then wore out, and finally snapped. Her other memories of the night were based on the gallery's photographs, so she became the person in them, dressed and celebrated and surrounded by her work, professionals, partner, friends, and not her mother. Once again, Lizzie wasn't there.

She had met a new man that week, according to Beth's brother.

'That's it,' said Beth, the only time she could speak about it.

'That's it for sure,' said Sol, nodding. 'I'm so damn sorry.'

Eleven

It was almost time to cross London to find Dr Bywater for Beth's first private session. She finished some work. She was now, at last, working, spasmodically, haphazardly. Tamara Bywater had given her that impetus. In painting *alla prima* in her larger studio, and making her hand move regardless of the result, she had started to inch herself through a barrier, and she had just begun to capture something that had eluded her in all her cosy, despairing procrastination. The banks hulked, forming from the river's contents: fungal growths, slums, coal-slimed like the alleys of home had been, and there was death in all except the slim shake of growing light, travelling to the sea, the unknown.

The face – so suddenly, like an apparition – looking out over Sefton Park.

* * *

Beth walked briskly from the Tube through the dying November afternoon, and got there just on the hour. Cleaver Square, with its age and cramped elegance, was a surprise: different from its north-of-the-river equivalents, more squat and dark-bricked, so she caught just the tiniest flavour of parts of Liverpool as she came off the square to the little street where Dr Tamara Bywater lived, in which the flat-fronted Georgian houses were dollish versions of the great Bloomsbury terraces she sometimes walked by. Here was stunted grandeur, a London still draped in gas lamp, cobble, horse.

She was about to see where she lived, for the first time. Number 13 was at the end of a row, with hellebore-filled window boxes and a front door painted a phthalo green that contrasted with the sooted brown of the bricks. Beth walked the few steps up to it to ring the bell and half-believed that no one would be there. She looked down at the area, where she thought she glimpsed movement behind the bars.

She waited. Her heart seemed to thump loudly. This felt like all she wanted: to be waiting, dressed up, exquisitely alert, about to see Tamara Bywater.

It was four on a Friday. The husband, giver of the wedding ring, whoever he was, would be out. The children – she was bound to have children; she would be a lovely mother: the sweetest, most comforting soulmate – might be inside, or imminently returning from school; or older, possibly. They must adore her.

'Beth,' said Dr Bywater, opening the door, and her expression was less guarded than in the clinical context of St Peter's. The smile enhanced the hint of off-centredness to her eyes.

She looked different. For a moment, Beth wondered whether she had got the wrong day, and Dr Bywater wasn't working. She was dressed more vividly than Beth had ever seen her in the hospital, yet in a more relaxed fashion, in slim trousers, and a patterned top, a necklace that was bolder than the silver jewellery of St Peter's, and her hair had an emphatic bounce to its layers. She was wearing more make-up than Beth had ever noticed on her.

'Might some sectioned lunatic at St Peter's pull you to his stretcher at the incitement of rouge?' Beth said, amusing herself, trying to stop herself saying it, but forging ahead and then blushing, though Dr Bywater laughed.

'Come through,' she said, and she guided Beth along a narrow hallway covered in a storm of paintings that Beth longed to study, rooms of miniature Georgian proportions in saturated colours leading off it: a cube of a sitting room in apple green with a pink lamp, an old French chandelier, a vast foxed mirror, again French in appearance; a portrait that Beth realised, with a start of recognition after passing, was of Tamara Bywater herself. She paused, tempted to stretch her body back to look at it.

'It's – well, it's a beautiful house. So much interesting stuff. All this colour! Not what I thought ...'

130

Dr Bywater's mouth twitched. 'Yes, I probably appear as though I should live in a library. Or a health centre.'

'I didn't mean that!'

She was led down a staircase that was unusually narrow for London, like a ship's to its galley, its walls silver, the metallic paint coating uneven plaster that glowed through the stairwell. Dr Bywater turned at the bottom, and raised one eyebrow, amusement still hovering over her mouth.

This was not what Beth had anticipated at all, only the house's smallness, its touches of economy, predicted. She had thought it would be more restrained and sensible, more ecru and white, with New Age touches, the odd bamboo object – the Mexican thingamabobs of *Lolita*. Not these convulsions of pigment, this throb of colour and cranny off a South London square. Though it spread further back and was less tall, it resembled her own house in its confusion of angles and its small rooms, a fact that was both disconcerting and pleasing, but the colours, Beth admitted with a pang of inadequacy, were better, bolder. An unexpected artistic eye was behind it.

They walked through a kitchen towards the back of the stunted warren, a run of quarry tiles leading past a narrow paved garden, the angle of the roof making her move to one side.

* * *

The consulting room was in a studio at the back: its pitched roof casting shadows, its one window looking out on a bay tree in the garden. Again, there was pigment that glowed, a gloom-dancing shade in which blue-grey-lavender variously emerged. Beth averted her gaze from the embarrassing presence of a couch along the back wall, but Dr Bywater gestured to her to sit opposite her in a red bentwood armchair, and lamps pooled about the room as they did at St Peter's, and there were pictures in frames, indistinguishable shapes in a row above her. Dr Bywater sat in front of Beth in a matching armchair in green.

'How are you?' asked her new persona in new clothes in the same run of a voice, but with a more conversational tone to it. She stretched back in her chair. She looked at Beth and smiled, held her eye, then she suddenly toppled into laughter, without excuse, and Beth laughed too. Every muscle in her seemed to flex to stand to embrace her, but she sat further back.

Dr Bywater touched her neck. Her nails were now burgundy, and she wore two large rings on her right hand.

Beth spoke to her for some time, and gradually her life seemingly ordered. The atmosphere of the room was more fluid than it had ever been in a therapy session: almost drowsy, but with that same calm shot through with the tightest wire of alertness, the combination reminiscent to Beth of something else, of those exquisitely paced moments before orgasm, that drop into profound relaxation.

They were back on to her mother. 'Where is she, now?' said Tamara Bywater.

'She lives outside Liverpool. She returned there. My father doesn't see her. We never even mention her, to save his feelings.' She twisted her hair. She tried to breathe steadily. 'My brother Bill won't have anything to do with her. She only tried twice, then left him alone. He doesn't think she deserves it.'

Dr Bywater nodded. 'A fairly standard male response. Have you seen her since?'

Beth felt her mouth loosen.

For some years after Lizzie had failed to turn up to Beth's opening, Beth could almost dismiss her; giving up meant a new sense of freedom, enhanced by Sol's ferocious protection. In those years before Fern was born, it was as though Lizzie Penn was buried in an open grave: her eyes alert, but she couldn't climb out to get her.

Only Aranxto, who enjoyed claiming that Mrs Penn was 'hot' or 'cool' or, infinitely worse, 'lonely': only Aranxto ever intermittently implied culpability. Sol, Ellie, Bill and Gordon Penn, the few who knew about her mother, were all unequivocal in their assertion that Beth should not see her. Yet while pregnant, Beth had had a premonition, the first for several years, that Lizzie would return.

'There is more?' said Dr Bywater.

Beth looked down. She nodded.

'I think I can help you,' said Dr Bywater. The rain of her voice in the deepening darkness. She glanced down at her lap. Her mouth twisted a little. 'I don't generally speak to anyone else like this,' she said rapidly. 'To my clients, I mean. It's different with you.'

'Is it?' Beth sat very still.

'Yes, and it happens spontaneously, but it worries me. There are boundaries to observe. You understand that?'

'Yes. Sol's analyst friend David Aarons bangs on about them.'

Dr Bywater paused, expressionless. She seemed to be forcing herself to speak. 'We should explore the transference that's going on here,' she said.

'I know about that. You mean,' Beth said flippantly, stiffening to ward away a blush, 'that I think you're my mum? My dad? That I think I'm in love with you because I've confused you with some past figure?'

Dr Bywater smiled then straightened her face.

'I think there are issues of transference and countertransference,' she said.

'I'll get researching,' said Beth, steadying her breathing.

'You know – much of the efficacy of therapy rests on what goes on in this room.'

Beth gazed at the wall behind.

'The relationship between the therapist and the client,' said Dr Bywater.

Beth nodded. She couldn't catch her eye. A heat and a suppressed smile were rising through her.

'But it has to obey long-established boundaries.'

Beth's mouth stiffened.

'We bond,' said Dr Bywater.

'Do we?'

'Sometimes I think too much.'

Dr Bywater suddenly reached for her diary, a Design Museum ring-bound book, unlike the sober desk diary of St Peter's, then looked at the clock. Abruptly, Beth twisted herself round to see the time. 'It's time to go,' she said.

Dr Bywater opened the diary.

'Sometimes I'm held behind at St Peter's. Could you come an hour later instead next session?'

Oh my God, Beth murmured on the street, baring her teeth in her hand mirror to check she had nothing stuck there, and she grinned to herself, the only way to siphon off the triumph, emitting Tourette's-like exclamations, knowing but not caring that she sounded crazy. She wanted to tell someone: Ellie, the world. Because by now, she was becoming certain. Surely, surely, Dr Bywater loved her back.

* * *

At home, Fern came downstairs, Sol clasped her confidently and she succumbed, while Beth failed to break through her resistance, and fetched her hot chocolate and a biscuit. She saw the scene through Tamara Bywater's eyes: the efficient mother, the art-strewn house, the subtexts at play. Sol picked out a few notes on the piano in passing. He told Beth she was beautiful. He shouted at a builder who had ripped them off, then Skyped his mother, full of consideration. He tripped a little as he returned. He would invariably, at some point in the day, bang into a stair or stub his toe on a cupboard and curse, play a few more piano notes, frown at a camera back, announce his love for the two women in his life.

The evening progressed. Beth did some work on the *Metropolitan Mice*, cleared up, and then hesitated outside Fern's room. She knocked, brought in Fern's clean washing and talked pretend-casually, sorting clothes for her as an excuse to avert her eyes, only a show of semi-indifference now making communication possible. Fern hardly spoke at all. She herself barely dared to say goodnight, let alone to kiss her.

Later, Beth yawned as she prepared for bed. Sol reached down and stroked her tummy; she tensed it reflexively, then relaxed it, and her skin responded as he moved upwards, webs springing to life and running to her nipples, and Tamara Bywater spoke to her, leaning towards her, the Vivien Leigh voice murmuring, *I wish I could be her friend*, again, and again.

'Let's do it,' she said abruptly, and laughed, and she pushed him back on to the bed, lifted herself on to his chest, and the lights were going past along the corridor, and Tamara Bywater was having sex with her husband across the Thames, across the night streets of the city.

When Beth came, she found her eyes were wet for a few seconds, for no reason.

Sol lay flopped across her on his stomach. She stroked his head.

'My darlington. Hello,' she said.

'Why, hello,' said Sol in the voice of a Hollywood lothario.

'Good evening, fine sir,' she said, pulling a face.

'Faint heart never won fair lady.'

They started to laugh, and old jokes emerged, released by sex, a huge hectic happiness washing over her.

'Oh, my love, what has been happening to us?' said Beth, snuggling against him.

He paused minutely. 'Just come back to us.'

She opened her mouth to question and protest, but nodded into his neck instead.

'What do you mean?' she said eventually, then cursed herself.

'You know what I mean,' he said.

She drew in her breath.

'I don't know where you've gone,' he said. 'Some-place else.'

'I—'

'I do love you,' he said suddenly.

'It's the "do" that worries me,' she said after a moment, and tried to speak more, but words were rolling out of reach. He said nothing, and held her, sticking to his skin.

I wish I could be her friend, said Dr Tamara Bywater.

* * *

The following morning, there was a whiff of coolness between Beth and Sol, the tightness of his mouth and her own guarded echo creating a film of tension that kept them at a distance.

'I think you are sidetracked,' he said in a low voice, and Beth's pulse speeded.

'You – you are still saying this?' she said weakly.

'You're not engaged with me. And even with Fern sometimes. That has never happened previously. Never for one minute.'

'What? I thought I was *too* engaged with her! "Helicopter parenting". "Give her space," you said – even when she's disappearing all over the place along the canal. I can't win.'

Snapping accelerated into a round of indignation and verbal blows, Beth's heart thrumming with the sudden knowledge that they had been blown out to sea when looking elsewhere, and every old wound was there, and raw after all, and new battles had sprung to life, along with the absolute knowledge, for that fragment of time, that they would have to separate.

Sol kept his impassive gaze on her, his expression further unreadable behind beard and glasses, and whenever she was indignantly in the wrong, he reminded her of a headmaster patiently waiting for the truth to emerge.

'And what do you expect?' she said, unable to tolerate his silences. 'It's almost as though she *hates* me. She can barely tolerate me, Sol.'

'Yes. True. But, Bet. Sometimes, in some modes ... like – now, maybe – you are not necessarily making the best decisions.'

'Thanks for telling me,' she said, and her voice was trembling. 'How can I when you won't discuss the real problems with Fern? I feel alone with this. So I just have to tell the shrink.'

Sol paused. 'David has some concerns about the psychologist.'

'I thought he didn't even know her?'

'Sofia does.'

'You wanted me to go to the fucking psychologist.'

He raised his hands in the air. 'True.'

'So what are you saying to me?'

'I am reluctant to say ... But I catch Fern's glances. Her looking at you with – sadness? Her expressions once you're gone. She keeps looking at the door. She thinks you're not with her either.'

'But, Sol! Have you been listening to a word I've said? If only. It's all I want. But it's impossible! She won't let me anywhere near her.'

'But maybe it's a vicious circle. Cycle? Circle? Which is it?'

'Believe me, I *try*. She can't stand the sight of me.' Beth swallowed.

Sol walked over to the architect's easel where he looked at photographs he printed out.

'You know what is mad?' said Beth. 'That the day after these rows, I often hardly know what the real cause – subject – was.'

Sol paused, and tapped on his phone. 'Uh huh. Me too. Crazy.'

'You keep writing things on your phone after we've had disagreements. Are you texting someone?'

'No.'

'What, then.'

'Making notes for myself. Reminders.'

* * *

The following Friday, Beth went to the dry cleaner's to collect a green 1940s dress she had pounced upon in Camden Passage while doing early Christmas shopping, and she glanced at it with something approaching gratitude. The taste for vintage dresses had sprung from periods of uncertainty about her father's ability to pay for new clothes, and she had taken to mornings of searching in charity shops with pocket money and later waitressing wages. 'Antwacky', they had called her at school.

She had bought the dress through a filter of Tamara, just as she made other choices through her imagined vision. It was beautiful; it curved to a tight waist.

'Oh!' she said when she came back to the house and Sol still hadn't left for work. 'Hi, darling.'

'You coming straight to the PV from therapy tonight?' he said.

'Yes.'

'Be there on time? I don't want to hang out with those people. Your appointment's moved to later, right?'

'Yes.'

'So on the basis of something that Sofia Aarons said, David showed me something that maybe I should show you,' he said, sounding hesitant. He lifted his iPad, brought up an attachment and tapped on it.

'What is it? It's sappy she took her husband's name.'

'Darn thing won't download.'

She leaned over Sol's iPad. The document was titled 'The Slippery Slope to Boundary Violation' by Dr Robert Simon.

Beth gazed, attempting to steady her expression.

'Is this some strait-laced piece of moralising the old workhorse has dug up?' she said after a beat.

Sol looked at her. As so often, a twitch of amusement crossed his face before he said anything.

'Got to go!' she sang out. 'Gonna be late.' She leaned over and kissed him.

***

Standing outside Tamara Bywater's in her dress and high-heeled sandals, she was struck by the fraudulent disparity between her self-doubts and the world she partly inhabited, that seemingly glamorous round of openings and private views. On Dr Bywater's instructions, she struggled through gnarled tumbles of jasmine to negotiate the yard that led to the door at the back of her consulting room, leaves sticking to her hair and coat.

'Good afternoon,' said Dr Bywater as she opened the door, then immediately turned and walked to her chair. She sounded formal. Beth hesitated. There was a silence.

'You shouldn't have to be working after a day of work,' said Beth.

'It's not a problem,' said Dr Bywater.

She shook out her hair and sat precisely, a notebook on her knee, unsmiling. She took off her jacket. She wore a blouse underneath, an antique froth of ivory.

She settled into her seat with her appointments book, asked some questions and made some notes. Shame was fingering its way towards Beth. The therapist was pleasant, and unknowable. Beth tried to make Dr Bywater laugh, but it didn't work, and humiliation broke over her. She was, she was coming to realise, just like the transference-riddled fools she had found on forums who conjectured, to the point of certainty, that their therapist desired them in return.

Even David Aarons had attempted to enlighten the preening idiot that she was.

They talked about her mother's legacy, and time went on. The evenings were darker and colder as midwinter approached. There was no sign of personal engagement. Dr Bywater would also be aware of her crush, gently guiding her through it, or even, apparently, using it therapeutically. Beth wanted to bury herself under the couch.

The dialogue seemed to grind to a halt.

'Is there something – wrong?' said Beth eventually, to break the tension.

Dr Bywater said nothing. She knitted her hands together, unusually ill at ease. She appeared smaller and older.

Beth swallowed. 'I haven't been bumping into you,' she said in a gabble to lighten the mood.

A look of self-consciousness crossed Dr Bywater's face. 'I thought … if I see you painting near the hospital, I should avoid you.'

'Why?'

'Beth. I'm your therapist.' Her skin paled, quite visibly, as though she absorbed her own words for the first time. She shivered. She twisted round and took a cardigan from the back of the chair, a deep rose cashmere threaded finely with glitter, unlike anything she had worn at St Peter's. 'There are rules – boundaries – to observe.' She shook her head. She touched her neck, glancingly. Beth turned. The clock hand was edging further.

'Oh, it helps your *patient*,' said Beth. 'Just come out equipped with a straitjacket and a slug of lithium, in case your boss catches you.'

'Don't make me laugh again,' said Dr Bywater, but she didn't laugh; she stayed looking down, the nervous movements abating, but an air of melancholy hung about her. 'I want to help you *so* much. I – I – for instance, I could handle – this wrongly.'

'What?'

'This situation. I have to say something to you. I have to … This – what we have been doing in the last few weeks – isn't therapy any more. We can't carry on talking like that. I – really don't talk to any of my other patients like this. To anyone much, really.'

A smile rose inside Beth and broke out on her face. Words to Ellie formed in her mind.

'Talk to me,' said Dr Bywater. She looked distracted. 'I should really still give you the odd worksheet.'

Beth laughed. A hectic happiness lifted her. 'I know you're changing the subject,' she said. 'No you shouldn't. They're too boring.'

Beth glanced back at the clock. She cringed. She had planned to leave on time, race back from Kennington, meet Sol at Aranxto's private view, and then go to Andrew Edmunds with him, dates either a romantic novelty or an attempt to reinstate normality after a row.

Traffic was a thrum. Hooting was sharp through the winter night. As they talked, more fluently, after the hour's end, Beth only half-registered the time, denial overlaying any awareness.

It was nearly twenty-five past seven. Sol was attending on her invitation, and unwilling to be in the gallery alone, impatient with the displays of affectation at such events, especially if linked to Aranxto. Beth glanced at the clock again and moved abruptly, feeling for her bag and jacket. 'I must—' Sweat sprang up on her forehead. She slowed down the clock hands, flexing her fingers against them until time stopped.

She felt for her phone. 'I'm sorry, I just need to ...' she said.

'Of course. You must get on with your evening.'

Beth began to message, blindly.

'Your friend has a new show!' said Dr Bywater, shaking her head and speaking more animatedly. 'His work fascinates me. Not as much as yours. *Bleached*, *Ghost Walks* ... I ... Is that where you're going, looking so beautiful?'

'Yes,' said Beth. 'How did you ...?'

'I am passionate about contemporary art. You know, it's just amazing to me that you know Aranxto, and others, so well. Well, you are part of that yourself. You take it for granted, but ... Beth, you look beautiful.'

'Thank you.' Beth looked at her lap to avoid the clock. Magic would make the hands freeze.

'We have an intimacy here.' Dr Bywater's forehead was tense. 'It can be a useful work tool, but this— So I need to say again, this isn't how I should talk to patients.'

Beth's smile grew. The air was thin. She was on top of the mountain.

'Excellent,' she said.

'Beth.' Dr Bywater shook her head.

'I just have to say. I owe you so much. My sanity,' said Beth, her throat contracting. Sol had disappeared. The clock had stopped.

'You're lovely. I think sometimes I become … a bit unboundaried with you. That's all.' Dr Bywater shrugged. She raised one eyebrow, her mouth self-conscious. 'We really *do* need to explore the transference issues.'

'*A phenomenon characterised by unconscious redirection of feelings from one person to another*, Wikipedia. Transference,' said Beth in a dull drone. 'One definition of—'

'Oh, this is hopeless!' said Dr Bywater, burying her head. She lifted it. She shook her hair back. She laughed.

'Futile. Quit while you're ahead, Doctor.'

'See,' she said. 'You're seductive. You wear me down – you're so engaged, you get me talking.'

Beth hesitated. She steadied her delivery. 'Excellent,' she said again, more emphatically.

'All right,' said Dr Bywater. She widened her eyes. She flung her arms open. 'I've tried. I've tried. I've done my moral duty. Now I think I'm going to tear up every page in the rule book.'

'That rule book is pulp anyway.' Beth looked at her phone, put it back in her bag and rose.

Dr Bywater laughed. She stood up and they wavered for moments that seemed to be as slow-moving and large-grained as an old film, and there were further hesitations in dragonfly jerks, in dips and retreats, before they wrapped their arms around each other and hugged, and then they both laughed to soften the moment.

'I – I feel I must just offer you a final choice, though,' said Dr Bywater, suddenly serious. 'Either I can – pull back. Stop talking to you like this. And carry on being your therapist. But much – much more distanced. Or we can – I think I'm prepared to – we can meet outside. We can be friends. We can talk *properly*. Equally, if you'd like to—'

'We will meet!' said Beth.

Tamara Bywater hesitated. 'Are you sure?'

'I've … I feel like I've been coming to the end of the therapy, really, anyway. How weird and wonderful it would be to see you in a café, a gallery, a real-life location where normal people meet. Do you exist in these places?'

'Yes. I'm a real live person. Flaws. Weaknesses. But … You know you will have to keep this quiet. There are rules. You know, don't you?'

'OK. I know.'

'No, really.'

'Yes.'

The clock had disappeared. An excess of triumph, so heady it was hard to define, was surging through Beth. It was reminiscent of experiences from long before that she couldn't quite identify: some sensation of coming top in her class, of pleasing her tutor, or something less concrete. She felt, in that moment, exquisite happiness, the kind of joy that was so raw and nerve-tingling, and yet so pure, it belonged to youth.

'It really *is* against the code of behaviour. If someone heard, they might put in a complaint against me.' Tamara Bywater pulled a face. 'I'm acknowledging a friendship that has formed with someone like-minded who is far from mentally ill, but one rule covers all ...'

'Who would I tell? Your boss? Sol—'

'Partners of my patients sometimes misunderstand—'

'I—' They interrupted each other. 'No, OK. Partners of patients sometimes what?'

'Oh,' she said. 'They misunderstand their partners' feelings.'

'You need my mobile number.' Beth stood. 'Look what I have yours under – "*Shrink*"!'

'No longer appropriate,' said Tamara.

Hello, ex-shrink. x, Beth texted her. She allowed herself to look round at the clock. 'Shit! Really shit.'

Tamara laughed at the time. 'You must go now, I know. Go! Hurry!'

148

Beth bolted out of there, trying to call Sol, but went straight to voicemail. *Sorry sorry sorry*, she texted, her hand shaking in the cold. *Got caught.* In what? Dr Bywater had delayed the start of their session by an hour? It would have to be that. Lying was becoming normal. *There v v soon. Really really sorry.*

* * *

She sent a hasty text to Ellie. *It was all fucking true.*

TWELVE

Beth dashed from Tamara's house. She took off her high heels and ran along the pavement. The bare trees were a swirl, yet picked out in precise light when she looked at them, her feet skimming, merely obeying her heartbeat, the cold making her cough as she caught her breath. Vertiginous swoop after swoop of disbelief came to her as she moved. There was no answer from Sol by the time she rocketed into the Tube. The lift on its way up seemed like a preposterous obstacle, so she galloped down the stairs, nearly falling twice in the heels she had put back on.

She changed trains, urging on the Central line, thanking it when it came in two minutes. She bolted into the gallery, whipping out a mirror to check the sweating state of herself, and paused in the commotion of the foyer.

'He's just left,' said Killian.

'What?'

Killian shrugged. 'He doesn't like this kind of malarkey, does he?'

Beth ran towards the cloakrooms. She tore back to the entrance, thick with press and guests. Jack Dorian was just arriving, and she waved. 'Sol!' she called randomly.

A head turned near the door. She ran towards it, lost it, stumbled and saw him again, his back a leap of familiarity. He was typing something into his phone.

'Thank God,' she said. 'Sorry. I'm really sorry. Don't be cross, don't be cross.' She fought for breath. 'Sorry, darling.'

He turned, his face drawn in and private, and she sensed in that moment what it would be to lose him, really lose him in a way that had never entered her musings, and it made her open her mouth. She saw him through a new lens, a telescope the wrong way round, as though he were a man with a life of his own. Not hers. Not with her. It was always that strange effect which encapsulated that moment for her.

'God,' she said in a squeak.

His mouth was straight, exactly as she had predicted it, the eyes unseeable.

'I'm so sorry,' she gabbled. She took his shoulders.

He stood motionless, then moved to one side. 'I'm just leaving,' he said.

'Oh, for God's sake. No. Sol. This is *ridiculous*. Don't leave.'

'It's late.'

'We're going back in. We're going back in. Give me your coat.'

He paused. Uncharacteristic confusion passed over his face, resolving into resistance.

'I really don't want to,' he said.

'No,' she said, grabbing his arm. 'It was the shrink's. The appointment—' Somehow, she couldn't lie. 'It started – no, it went on. I've run here as fast as I could. Please.'

He paused again, his iciness overlaying a more worrying drift of sadness. 'That was your choice.'

'Please. I want to be here with you more than anything. I love you. You idiot. You're a pain in the arse, but – but, so am I. I know I can be. No, you're not. I need to see you. I want to see you. Let's go back in.'

He gazed at her.

'Look, I'm covered in sweat!' She lifted one arm and pretended to press herself against his nose, laughing to smash the mood.

He smiled faintly. 'You smell.'

'Exactly.' She laughed with relief. 'I'd better go and chuck some soap and water under my pits,' she said. 'But then you might stomp off like a grizzly old bear.'

'You push it sometimes, Bet.'

'You love it,' she said reflexively, and immediately knew that this was now the wrong approach to take.

'You know that?' she thought he said, but she was running to the cloakroom. She looked at herself in the mirror as though she were an alien being: dis-ordered, chosen.

* * *

Sol was talking, head bowed, to Aranxto's tiny brother in a gesture of independence. Beth mimicked shoot-ing herself to Killian who rolled his eyes, then she struggled through the crowd to find drinks. Tamara Bywater was there like a reflection in water, overlay-ing all else.

Beth could never do what Aranxto did: his self-excoriating explorations of the inner workings of his own fantasies, his childhood, his rectum. A fountain installation of his penis, moulded in crystal glass, the water bathed in different-coloured lights at different times of the day and entitled *Mood*, had just sold for almost a million dollars, while a film of him cutting his thigh showed on a loop at MoMA. Should she, too, finally try the conceptual route, that usually female preserve of self-harm and the confessional? It would be an entirely cynical move, she knew.

She took Sol's arm. He resisted for a few seconds, ignoring her, then nodded at Aranxto's brother and followed Beth through the squash of press, models on such exaggerated heels they hovered inches above him, until they found a place among all the hubbub beneath a neon piece no one was looking at. They were photographed. Beth looked up at the flash, but she and Sol were merely civilians invisible to the gawkers as Aranxto processed to that end of the gallery with some of his cohort.

'I owe you the most grovelling apologies,' she said. 'I realise I was maybe an hour late—'

'An hour and nineteen.' He winced as a camera flashed right by him, and turned to avoid more. They were jostled by the crowds. 'Don't tell me now,' he said, stiffly.

Jack Dorian was standing nearby, talking into a journalist's phone. Sol ignored him.

'What is happening?' he said.

'What do you mean?'

'I told you. You're on some kind of a high. As well as low. Most times high. Look at you right now. Jesus, Bet.'

Beth paused. 'I know what you mean,' she said, trying to be truthful.

He nodded, solemnly. 'On edge, excited. You're telling the shrink all about it?'

'What?' She looked at him. 'Oh, God. I know that face.'

Beth took him into her arms with an appearance of confidence. The elation of Tamara Bywater rose then tipped. Sol. A punch of loss. People left her. Her mother in Sefton Park. Anger, yet guilt. All dark, dark, shining dark. And the shrink, Tamara Bywater, her fragrance, her skills. Beth's knees were unsteady.

'I love you,' she said rapidly to Sol, as though shouting through the fog. Tamara smiled at her.

He didn't react. 'Don't jerk me around like this because I don't know if I can—'

There was a rising clamour. Success and money were out in force, and Beth and Sol were pulled into a crowd. Beth smiled as she steadied herself on Sol's shoulder, leaning into him to whisper an observation into his ear, and there were several flashes around them, press and gallery photographers circling the artist and friends.

'You appear to be very willing now to go to her. You're telling her in confidence whatever is going on?'

Beth frowned. 'No,' she said.

He exhaled through his nose. 'Then what?'

'Really, just about you and Fern, and Lizzie.'

She looked steadily at him. Her heart was thumping hard.

'I'm concerned she's not the best person to be—'

Beth swallowed, caught saliva in her throat, her words tangling. 'Well if a professional psychologist isn't, who is?'

'Another therapist, maybe?'

'Where's all this coming from?'

'I think Sofia is concerned.'

'Why?'

'I guess …' He touched his temple. 'She doesn't like her.'

Beth began to laugh.

'That sounds dumb, doesn't it?' said Sol. 'I'll find out more details. This was a passing remark.'

Aranxto came past, shrugging into a snakeskin jacket. Sol tilted his head towards him. 'You always need a bit of excess,' he said to Beth.

'Do I?' she said, arching her back, directing the expression in her eyes at the ceiling instead of him. All was possible now. She could bring Tamara to the next private view, Tamara who was fascinated. She could introduce her to Aranxto, that week even.

'You – you, Bet – are attracted to extremes. It's just you don't notice it. Your tolerance for oddballs is off the scale.'

She laughed. 'If you say so. Most of my good friends are sane. You mean the outer circle.'

Aranxto was posing poker-faced amidst cheers in front of a wall projection of the infamous glass penis, and in the commotion, Sol came closer to her. There was the faintest twist to his mouth. Then, wordlessly, they hugged each other. He put his arms around her and looked into her pupils so intently, her forehead resting on his, that they were in a cave of owl eyes.

'He is unfortunately developing tosserish elements,' she said into his ear.

'Developing? I love you too, Bet. Make life easier for us. Please.'

You make life easier for us, she thought, and would have retorted aloud on any other occasion, but with great effort she stopped herself. She kept close to his neck, her radiance hard to hide.

'The secret life of Elizabeth Ellen Penn,' said Sol, and, though she laughed, he wasn't smiling.

* * *

In the night, Beth felt as though she had drunk caffeine after MSG, or taken coke, her heart rate rocketing. Worries about Sol's conversations subsided as the puerile triumph she felt coursed through her, Tamara's Bywater's words and gestures played and replayed. In the early hours of the morning, the elation started to become stained with panic. No more shrink's appointments. Just like that. She was dry-mouthed. She got up, peed, downed a glass of water and then another. Tamara loomed, leaning towards her, giant and distorted. The princess looked down from her throne and winked straight at the lowly Beth in the crowd.

She couldn't sleep.

She had wilfully lost her therapist. The prop of her sessions, kicked away. She should have kept her, not agreed to some half-hatched notion of friendship, in which there was a now undeniable flirtatious component that she couldn't process, and that unsettled her even as it electrified her. The sweat ran down her chest in cold streaks.

But in the panic, a new path opened, queasy, night-covered: a tunnel on a roller coaster. She would meet her. She would finally assuage her curiosity and encounter the real Tamara Bywater. An almost bilious excitement snaked through her.

Still she couldn't sleep.

The shrink leered, her image skewed, but there she was, and there was Lizzie. The image of her mother in a hospital bed. Lizzie quoted poems at Beth, once known in childhood and now grappled for, and Beth tried to shake her off, like a succubus.

* * *

At seven in the morning, Tamara Bywater slapped into Beth's thoughts in a shock of disbelief.

She went to the studio as the only way to escape her distraction, the tentative paintings coming to her – rivers in which gills and hair were emerging – and she had an uneasy awareness of her phone, because no text had yet arrived from the shrink. From Tamara. It sounded fraudulent. Dr Bywater had possibly changed her mind. Beth shuddered and glanced at the time. It was not yet ten and it was a Saturday. Tamara would be in her husband's arms in Kennington, shoes strewn somewhere on the floor, a chance for quick sex before she ran down barefooted to make her children breakfast.

Hi ex-shrink. Let's meet!, Beth wrote, cringed, deleted it. Somehow she had to wait, to prove she wasn't a stalker. She worked, then bussed back to make lunch. Fern's music drifted down from her bedroom. Smoke from the *Mary-Lou* was covering the air, like a thin layer of hessian, and beautiful scuzzy girls, middle-aged women in military jackets and men in steel-capped boots disappeared inside or crouched on the roof, smoking by log piles and dead geraniums. All afternoon, Beth jumped at texts.

* * *

Beth kissed Fern that night, hair squeaking shampoo dampness, the clamped face turned from her. She chirruped at Fern's coldness, and suddenly she felt old and simply unable to communicate. She hesitated by the door to try again, but Fern's back was facing her and she forced herself not to. Such counterintuitive restraint made her almost dizzy with effort.

'You, like, always stare out of the window,' said Fern suddenly, just as she was about to leave.

'What?'

'So, why are you *like* this to people? Mum?'

'Darling,' said Beth, walking back over to her. 'What? You've said this before. What do you mean?'

'Yes. So basically, you – you don't speak to your own *mother*, and now you don't speak to …'

'Who?'

Beth waited. But Fern had turned with a rapid movement and buried her face in her pillow.

'Who? Baby? What—'

'Me,' said Fern, possibly, into the pillow, but she would say nothing more, however gently she was asked.

Sol was downstairs editing his photos on his computer. He and Beth cleared the house, approached the pile of paperwork sliding over the table and began one of several washes. She put on some Pachelbel and gazed and gazed out at the canal, as though Tamara Bywater were likely to be strolling along the towpath, and sometimes she thought she saw a man there, but the twists beneath the choke of plant life were indistinct. Where was she? Beth felt alone. Aged thirteen, she had wondered whether she could follow the Mersey to its source by hitching a lift with one of the tug pilots, who would ask no questions, then continue down canals, crossing the country by waterways to find her mother with her boyfriend.

There was no message all weekend. She could discuss the unexpected grief at her session, she thought, and then she remembered.

* * *

Where was Tamara?

Beth went to The Dairy and taught the Lower Fourth in the gloriously large Art Three, goading time-wasters through their expensive installations. Having sought mechanical advice from the DT department, she helped a boy she liked solve a problem with an outsized sculpture, and goaded the class to finish their projects before the Christmas holidays.

It was only a matter of time before someone decided it was original to dismantle a doll, rearrange its limbs in sub-Chapman fashion, or use its face for shock value, to coos of admiration from classmates. Bleeding objects, self-mutilation videos and barbed-wire motifs would inevitably shortly follow. Beth felt her phone buzzing in her pocket several times, but again these were phantom vibrations, and the phone stayed text-free. She edged it out and propped it on a windowsill as she taught. She breathed deeply, using Tamara's CBT techniques to challenge her thoughts, to distinguish assumptions from reality.

In the evening, she had to put her phone upstairs so she couldn't hear it. Even *No Caller ID* no longer contacted her. Laurie arrived with a battered *Standard*, pointed to a photo and laughed. 'You look like an old git, Dad,' he said.

There they were in a group of artists at Aranxto's private view, Beth in profile, whispering in Sol's ear in amusement while he smiled at what she said: a couple caught in a moment of communication. It was flattering. Beth's only thought was a hope that Tamara had seen a rare good photograph of her.

By Wednesday, Fern had told her that there was no point in her coming to say goodnight, Sol was guarded with her, and her phone was still blank. Two more days passed. The Dairy term ended. As she dutifully hung Christmas decorations, Beth ached for the Tamara Bywater of old.

And the flavour of waiting reminded her of those years she had longed for the sweetness of her mother. A longing that was replaced in adulthood by aversion, and ultimately by a fear of contact. And then, just as Beth had anticipated, when her daughter was born – how had Lizzie known? She and her ex-husband Gordon hadn't spoken for years, but there were still other Liverpool networks – the requests had started up again. There had been a message via Beth's gallery, followed by a postcard on Lizzie's behalf from her half-brother in Liverpool, to which Sol had replied with a furious letter.

A few weeks after the postcard, Sol had just left for the day, and Beth was feeding the baby in the glow of astonished love, unwashed hair falling over her breast as she breathed in the miracle through a pall of exhaustion. How had she, they, produced a perfect thing? *The* perfect thing? The traffic on Beck Road, the builders' radios, were a dreamy backdrop and she was an animal, her stomach spongy, her body producing food for her beloved: the cleverest thing it had ever done.

Fern was a baby fern. A rosebud mouth on a heart, a dormouse. How had anything so exquisite ever landed on the planet? Beth wanted to retch with tiredness, but in the dips between the waves, she knew magic.

The doorbell rang.

Beth hitched Fern to her shoulder but there was no one there. One of the artists from the studios along the street addressed her and admired her baby, an early winter Hackney morning rose, and Beth decided to take Fern out. She changed her, tucked her up, kissed her and walked along in an old coat, her hair bright against grey wool, stopping the buggy just to look at her baby, check on her, kiss her. The little peach of a cheek in a blanket, fathomless smudge of eyes gazing at the sky.

Someone came towards her but she barely looked up. They passed. The sun was a chilled haze; she bought some apples, stroked Fern's forehead, saw her blanket filling and falling with new sleep.

'Bethy,' came a voice, and there was a smear of awareness, but the name was a thing of the past. For a few seconds she could dismiss what she might have heard, people walking down the street talking; and then there came, 'Bethy?' like a croak, both familiar and confusing.

She whipped her head round.

There she was, clearly Lizzie Penn but older.

Beth took in the hairs that wired independently in metallic strands above the brown, the pleats forming below Lizzie's eyes, the flickers of almost tan-coloured striation in the beds of her irises, the flecks of dandruff on her shoulders: fragments of her mother, those human signs that the young Beth would have died for. The bird's-foot patterns angling from her eyes were more deeply grooved; the gamine look of hers had filled out a little, broadening her face and waist. Lizzie's mouth was concertinaed with creases that bloomed and sank as she talked. Beth held the buggy handles, her jaw slack.

Lizzie said nothing. She was a straight-spined statue of a ballet dancer standing there: the Degas sculpture draped in work clothes instead of a dead girl's grubby tutu. There was nothing readable behind her eyes. What was she doing in London?

'Can I see?' she said eventually.

* * *

And these days, Beth feared that the thirteen-year-old Fern would again mention her grandmother. In Fern's earlier childhood, Beth and Sol had instinctively underplayed the issue of Lizzie leaving, though they told her the facts. Fern had simply nodded, puzzled. Infant acceptance had been followed later by a curiosity inspired by abandoned-animal and orphan novels: questions about clothes, diet and wickedness that were more appropriate to television drama than real life.

Beth almost texted into Tamara's silence, several times. Instead, she made herself return to her river series: leaves and crabby brickwork, the buildings increasingly haunted; fungus, desire; the loneliness of a search. She put a final wash over a backdrop built up with wax beneath oil, the river's muscular heave lifting detritus through the paint layers. She was painting intensely again. In all the turmoil, Tamara Bywater had returned her ability to her.

She came home from work and hugged Sol, wrapping her arms round him so he looked surprised. His steady love and stringency seemed at that moment the best qualities in the world. They drank some sloe gin from her father, the sloes picked by Gordon Penn with his son Bill's twin girls when he took them fishing and exploring in New Brighton and beyond. When he came to London, or, steeling herself, Beth visited him in Liverpool, Fern had always clung to him and danced around him, and he was intensely proud of his three granddaughters. Bill had returned to Liverpool after college, married and had his twin daughters six years to the day before Beth gave birth to Fern, so the three girls called themselves triplets.

'Look,' said Beth, and nodded at the bottle, smiling as she swallowed a tightness in her throat. 'We must call Dad.'

'He doesn't like it, Bet.'

'I know, but he wouldn't like *not* being called. I'll just chat at him. I'll send him a Fern picture.'

'You're a good daughter,' said Sol.

She shook her head against a needling in her eyes, and poured them more gin.

A beep came from her phone, and she looked at it when she stood, weary with hope. *Tamara B.*

***

Dear Beth. I'm finally letting myself write to you. How are you? I'm sorry I couldn't write to you before but I was too afraid. I dithered, didn't know the best thing to do. But I didn't want to let you down. For the next few months I won't contact you again in written form. Just to be safe and in case you change your mind which you can do, of course, at any time. Just want everyone to stay safe. Xxx

***

Beth murmured in a small meow that she turned into a cough she then exaggerated. She wanted to leap, to grin, to yelp out loud. She read it again.

And yet there was nothing to answer. There was no suggestion of meeting. A sense of rejection quickly filtered through and settled in her stomach. She messaged Tamara the next day, waiting until the evening, when she was laughing with Sol and suddenly felt warm and certain. *So bonsoir, ex-shrink. How are you? Let's meet x*, she wrote.

There was no answer.

On Friday, she painted, doggedly, and as she worked, she cringed at the text's whiff of desperation.

She had started a new river painting from a lower point of view, in which she found that the water only swelled between the thickets of detritus, and she added a translucency of French ultramarine to the mud. There was more surfacing through the top layer of her paintings now: oiled feathers over hair, quite possibly flesh.

Her phone rang, and she jumped, with a rocketing of her heart. She almost knew it would be Tamara Bywater. Instead, it was *No Caller ID*. Her hand shook. She waited.

'Hello?' she said warily.

There was silence, but this time there was no echo of space or breath.

'Hello? Hello?' said Beth rapidly. 'You a fucking PPI company?' she snapped into the void.

The bathos hit her with shame. But of course it wasn't her mother. Of course it wasn't. It never was. Or was it? Perhaps, just once, just once in her life, it had been: the face overlooking Sefton Park. The shock of her mother's face framed by a window, mere streets away from her own home.

She had been fourteen, nearing fifteen. The day had been unexceptional, Beth trailing home in a group of girls, grey uniforms like rain; pigeons, clouds, the gut-tearings of unhappiness subsiding into a growing awareness that this was now normality: the boredom and guilt of sitting with her father over dinner with so little to say, the waiting to bury herself later in *Lives of the Great Artists* and *Just Seventeen*. The house containing the woman had cracked rendering, the face appearing as an impossible vision above a row of bird deterrents. Momentary only, looking out.

'Just a min,' Beth said, but these were mouthy local girls who converged on the way home rather than close friends, and she hesitated, then she ran across the street, almost stumbled, pressed the middle bell, then again, then the top and bottom in rapid succession, but a couple of the girls were looking at her and frowning. She knocked, very quickly, the calls of 'Antwacky' and 'Divvy' barrelling over, and there was no answer, though the woman was there.

THIRTEEN

Fern stiffened as Beth went to hug her as she left for work, and so Beth forced herself to turn, blow her a kiss and then go.

The riverscapes were more vivid now, burping bubbles, writhing with life: mussel blood, fish roe, seaweed like glans in the diesel. Beth loved working in the large studio; she loved working on location, however unusual it was, in layers and coats and fingerless gloves. She mixed Alkyd medium with French chalk, or sand, or even sawdust to create such surfaces. What was emerging disturbed her, but she barely questioned it, and simply followed the disarming progress from landscape to narrative. At the side of the canvas, there was, perhaps, a figure in a window. Or was there? A woman. Or was it just a shadow? The shape the curtain made?

Finally, later that Friday afternoon, a text arrived. Beth stared at the sender, the name from the hospital on her screen surreal under the clouds. *Tamara B.*

* * *

So – madly – I can see you TONIGHT! Could you? Say you can. Early eve? Early as poss. I'd love to see you. This is my only real chance for at least a fortnight, with all the Christmas nonsense, X PS This message should spontaneously combust after reading ... T

* * *

Beth stood there, and the clouds that had been sinking into the river raced back into life.

* * *

'Why are you carrying that?' she said to Sol when she arrived home, smiling at him.

'I was just about out of here.'

'What?'

He turned, put his hand on her shoulder. 'We've always said the Tube is the easiest?' he said. 'Cheapest. The good Lord bless the Piccadilly line.'

She watched him, her mouth moving minutely.

'Picca— yes –' she said. She frowned. 'Sorry, I ... Heathrow. Yes.'

His eyebrows knitted.

'You had actually *forgotten*, hadn't you? Bet.'

'No.' She coloured. 'Yes.'

'Kahramanmaraş mosques,' he said impatiently. 'You've known about this for a while.'

'I'm so sorry, I'm just—'

'Busy,' he said, looking straight at her.

'Well, I am. Where's your bigger case?'

'I'm only taking this. Pernille has the equipment. I need to pee.'

Beth grabbed a pen, scrawled a note and slipped it in his hand luggage, as she had done in the early days when he went on potentially dangerous jobs.

'You're going *now*?' she said.

'In five.'

'It's just – yes. I need to go out tonight too. Fern can ... I'll organise something.'

'Mum,' said Fern immediately. 'Jemma's.'

'Laurie,' said Beth at the same time, rejecting outfits in her head. 'We can see if Laurie can come round?'

'Unlikely?' said Sol. He waited.

'The shrink,' she said at the wrong moment, just as she was calling Laurie. Fern was pulling her shoulder. 'Oh,' she said to Sol, 'he's already out.'

Fern made her eyes wider.

Beth leaned over and kissed Fern, dashed into the downstairs loo and began to brush her teeth and hair at top speed.

'You *are* smart,' she said to Sol in a toothpaste voice.

'Reception as soon as I'm out of Atatürk,' he said.

'Oh yes. This was already arranged. I can't really cancel my—'

'Who?'

'You can get going,' said Beth, kissing him through toothpaste. 'Oh, and you *smell* nice too. Huh,' she said in affronted tones. 'Watch out. That Pernille.'

'And her boyfriend. What about Fern?'

'I'll sort it.'

'Can I go to Jemma's?' said Fern brightly.

Beth groaned. Sol stood there saying nothing, emanating disapproval that made Beth want to shout out loud. Sometimes I hate you, she thought.

'You are happy with her going to Jemma's now, after all?' he said eventually.

'Yes,' snapped Beth.

His face was blank.

'Where are you going at this time?' he said. 'Shrink? Why? After work hours?'

'Oh, she could only see me late,' said Beth.

'What?' He took out his phone and stared at it, his fingers doing nothing while Beth watched. 'What is it with this shrink and lateness?'

'I'll – I—' she said, floundering.

'In the evening?' She could hear the frown in his voice with his back to her. 'Is that pretty crazy? Departments open? Well, I guess David does, but that's private.'

'Oh, I'm – she can see me then. Privately. Remember. It's private. I – I don't know. It's a bit late; it must be the only time she can do. She works, so she has to fit her private clients round that.' She was speaking too quickly. There was a small silence. Just tell him, she

172

thought; tell him, despite what Tamara had cautioned, about their new friendship.

His mouth was invisible behind his beard. His chest moved up and down in a new shirt. 'Well, you omitted to tell me that it's private.' He fiddled with his phone again. 'OK. You pay for it now. So where do you meet her?'

'South London. Just across the river,' she said, the ease of lying carrying fresh pinches of self-disgust.

'Enjoy yourself.' He had the Notes page of his phone open.

'Well, that's hardly—' she began. 'Aren't you late?'

'Probably.'

'You – you go.' She started to clear up swiftly, holding an earring between her teeth. 'I'm really sorry I forgot. Duh. I hope it's good. Good work I mean,' she said.

He watched her. One eyebrow travelled minutely upwards. He patted his pocket for his wallet and keys, but didn't leave.

'You look like an incredibly annoying teacher when you do that,' she said.

'Uh huh.' He stood there, waiting. His navy shirt was done up to the neck, no tie, one of his professorial grey tweed jackets over his shoulder.

'Go,' said Beth. 'Just go. You also look sexy dressed up. I'll sort out Fern. I may not even go.'

'You must,' he said semi-gruffly, and a contraction of guilt made her look down, then smile at him.

They kissed briefly.

'*Take care* of yourself, Sol. We need you.'

Fern flung herself at him, holding him for long moments and then rubbing her head against his neck like a Disney faun with its mother.

'I love you so much,' she said in a hoarse whisper in his ear that Beth could hear.

I love you more than anyone, ever, in the world, she thought, looking at the dots of Fern's freckles.

* * *

There was a text: *Tamara B*. Beth looked at the name. *Hurry hurry hurry! I'm missing you.*

'Mum, go. See you later,' said Fern on Peyton Street, where Jemma lived. Fern looked up as though inviting affection, then cut her gaze, and Beth had learned through pain and discipline to detach herself as required. She let her hands drop and didn't hug or kiss her goodbye.

She increased her pace from the Tube, slowing just before the restaurant, an understated modern Japanese off Greek Street she had once been taken to by Aranxto's gallery owner after a show. She disappeared into the gloom of a run of rooms resembling a series of drawers, with screened and walled alcoves, blue-lit orchids, as she was shown to a tiny room of three tables placed awkwardly close together. Despite Tamara's text, she wasn't there. Beth angled a candle to read the menu. Her stomach felt unsteady.

She examined her teeth in a metal chopstick holder, adjusted her hair.

A couple arrived at the table next to her, and there was an obligation to acknowledge each other in their proximity. She sat there for a further few minutes. It hit her. She was sitting here waiting for Dr Tamara Bywater, the NHS professional randomly assigned to her, with her worksheets and her skills.

There was movement at the opening to the room, a man who was clearly the manager himself gesturing to her table. Beth's eyes were drawn downwards and she saw heels behind him, slender-strapped and clearly expensive sandals that rendered the legs they supported disproportionately thin, and a dark satin cheongsam that fell just below the knees. Beth registered the woman's face, then deregistered it in a moment of confusion, a crudely executed double take, before understanding, as the woman bent down and swiftly kissed her, catching her temple, that this was indeed Tamara Bywater.

'I'm so sorry, I really didn't mean to be late.' Her voice was the dove swoop in Beth's ear. Through the darkness was the radiant smile, lipsticked, hands settling calmly on the table. A different ring.

Beth gazed at an enhanced version of the woman from the consulting room. She looked striking in a way Beth had never previously perceived her to be, yet her appearance was disquieting, not altogether appealing. Her eyes now seemed, if such a thing were

175

possible, over-large, her features exaggerated, the heels changing her proportions.

Tamara smiled at Beth, scanning her face, and the disconcerting aspect of this new version of her resolved itself in that moment into what could only be viewed as beauty. The transition took Beth aback.

'I thought you were here ...' Beth said blankly.

'Oh,' said Tamara, and despite the unnerving gloss of her appearance, that smile alone wrapped Beth in softness, as of old. 'I had to take a phone call.'

Who? Beth wanted to say.

The man at the next table nodded at Tamara – now Tamara, quite different from Dr Bywater – and she smiled, whereupon he addressed her with flurries of outdated gallantry while the woman opposite him remained immobile.

'I need a drink. Do you?' said Tamara finally in an aside. 'Save me from him,' she muttered.

She turned her neck and smiled straight at Beth. 'We can talk ...' she said. 'Unbelievable.'

There was a slight pause. 'You look – different,' said Beth awkwardly to fill it.

'This is me.' Tamara looked to one side, then she gazed at Beth in a stream of focus. 'You think I'm a besuited social worker in my real life?' she said with a run of laughter through her 1940s delivery. She reached out, but instead of touching Beth's hand, she took some edamame, the impenetrable doctor eating like a human.

176

'My friends sometimes laugh to see me in my nun's weeds,' said Tamara. 'I suppose – yes – you've only seen me in disguise so far … I forget that.' She smiled again. She tapped the table with her fingers in sequence, the nails sufficiently exquisite to be the sole source of beauty. 'How –' she hesitated '– strange that is when I've met you in my mind so many many times outside the office.'

Oh God, Beth stopped herself saying.

'I think I'm still hiding from you a little bit,' said Tamara, and there was a nervous play of her hands. 'I'm not allowed to do this. Do you understand?' She swallowed. 'I don't think you could.' The light caught the hollows below her eyes, beneath the concealer, powder she had never worn at St Peter's. She twisted, running the tips of her own fingers through her others in turn. 'I can't tell you how many times I nearly called and cancelled this – this and any other contact. I had fears. I didn't sleep well. I'm doing something very wrong. But I'm not. I know you enough to know that seeing you will do you no harm. But – I could actually be struck off for this.'

Beth's mouth opened slowly. 'We will, though?'

Tamara paused. 'Of course. How could I not? I gave you the choice.'

'Yes.' Beth smiled. The flowers on Tamara's dress were flattened into grey-reds under the lights between fretwork. 'I'm no longer your patient,' she said. She cleared her throat. Without thinking, she laid her hand on Tamara's. The hand stayed still. Beth removed hers.

'That professional rule book wasn't made with any real human emotion in mind,' said Tamara.

Her face was half-shadowed, its highlights exaggerated like a screen print. Beth wanted to capture her in paint or as a few saturated seconds of film noir. She was also Dr Bywater. A queasy excitement lay in the disparity between the images.

'It's not relevant. There's a time issue with ex-patients. But – I had to dare myself to come here. If we don't take risks, challenge ourselves, especially at this stage of life ...'

'You think? Yes. Well.' Beth cringed at herself. '*Tell* me things,' she said rapidly.

'What kind of things, Elizabeth Penn? Sitting right opposite me!'

She picked up Beth's hand and kissed it. A lipstick mark remained.

Beth laughed.

The waiter appeared, hovered and left them again.

'If we're seen here,' Beth said, 'you can claim I'm a craven patient who's stalked you at dinner.'

Tamara laughed. 'I'm happy to be stalked by you. How are you?'

'I've been—' she said, and suddenly they were recalling moments from the past months, of awareness or curiosity, replayed and reinterpreted, discussed with leaps of recognition, and nothing, thought Beth, could ever be so satisfying, or so illuminating, as they interrupted. *Do you remember when …? What did you think when …? What did you mean that time …? Do you know how much I dared myself to say …?* They forgot to order, the waiter appearing, disappearing, reappearing.

'So now I can ask you,' said Beth self-consciously, 'everything. About you, I mean.'

'I can't think what you'd want to know. It's you who has the much more interesting life.'

'That is rubbish,' said Beth. She watched Tamara's mouth as it formed those Pinewood enunciations. She was not real: a celluloid creature momentarily materialised. 'So you have children, right?'

'Yes. Girls.'

'Oh. Lovely,' said Beth. 'What age?'

'Oh. Miriam. She's seventeen. His – he married quite early. She's my beloved. And the younger one's eleven. Francesca. So –' she smiled, as though to herself '– I have a little more time now. Not much, but a bit.'

'Good,' said Beth. 'Eleven is sweet. Before it all changes.'

'You and I both gave birth to one girl. And we each have an older stepchild. But I could never tell you such things. It was so frustrating.'

'So …' said Beth, leaning on her elbows. 'Where – where do you come from? Who's your family?'

'I don't see them very often.' Tamara gave a small smile. 'You see, all families are complicated. I think

179

working out my own past was what drove me to psychology in the first place. Making some sense of a dysfunctional background.'

'Where did you grow up?' Beth asked.

'Norfolk.'

'Oh.' Beth paused. 'I wouldn't have thought that. I tried to ask you.'

'And I could say nothing.'

'What was it like?'

'Leaking rented section of a huge house. The parkland was all soggy. No money. School fees unpaid. Mud, salt marshes, asthma, sisters, etc. That's about it.'

'That's so not what I imagined either.'

'I know. I look too un-English. My – Angus – husband – always says I could come from anywhere but the Norfolk marshes. Actually, my mother was Ukrainian-East Anglian. Trouble.'

'What else?'

Tamara shrugged. 'God. I don't know. This kind of rackety grandeur, all unpaid. Lecherous odd-job men. Nannies left because of lack of food. Private schools while we went hungry.'

'I could tell you were a bit of posh,' said Beth eventually.

'They couldn't pay for their lifestyle. My mother was virtually brought up as a hooker, it seemed to me later. East Anglian-Ukrainian bred to catch minor aristocracy like my father.'

180

Beth gave a slight laugh. 'Your husband?' she said, and paused. 'I – what does he do?'

He's an architect. She heard the answer before it was said.

'Nothing much,' said Tamara.

Beth laughed again. 'Nothing much of what?'

'He's a financial adviser, he has a few clients, but he's very involved with the girls' upbringing.'

'Right,' said Beth.

'It's hard to know how to say this,' said Tamara. 'But he – Angus – is not like you or your friends. Not of your world, with all its creativity. That intrigued me, from the beginning ... You're talented. That's precious, you know.'

Tamara's eyes slid away, then landed back on Beth and bathed her, and she could do anything while basking in the persona manufactured for her, in which her good qualities were magnified and her flaws ignored or unseen.

'Your life to me – and I know,' she said gently, 'that you've suffered much grief – but your life really does interest me. If the therapist can project on to the patient as well, perhaps I have, but anyway, I picture it all. Your friends, your house. Camden. Those openings. I picture Fern.'

'Fern!' said Beth, jolting. 'I must check on her.' She reached for her phone.

'You're the creator,' said Tamara, as though she hadn't heard. 'I'm just a collector, an enthusiast. In

181

another life … But I always wanted to help people too, or work them out. So as it is, I only decorate my house and myself.'

'You must come round to mine some time.'

'But …' The flash of anxiety passed over Tamara's face, adding vulnerability. 'I can't ever meet your husband, be public …' She tailed off. 'Anyway, I'm not sure I even want to meet him.'

'Oh you should.'

'I saw you two in the *Standard*. I got very jealous. But you must get on with your evening!' she said suddenly. 'You don't want to sit here listening to all this.'

'But—' Beth's throat tightened into a cough that took several attempts to eliminate, worsening as she tried to ignore it. 'This *is* my evening.'

Tamara smiled to one side and her neighbour was all attention once more. Beth made a few comments that failed to elicit interest. There were silences.

'Let's order,' said Beth stiffly.

'Isn't Sol wondering where you are?'

'Yes, you're right. I'll go and phone him,' said Beth in a cold tone. She could find nothing to say. It had all changed. The real Beth Penn was a tedious disappointment. The humiliation made her clench her muscles. She rose and walked outside, where Christmas lights were painting the street and taxis came and went. She phoned Fern instead, who was happy and occupied and wanted to end the call.

182

She returned to the restaurant. Tamara was ignoring her neighbour's body language, his girlfriend stiff-backed, and she appeared smaller than usual, shrouded in her own thoughts. Beth wanted to reach out and touch her.

'Yes,' said Tamara.

'What?'

'Yes, you can touch me.'

Beth started. 'Oh, God, I—am I—?'

'I can read you. I think I always could,' she said, and with the effects of a little wine, with great effort, Beth made herself dare to lean across and hold Tamara's shoulders, her arms, and Tamara bowed her head, then tilted her face up to Beth so she was all eyes, black-framed, neon-blued, and they gazed at each other without embarrassment. Beth had never in her life looked at a woman this way. There was something else faintly discordant, off-kilter, that Beth could detect beneath the confidence. She couldn't identify what she meant.

The couple at the adjacent table started to leave, and an object appeared between them. Tamara picked it up.

'His card,' she said, pulling a face.

'Bloody cheek!'

'I have dozens of these,' she said, bending it idly between her fingers till it jumped on to a napkin. 'I put them all in a jug.'

'What for?'

She shrugged. 'They might be useful one day. Probably not.'

'You know, I have to leave,' said Beth, glancing at the bill and paying.

'I know you do,' said Tamara. She gave Beth a wry smile, and Beth felt the warmth of her breath on her. 'We will meet. Somehow. We have all of each other to discover.'

'Me to discover you,' said Beth.

Beth kissed Tamara goodbye, and she was passive and held out her other cheek, barely tilted, for a second kiss, and Beth took in the little chemical motes around her and a charge shot through her that she didn't expect, like static. That cat smile of old curved Tamara's mouth. 'You must behave,' she said quietly. 'Be good. A good little wife ...'

Beth laughed. 'Don't say that.'

A group of pre-Christmas revellers poured from a taxi on to the pavement outside the restaurant and, without hesitation, Beth stuck her head through the cab window and secured it for Tamara, then stepped back as Tamara got in and drove off, not turning to look at her once more, and Beth stood there and gazed while people milled round her, and she watched the space on the road where the taxi had been.

Fourteen

'You don't need to stay in with me any more in the evenings,' said Fern three days later. Her mouth was a tight pout, baby giraffe legs in tracksuit bottoms. She had largely stayed in her room while Sol was away.

'Of course I do.'

'Then you don't need to put me to bed.'

'Oh?' said Beth. She made herself turn around. Her voice seemed too loud. Ducks suddenly chattered. A lorry roared somewhere further off.

She turned back. Fern seemed to be eyeing her thoughtfully.

'I only really come up and kiss you goodnight now,' said Beth, tucking a piece of hair behind her ear, then hummed, unnecessarily moving some papers.

'You don't have to.'

'You'd rather I didn't.' She focused on the table. There was camera equipment Sol had left behind, Fern's Kindle by the perpetual pile of paperwork at the end, Fern's felt tips.

The tense shoulder blades turned, emanating something close to disgust.

Fern shrugged, nodded.

Beth's neck tightened. 'OK.'

Fern blushed a little. 'Then you can be dreaming with your pencil held in the air while you're doing *Mice*,' she said. 'Or on your phone. Don't worry, you can.'

'Oh, *Fern*. Don't be ridiculous.'

Fern watched her, as though through a coating of ice.

That body had been wrapped in Beth's arms, head rubbing, finding patterns in the luminous stars on her ceiling, Fern begging for more time, kisses sipped, scalp warm, cheeks almost downy: the earth-shaking pouring of maternal love. At the same time, in truth, Beth's neck aching, fighting through the tiredness of the day, dinner calling, wine if they let themselves, adult chat with Sol, but always the wonder of the human beside her whose voice tone, skin smell, was boundlessly pleasing.

'OK,' said Beth with apparent calm, her heart racing, 'I'll say goodnight down here. Of course.'

* * *

'Are you all right?' was the first thing Beth had said when her estranged mother had appeared in Hackney over a decade before. 'Why are you in London?'

Lizzie stood there on Beck Road by the buggy, as poised as an ageing ballerina. She hesitated, then nodded. 'Can I see?' she said, and didn't wait for permission, but dance-plunged as she always had to the buggy head and bent over to look at the two-month-old Fern.

Beth gripped the handles.

'Oh, Bethy,' Lizzie said, on a draining out-breath. 'So beautiful.'

Beth stood there. Certainty was quite gone. Seconds were shunting past.

'A boy or a girl?'

Beth paused. 'A girl,' she said stiffly. Lizzie's looks were softening into old age; she seemed to be alone. No wedding ring. There had always been a man attached to her.

'Beautiful. A beautiful baby, Bethy,' said Lizzie, peering into the pram, and Beth stared at her mother's head with the defenceless spray of a crown, and fury started to rise: a storm of uncryable tears.

'I'd love—' said Lizzie, reaching out to Fern's cheek, a witch's finger on the peach skin. 'Please can I see her?'

'Well, no—' Beth began. She pulled the buggy towards her. 'Sorry,' she said. Lizzie stared at her, all eyes of need, assessing and age-clouded.

Everything in Beth wanted to cry, throw her arms round this mother and protect her, this spiky vulnerable woman, the burden of responsibility on her own shoulders – only hers; her brother and father absent – and she would bow down to the ground to her, minister to her for life, have her back.

And yet lying below her was an innocent with that witch's finger on her. Beth jerked away the buggy.

'You couldn't even be bothered to turn up,' she managed to say.

Beth walked off, trembling more violently than she ever had in her life, and after a few steps in silence, she turned, because what if she had killed her mother? It was the expression of Lizzie's which always returned later when she hated herself: a mouth round in a face that was a deflated balloon, pouched with grief. Her mother had now been abandoned. The shaking brought a rush of saliva to Beth's mouth, and she walked faster.

'No. No,' Beth had begged Sol later when he had written to Lizzie care of her half-brother. 'Not like that.'

'Ungrateful,' Lizzie had called to Beth's retreating back.

* * *

The following week, Fern shrugged her way out of a jumper covering a skimpy top, and put on her favourite hoodie that, touchingly, bore the simple legend *London*. Beth caught sight of her waist, her belly button thinning as she stretched upwards, and the slightness and thinner face filled her with a leap of protectiveness.

Fern seemed to stare back at her, then a small smile twisted her mouth.

'You *really* don't need to stay in for me any more. Remember.'

'What kind of bonkersness is this?' said Beth.

'Go out again tonight.'

'I don't want to!'

'You can,' said Fern. 'I have a rehearsal. I'll go to Maia's first.'

'For what?' said Beth. 'Can we talk about—'

Her phone started to ring in her bag.

'My play. Remember. I'm Dulcie.'

'Yes,' said Beth, scrabbling for the phone.

'Beth,' said Tamara Bywater.

'Hi! Just one minute …' She held the phone to her palm. 'Let me just talk to you in a minute?' she said to Fern.

Fern turned her back. 'I don't think you care about anyone,' she seemed to say.

Beth was slack-jawed. 'Did you just say that? Fern, I love you and care about you more than the *world*.'

Fern gave a scornful laugh. 'Legitimately, bullshit,' she said.

'Good God,' said Beth to Tamara. 'Did you hear that?'

'Not really. Some teenage nonsense?' said Tamara, the low-level voice from the consulting room on her mobile. 'You have to ignore a lot of these dramas going on in their own heads at this stage. Because you become the scapegoat. Beth. I needed to hear you.'

'Oh. How – yes, I'd like to hear you too. That came out wrongly. I'm talking shit.'

A laugh.

'That reminds me exactly of you! I'm not supposed to see you but … I miss our sessions even. At least then I could see you every week. Was it a mistake to stop?'

Beth paused. She opened her mouth. 'No,' she said.

'So let's make another plan.'

Fern came quickly through the door.

'You're going out?' she said, triumph lifting her voice.

Beth shook her head and pressed her finger against her ear. There was a pause, silence on the line, Fern circling.

'I was rash, wayward; I put my job on the line. Yet I want to see you.'

Beth could hear, to her surprise, the wobble of a battle with emotion that Tamara wanted to hide from her.

'I'd like that.'

'Go out as long as you want,' hissed Fern. She shrugged.

'I can see you tonight,' said Beth. 'Early?'

'Yes,' said Tamara. 'Yes, please.'

Fern was looking up at her, her mouth parted. Her eyes were light hazel circles, freckles pinpoints against the pallor. 'Only while you're out,' said Beth.

'No, no, stay out all evening,' said Fern.

'I wouldn't do that!' said Beth.

'Ah, but you can, Mother, you can.'

'Fern, you're now sounding extremely odd!'

'The fucks I give are zero.'

There was a small laugh from Tamara on the phone. 'The hormones going berserk, the new brain connections haywire, the world grossly unjust.'

'I love you,' Fern muttered, then left the room.

'Did you hear that?' said Beth. 'All over the place. And yet, fool that I am, it makes me instantly happier. Bar at Moro? Seven possible?'

'Yes. Six thirty even.'

Beth made rapid mental adjustments to her schedule, ended the call and grinned at herself in the mirror, stretched her mouth, pulling faces. Her mind raced through outfits, options for greeting Tamara.

She found Fern, broke through her teenage force field and put her arm more confidently around her as Sol always did before she left for school.

'I don't know what all that was about, but I love you more than you can ever know.'

Fern nodded, her eyes cutting away from Beth. 'Rehearsal finishes about eight so I will be back by eight thirty. Like you can check with Maia's mum if you don't believe me.'

'Of course I believe you. No later than eight thirty.'

As Beth turned, she caught sight of herself in the toaster, in her own kitchen with its known utensils and drawings by Fern, and she realised in a sharp moment of clarity that she had another chance to stop it all. Stop what? Halt some trajectory that was dangerous and keep it all as it was. She could change the course now. She could arrest it.

* * *

After skipping a meeting, Beth waited inside Moro, the restaurant already full, a queue trailing out of the door. She had let her hair dry in a tumble. She wore a muted pink cashmere over a long tight skirt, red lipstick and her favourite small emerald earrings that Sol had given her years before, in a different life, to set off her hair, he said, her dark eyes. The minutes of waiting, of rearrangement and mirror-checking were there to be played with. Anticipation made her feel mildly queasy. This was what being in love was like. Was she in love? Yes. No. She didn't care. Tamara washed away the guilt.

The minutes ticked by. Beth looked round for something amusing to WhatsApp to Fern. Possibly it merely irritated her now. Tamara Bywater appeared in the door before she attached her photo, and she didn't send it.

Tamara paused, hovering on one foot, a waiter attending. Was there a way in which she moved – a level of strangeness even, a desirability to her very flaws – that caught the attention? Her manner was more beautiful than she herself was: there was the momentary charge of a Hollywood actress arriving. That shine was switched off in the consulting room,

She appeared close to Beth and grazed her cheek against hers.

They stood together in the queue for seats at the bar, jostled by media-employed strangers.

'How are you?' said Beth uselessly.

'Better for seeing you. Tired. Knackered.'

There was a small silence.

'How have you been so busy?' said Beth, awkwardly.

'Oh, I always am,' she said. 'Ann Penrose is a slave driver. The thing is, I'm obsessed with my work; but if I give it everything, life gallops by …'

She addressed a tray-bearing waiter, who paused in all his haste, and within moments they were sitting at the bar ahead of half a dozen queuing people.

'How did you do that?'

'I don't know,' said Tamara absently. 'I just cared about the poor boy. They're so underpaid.'

They sat in a crush on bar stools, and there was a party atmosphere going on, noise and jostling, but they were in a hollow of their own, Tamara's flimsy gloves appearing like underwear on the counter, the staff placing olives, drinks, carefully around them.

She gazed at Beth for some off-centre moments. 'I think I do need you,' she murmured.

'You do …? Yes. I'm confused? Well. So how are you? Oh, I'm all—'

'Be calm, Beth! You're jumpy. Are you nervous?'

Beth's mouth opened. 'I— Yes.'

'Of course. So am I.'

'Are you?'

'You know, don't you, that I'll always help you however I can? We don't need a silly restrictive consulting room for that. You have so much going for you. I don't think you realise.'

'Thank you. Tell me more about your husband,' said Beth abruptly.

Tamara looked away. 'Angus. He's – good. To the girls, to me. He's a good man.'

'Yes? Good.'

'He bores me. Quite a lot.'

Beth laughed, but Tamara remained still-faced. The journalists chattered among the terracotta.

Beth threw the questions at her that had always been forbidden, and with prompting, dismissal, the world of Tamara Bywater span in front of her, resetting itself: a colourful, somehow awry existence in which a psychologist's work seemed to involve multiple challenges with colleagues and patients; a social life that appeared impossible to categorise; but, glimmering between Tamara's words, there was a sense of some badly behaved netherworld that both excited and unsettled Beth, jealousy gripping her even now.

Tamara wore a gossamer covering of tights only. The old Dr Bywater was disconcertingly recast. Beth had a long-ago memory of a heel under a desk, dismissed.

Beth lifted her gaze and a woman was looking at her. She caught her eye and the woman gave the awkward smile that the moment of interaction demanded, then looked down.

They talked of their daughters, of American politics, of British MPs, of foundation and Brora sales, of artists, of perfectionism and self-doubt, of sibling relationships and work pressures.

Full absorption of the fact that here was the NHS mental health professional out in the world, was still impossible. Periodically Beth invoked the past, the boundaried doctor listening in her chair, and with it the retrogressive thrill of the taboo. It was as though she, a pupil among many, was out with the headmistress.

'We had this soulmate thing going on,' said Tamara in an uninflected voice that Beth had to strain to hear.

'How can you tell in a consulting room?'

'I can tell.'

'I hoped, I thought, I didn't dare be certain,' said Beth, blushing. 'Transference—'

'Transference schmanference.'

Beth laughed. '*You're* not supposed to be the one saying that.'

Tamara shrugged.

'What does your supervisor say about you seeing me?' said Beth suddenly into a silence. She bit her lip.

'I won't talk about it to my supervisor.'

'Why not?'

'He'll tell me not to.'

She leaned over and Beth breathed in her scent. She was tapping out something, a reminder note, on her phone. It reminded Beth of Sol, frequently on his mobile's Notes. She checked her phone for Fern. Tamara was still writing with one fast nail, making no excuse. Beth glanced at the patch of puckering that formed above her left eyebrow mid-contemplation. She wanted to kiss that mouth.

'Is this all there is?' said Tamara. 'In our lives.'

'What do you want?' said Beth.

'More *life*? Something, someone.'

'You need someone else?' Beth laughed, self-consciously. 'Something else? Travel? Well – what?'

'Yes. Rawness. Risk. As you once said yourself.' She looked away, picking up a cocktail stick and playing with it, bending it till it pricked her finger and drew a tiny spot of blood. 'There's always something. Professional rules to abide by. Other people.'

'Well, yes—'

'None of us should ever be afraid to live a life on the edge,' she said.

Beth held her phone tightly. She glanced at her Uber app. There was silence. 'But – but – what do you mean?' she said uselessly, to fill it.

'Rules are for little people.'

Beth laughed. She strained to hear every word, Tamara almost inaudible above the crashing of tapas plates, the scream of the Gaggia.

'I must get back to Fern,' said Beth. 'Sorry. It's too short.'

'Don't go,' said Tamara, and she grabbed Beth's hands then dropped them.

Beth took a gulp of alcohol and relaxed her shoulders as it fanned through her. She pushed herself, felt the movement of her arms as she pulled Tamara into them, there at the bar, drawing her to her whoever might see them.

'You can't do that,' said Tamara.

'No?' said Beth, but it came out as a cough.

'I'm married,' she said primly. 'And I'd be struck off.'

'We're both married. This is very weird.'

Tamara moved a strand of Beth's hair from her face and tucked it behind her ear. 'Treacle colours,' she said. She moved her mouth closer to Beth's ear. 'I love it that you don't just do what you're supposed to do. You're naughtier than you let on.'

'I think I'm very well behaved.'

A laugh.

'Too dutiful. I had to be,' said Beth.

'Shall we run off together?' said Tamara, whispering, her face close to Beth's.

Beth smiled. She opened her mouth.

'We can pretend,' said Tamara. 'We can pretend at least,' she murmured into her hair. 'Fantasise. That would keep me happy for a little while.'

Tamara stayed there and Beth held her, felt the intimate indentations of her spine; they pressed their faces together, their mouths talking and brushing each other's between words, and everything Beth could summon stopped her from kissing her properly. All Tamara's scents mixed with her hair, and they held each other, a pool of silenced talk around them.

'How many times did I long to do this through those sessions,' Beth said.

'Me too,' said Tamara, sinking her head. 'So much.'

FIFTEEN

It was later than Beth had thought. The traffic was heavy, rain falling in sharp streaks on the windscreen and distorting the white Christmas tree lights above the street. She rang Fern, went straight to her voice-mail, texted *Home soon xxxx*.

She caught sight of herself in the taxi mirror, rose colours, eyes dark with stimulation.

When you back?xx, she texted Sol. She added a heart. The taxi was piteously slow. She pressed her hand into the seat. The driver had to take a detour. 'Shit,' she muttered, and called Fern, but it still went straight to voicemail. She texted again.

She stopped the taxi early for greater speed and raced up Camden High Street, where she ran straight into Sol, lugging his bag and equipment.

'What?' she said, her voice high with surprise. 'Hello!' She hugged him, pressing her face against his neck and hiding from him. 'How was it?'

'A date?' said Sol. He looked her up and down.

'Oh I – don't be ridiculous! You haven't even said hello to me!'

Sol waited.

'How was it?' she said. 'I'm so glad to see you back safely.'

'Then what? Who?'

She opened her mouth. 'I was seeing the shrink,' she blurted. 'I mean I—'

'Like that.' He nodded at her clothes.

'Yes. A drink.' She blinked away the rain that fell on to her eyelashes.

Confusion passed in a wave over Sol's face. 'You were also seeing her the night I left. I thought you were seeing her for private sessions.'

'Oh. I was. But we've stopped now. We have to hurry back. Fern.'

Sol looked at her with the assessing expression that made Beth want to push him away. Her face was even hotter, barely cooled by rain. He walked ahead. 'We must discuss this psychologist at some time.'

'Why?' snapped Beth, accelerating her pace.

'It's the feeling of shifting ground that gets to me. It's becoming clear that all is not, uh, by-the-book with her.'

'You know,' said Beth, catching her breath. 'She's a consultant. NHS mostly, a bit of private.' She paused. 'So would you—' She scrabbled to fill the space. 'Yes. Listen, my – my taxi was late. I told Fern to be back by half eight.'

'Bet. It's way after. David's dropping by after nine. Must be that now.'

'Is it? I know. It's – oh God.'

She began to run and walk in turn.

'Just message her you're late,' said Sol.

'I have.'

They ran down the bridge steps. She tried to hold his hand, but he ignored her.

'The water reeks,' he said. 'You are dressed up. He—'

'Jesus, Sol. Do you think by repetition ...?'

'Who, then?'

'I *told* you. The shrink. Well, not my shrink. Therap— Tamara,' said Beth, as she paced by the canal.

'You don't normally stop therapy that abruptly. Right?'

She feigned an ignorant expression.

'David has told me about this,' he said. 'When he had a needy patient. You set an agreed future time together to terminate it.'

'Oh, therapese,' said Beth. 'I know. Anyway. That's analysis. Freudian couch wanking. But I'm fine. I don't feel as though I need any more.' She swallowed.

Sol glanced at her sharply as he hurried. 'You don't look so certain of that. I'd consider you do. Anyway, she should decide on that. Can you see therapists *socially*? Seriously unorthodox, right?'

Beth said nothing, biting her lip.

'OK,' said Sol, his shoulders lifting as he walked. 'Go off and see your therapist for a drink. Crazy move. You know what you're doing.'

His glasses were on his head as he tapped his phone, still striding, and turned into Little Canal Street. He opened the front door and Beth followed him. Only a low light shone from the floor above. She ran up. There was Fern, sitting cross-legged on a chair, gazing at her through the semi-darkness.

'Oh darling, I'm so sorry I'm late,' said Beth, pulling her towards her. 'Why haven't you put the lights on? It's cold in here.' The usual unbending posture, only a head to kiss. 'I'm sorry.'

Fern gave a small smile. Her eyes were shining in the gloom.

'I told you,' she said finally.

'What?'

'I told you,' was all Fern said.

* * *

The thump of the front door was followed by Sol's voice, the stairs to the first floor creaking with the bass of two pairs of footsteps. Fern was now ignoring Beth and picking at her nails. Beth's mobile began to ring from the side table at the entrance to the room, and she ran over to it. Fern followed, throwing herself into her father's arms.

The phone stopped ringing as Sol reached out and handed it to Beth in silence. *1 missed call. Tamara B.*

Beth feigned disinterest, glanced at David, who was behind Sol, and smiled. She put the mobile in her pocket.

Sol's expression was blank. He brought out his own phone. 'Drink?' he said to David, and they wandered into the kitchen, Sol tapping.

Beth took her mobile into the corridor. 'I just wanted to hear your voice.' A pause. 'Love love love,' echoed straight into her ear.

'Did you call her back?' said Sol from the doorway. 'Who?'

'Well, I'm guessing you're telling her stuff, confiding in her. If it's not about some man – the Jackass? – then who … beats me. So maybe you can inform me?'

'Oh, Solomon Brierley, you are so wrong. Shhh, anyway.'

'This is serious. David is concerned about this, says the patient shouldn't be talking to the therapist at all outside therapy.'

'David's still in the kitchen …? So keep quiet!'

'Why? This is not boundary-keeping at all – David,' he called, 'tell Bet what you—'

'I don't want to get involved,' said David in the work mode that Beth could usually pierce by making him laugh.

Sol's voice had tightened. 'Does this woman think she can solve everything?'

'Boundary issues here,' said David. 'I'm off.'

'See you Thursday,' called Sol as David left.

'What the fuck?' Beth said to Sol. 'Why did you tell him? Jesus! She could get into real trouble.'

'Then she should not be contacting you. I didn't need to tell him a damn thing. She did it all herself.'

'Oh.'

'What effect is this woman having?'

'Uh—'

'She is encouraging something in you, outside your regular life. I'm not dumb.'

'Because she is not restrained, she knows how to be free,' said Beth passionately. 'So, yes, she improves my life! Because she is kind and wise and knows how to help. So you should be glad. You wanted me to get help. I did. She still helps me. A lot.' She took in a deep breath. 'It could affect her job, this, this talk. Please. I mean, yes, she's aware it's a bit irregular, but she, but she – she thought it would help me.'

Sol nodded, slowly. 'Honey, she's helped you. I'll give you that.'

'Thank you.'

'So I'm being too cynical here?' he said, stroking his beard. 'She's calmed you down, made you happier, so maybe now I'll shut the hell up.'

'Never shut the hell up. I find you fascinating.'

'Hmm.'

Beth bit her lip. 'Is she – Tamara – going to get into trouble?' she said in a small voice.

'He won't say anything,' said Sol dismissively. 'He's not interested in her, and anyway, he'd protect Sofia. It's only concern for you that made him raise this.'

'You're such good boys.' She smiled at him.

Sol shook his head. 'And good boys are not fun, right?'

'I didn't say that. Of course not. You're *my* beloved good-boy-not-always-good.'

'Go back to the Jackass or his replacement if you want flowers every day and never knowing if your boyfriend'll show up.'

Her phone beeped in her pocket. She smiled again. 'You're right. That's exactly it. Not in a century would I go back to the Jackass or any man like him.'

* * *

Nights were disrupted. Beth was a sick woman, a creature of nerves and daydreams. Fantasies proliferated: Tamara in the Little Canal Street kitchen, implausibly sipping tea in work hours before Fern returned from school; Tamara kissing her in her office in her lunch break; Tamara in a boat with her, rowing to the tangled half-islands on the canal shore and lying there together; Tamara in the small room used for storage and guests, sneaking in after Fern's bedtime.

Beth pictured the books, paints and neglect up there and hastily cleaned it all in her mind, washing white curtains so that they danced in the wind over the canal light, the flight of swans, and all love was in there, high sky, wet bodies. The room had only a single bed – she tucked in the sweetest sheets she had, innocent and sprigged – and they made love together, however that happened, her legs weakening even as Fern was hissing some new accusation.

'Sleeping,' Fern said when Beth went to her room.

Beth backed away. 'OK,' she said. 'Don't worry. I won't even kiss you. But I love you.'

She had recently written Fern postcards and a letter stating her love, acknowledging Fern's anger, expressing a desire to understand any mistakes she had made and carefully refraining from asking questions. There was no sign Fern even read them. Fern's back was hunched against her, her face turned to the wall and covered with hair.

'Goodnight, anyway,' said Beth softly. 'I love you,' she said again, before she could stop herself.

* * *

Winter sunlight grazed the walls in the morning, ballooning with the canal's movement. The boy who wore a hoodie was out there, and Beth stared down at him from the window, but this time he passed by without turning. She looked around for a note from Sol, his X or scrawled heart on the back of an envelope, but there was nothing, and no text. Fern had gone with him. The restrictions on Fern were being gradually lifted, and she was permitted brief holiday outings with friends, though her apparent fury was growing rather than abating. Tamara was with Beth, day and night. But two days passed, and where was she? Her last words at Moro came to her: '*Me too ... so much.*' Beth rang her and leaped straight on to voicemail, every breath and tonal undulation pouring amplified into her ear.

She walked to the bus stop, to work in her studio. The light shone in the rare angle that allowed a glimpse of the canal bottom, only visible on early winter mornings, sun now illuminating a trolley, a car wheel, sediment-draped objects that were less definable. A fish silvered through a glare of weed, a disturbance of mud, and suddenly there was Lizzie. A memory of her in Hackney that made Beth's stomach plunge.

* * *

Beth had feared that Lizzie Penn would make another attempt after her approach on Beck Road. Her baby was so newly minted, with her precise little features beneath a slant of hair, her brows pen marks; and Lizzie had always, Beth later realised, been a determined person.

It was winter when she saw her again. Beth was on her own, enjoying the novelty of a walk with unencumbered arms, and mentally preparing Fern's supper, a backdrop of work ideas just beginning to stir, and there was Lizzie Penn, not back in the North, but at the top end of London Fields.

Beth turned sharply, but Lizzie was already calling. Beth carried on walking, her head down, though the voice of her mother made her heart a sagging organ.

'Please, Bethy. Can I – can I see her?'

'Sorry,' said Beth loudly, walking faster, but Lizzie had caught up.

'I'd like to see little Fern,' said Lizzie in a voice carrying an edge of ownership.

'Oh God,' said Beth. She glimpsed Lizzie's face with its wobble of indignation, the tears marbling her eyes. 'No. You didn't want— Why should you?' she said, anger giving her strength.

Lizzie recoiled as if slapped. The tears welled, hesitated, then spilled over.

'I'm her grandmother,' she said in a voice that expected a response.

* * *

And yet, all those years earlier in Sefton Park, Lizzie had been there. Her mother had *been* there at a certain point, back in Liverpool. Beth had rung those doorbells, her school companions calling, and there was no answer, and the face had disappeared. She knew she would go back the next day, or even that night if she could escape her father.

* * *

In the studio, the new space heaters Beth and her colleagues had succumbed to barely dented the sun-hazed cold, and they still clustered around the old stoves, even warming their hands by the bare light bulbs. Jack Dorian, no longer invoked to generate arousal for marital sex, was affable, cheerfully flirtatious, and part of the daily scenery. She ignored the chat. She wanted to fly through the smeared skylights to soar in the sun above Finsbury Park. Tamara must be only three or four miles away, breathing and moving so close to her.

Where was Tamara? Where were her texts in answer to Beth's?

And Beth was back to being Bethy, with the heartbreak of other people's mothers' kindness; back to relying on Ellie for tampons, to having an embarrassing home containing a man and adolescent girl, to love so strong for her father it made her insides plunge. She was a girl who had started to throw her misery into painting.

She had begun to choose all her own clothes by necessity, and so she had gradually invented herself without maternal guidance, although Ellie's mother occasionally tempered her odder choices as she stretched her small budget in second-hand shops, the interesting and the surprising used to disguise her awkwardness, and she was teased at school and admired at art college. Although her brother Bill had cut himself off from Lizzie after her departure, when he returned to Liverpool from Brighton, he was an armoured hunger of spiky hair. It turned out later that he had been starving himself.

Gordon Penn paid a neighbour, an old widow, to sit with his daughter after school until she was fourteen; yet in the first months, Beth still believed that Lizzie was coming back. She looked through the trees and detected her face in the sky; or she saw messages in the clouds. They were symbols. If she kept up the search, then Lizzie hadn't gone, and the light would be on in the kitchen when she got home after school, her mother's hair blurring past the window, and everything back, back to what it was, the overwhelming happiness of her return. The truth dawning in the mornings was a repeated shock.

* * *

And where was Tamara? Two more days went by, and in the frequent absence of Fern and Sol, Beth worked on the *Metropolitan Mice* during The Dairy's Christmas holidays, and painted in a fever. Sol had begun to keep his distance in a way that was objectively worrying but afforded Beth mental freedom, a new technicoloured life flowing above the problems of reality.

On December the twenty-second, Beth picked up a call from an unknown number and jumped at the voice of Tamara Bywater. 'I have been so longing to hear you,' said Tamara. Beth made a small sound. 'I'm using someone else's phone ... oh, hello, just a moment ...' A background of people talking, of work, of static, Tamara in a hurry yet soft, the voice travelling through and down Beth. 'Oh, darling. I'm in terrible trouble ... Tried to explain, but then a colleague came in ... my boss Ann Penrose is after me, would love to get rid of me. We were spotted ...'

'Spotted?'

Tamara greeted a probable patient in the background. 'At Moro. Someone who knows Penrose spotted you, from the *Standard* or something, Penrose worked out it was me from my *handbag* ... her menopausal rampages ... Christ, I have to go. I love you. I don't think we can see each other. It's awful. I've been crying—'

'Can't see each other?'

'Of course not. I'll be struck off ... Just coming, so sorry ... Need to lie low ... If I'm caught again, there goes my career. Got to go. We are for life, you and I, in whatever form.'

The line went dead.

'Tamara,' said Beth into nothing, only now absorbing a fraction of the loss that would then follow, and tears that she hadn't noticed trickled down her face into her ears.

'No,' she said, to her phone, to herself.

* * *

There was a purity to it. Her daughter would no longer speak to her. Sol was absent. She had driven her mother away. 'It was not your *fault*,' came Tamara's voice of old. 'You have internalised this, Beth.' Christmas was a numb echo of Christmases past, the rituals sustaining any semblance of levity, Boxing Day sagging into relief.

Sol spent the school holidays working, taking Fern on safer freelance jobs when he could, and he bought her YA novels with blocky fluorescent jackets that she read as he worked, and bubble tea in shops she led him to. They went off to ice-skate when Sol had time, eating at the Lock, and shooting a film together with Fern's friend Soraya, the 'rushes' viewed with shrieks of hilarity or disgust each evening.

As late December and then January progressed, it was only work that brought Beth back to the absent Tamara, to Lizzie, to thoughts of death, the tar and silt clogging the underlayers, so at times the paint was built to a depth of several millimetres in bulbous swirls beneath a translucency of wash. Memory after memory in unwanted flashes: Lizzie almost unrecognisable in her Liverpool hospital bed, face pulled into rubber distortions. A maw of need. The Tartar features plumped and skewed, covered in tubes.

After some hours of *plein-air* work in which she studied the river, Beth hurried along the north bank and, like an animal into its pen, walked straight into the hospital.

She stood in the rattling lift in a fug of heat, her hands thawing, and she was back there, back in the place she had found deliverance. There were the double doors; the disinfectant fumes of salvation. She wanted to live there, crouch in a day room with her own Thermos, a row of plastic padded chairs to sleep on, a river view in all its moods. Scarcely needed at home, she would be quite happy, waiting for Tamara to finish work and then bandage her mind.

There was no one there. Already, the department had gone. The receptionists' area was closed, the window shut over their booth. Their stacked post and leaflets, their computers, the filing cabinet behind which they had stored Beth's wet painting carrier, were all gone, a few notices still stuck there, a pile of magazines left on a chair. She spun around. A light flickered with a neuralgic buzzing, but no one emerged, and she ran through doors to the corridors to where Dr Bywater worked, every detail so known, so loved, it felt almost owned by her. She stormed along, names, familiar to her now as a forgotten dream, emerging thick with loss. She got to their room. *Dr Tamara Bywater, Consultant Clinical Psychologist.* She tried it, but the handle wouldn't even twist. She rapped on it, its varnished wood dulling the force into a feeble tap. She sobbed against it. *Dr Tamara Bywater.*

She ran back along the corridors, her mouth a strained rhombus, her feet slapping on the floor with no one to hear. A cleaner was out there, shunting round an industrial-sized machine with the indifference of a mule.

'Where are they?' she said.

He gazed blankly and said something Beth didn't understand, and she nodded then burst back out through the doors.

'Where did they go?' she said to a doctor who was walking in the other direction.

He glanced back. 'Psychology's moved,' he said. 'Out to the Wilton Centre.' He paused. 'Do you need some help?'

'No, no,' said Beth too loudly.

* * *

The dawn was to be got through. She was thirteen again and she was vermin. She was one of the rats that, if she stayed through dusk to paint at the river, she saw running up the sidings. She lay in bed. She still checked her phone, then again. The self-loathing possessed the calmness of snow-sleep. She was where Lizzie had left her.

Fern's banked-down disgust now turned to fury. She would barely speak to Beth, giving her assessing gazes before she turned, or casting her baleful glances that were so exaggerated, they verged on the comic, and Beth did not comment but forced herself, with an effort of will, to wait for her to reveal further sources of abhorrence.

* * *

The weeks without Tamara were muffled. Signs of life in February were now only there to torment: the alder catkins, wild arum leaves, sudden gulls in evenings, blackbirds pecking on the terrace.

'You are completely distracted,' said Sol.

Beth hesitated. 'I know,' she said in misery.

'Are you having an affair?'

Beth paused. '*No*,' she said in a staccato voice. 'Are you?'

'Of course not. An emotional affair?'

'No,' she said, stiffening against the heat that began to rise.

'Where's the therapist?'

Beth's back tensed. 'I don't know.'

'Well.' Sol shrugged. 'Something. A – a breakdown?'

'No. I'm happier,' she said dully.

'What, then?'

She paused. She pressed her big toe hard into the bottom of her shoe. Sol's mouth was ominously tense. Beth shrugged and pulled a face, and he remained motionless.

'You think I will just carry on, like this?'

Her phone rang. *Tamara B.*

'Take the call,' he said, and walked out of the room.

Sixteen

As the weather started to become warmer, the mayflies
and coltsfoot emerging, there were more walkers on the
Regent's Canal towpath, their shapes moving blots in the
night. Dusk was best for those apparitions whose outlines
were blurry with gold that dipped into shadow. The one
time Tamara had rung Beth, the line had gone dead, Beth
had gone straight to voicemail when she called back, and
then Tamara hadn't answered her text of enquiry.

Beth now attempted not to ask Fern questions,
making suggestions and dredging her mind for anecdotes or quirky facts instead as Fern shrugged.

'No touching,' she said as Beth approached, then
hesitated, in preparation for a hug before work. 'No
touch,' said Fern. She held her palms up.

Beth lowered her chin. 'OK,' she said, and lifted her
bag without turning to say goodbye.

'Like, she's not even saying bye to me now?' Fern
spat out. 'Such dumb shit.'

'Don't be so rude to your mother,' Sol snapped.

Fern blushed. 'Sorry,' she said, and as Beth was leaving, she flung herself at her father and they hugged.

'You smell of teddy bears and the clothes dryer,' she said to him.

* * *

Beth had tried to return to Sefton Park the night after she had seen her mother in a first-floor window, but Gordon Penn was watching TV all evening, and it was impossible for her to sneak past him from her bedroom. Then when she had gone through the park again, shaking off the girls who walked home with her, she was uncertain which was the right house. There was the vast terrace scabbed with gull excrement crusting soot and rain, and there was house after house, divided into flats.

She saw a boot kicking her, and it was her own foot slamming into her own shin in self-loathing for not remembering. How? What idiot would fail to notice the number of the house that seemed, inexplicably, to contain her mother? Had it been the one with a bird barrier, one with a ribbon tied to the railings, one with cat food flaking in a pool of rain in its basement area?

'*Mum*,' she said out loud. 'Lizzie,' she tried hesitantly.

* * *

The evenings were longer now that the clocks had changed. Bird sound bled its mechanical chirruping. Could that be Tamara? There on the towpath in April at dusk when the flickering of rose and black was like a photograph of the long-gone past. Beth saw her in all places: Tamara Bywater, as unreal as a geisha; as absent as the dead. Any possible sighting by the canal was a chimera on which to pin hope. The sop of the substitute was better than nothing.

Now, on Saturday morning, the tourists and cyclists were already filling the towpath, mallards calling, and there among them she was; there she was. Tamara Bywater.

Beth kept looking. She felt sick. There was the buzz of a text.

Sol found his phone. He wandered over. He looked out, seemed not to notice.

Beth took hers out. *Tamara B.* She dropped her hand as Sol came back, and it shook.

She couldn't look yet. She put the phone on Silent mode. She glanced round the kitchen. They were to have a family day out, Fern persuading her parents to view Camden Lock as the focus of all their activities. Fern now sat reading and mindlessly eating yoghurt in her sleeping shorts, her washed hair in several plaits for crimping purposes.

The phone vibrated. Beth sneaked it out, watching Sol. His hand rested on Fern's shoulder while he shook a frying pan to cook her egg as she liked it, addressing her as 'sweetcakes'. The night before, he had made Beth a hot-water bottle as she bent over with period pains.

He gave Fern her egg to a mutter of thanks, scrawled through photos on his phone in a towel and began to do his usual back exercises stretched against the door-frame, still frowning at his work.

Beth's phone was dangerous treasure in her hand. *Tamara B: You there?! Delete.*

'Darl—' she said to Sol in rushed words that collided with a cough, 'your back's hurting?'

'Only a little,' he said, not looking up.

What are you doing? she tried to text with her thumbs under the windowsill, but she hit the wrong keys. The ducks paddled idly, a tourist boat chattering past, the *Mary-Lou* absent in the face of the Saturday police, and the spring crowds choked the bridge.

What am I dot giving?!! Tamara texted, and lifted a hand. *If I can't see you, I have to come and see you. Forbidden?*

Fuck Ann Penrose.

'You are a texter,' said Sol.

'A bad habit.'

Can we see each other? I couldn't stay away any more. It's been so so long. Please please delete, texted Tamara.

How? Yes. Where? texted Beth, and walked away from the window. Sol caught her eye.

'Sorry, it's rude,' said Beth.

'Hey, girls,' said Sol, 'if we don't push off now, we're going to miss a table at this Bar – Flamenco? Hasta la Vista? … Cinco de Mayo?'

'Bar Arriba,' muttered Fern, undoing a plait.

'You seem more cheerful,' he said to Beth.

'My period pain's gone,' she said blithely, the ease of lying followed by a flash of remorse.

'Apologies for your wimmin's suffering,' he said with a straight face, and beat his chest. She laughed. She began to brush her hair.

She looked at the silly Barbapapas calendar on the wall that Ellie had given her.

'I can't,' she said in a blurt that turned into another cough.

He looked at her with his steady brown gaze. She swallowed.

'I mean I—' She smiled. 'Need to do a bit of work. Can I meet you in a bit?

He got out his phone, paused and made a note, as she had subconsciously known he would. Fern steadily ignored Beth.

'Your choice,' said Sol, and she caught a glimpse only of his expression.

* * *

Looking back later, this was still a time of comparative stability, or so it seemed, when the family was in the house, and Beth was working well at last, even Lizzie temporarily subdued; but her daughter no longer spoke to her, and the house was straw and she didn't know it. All she knew was that her life was infused with magic.

Tamara glittered. In the few snatched encounters Beth now had with her between frequent texts, she shone with more spirit than Beth had ever seen in that consulting room. They would meet by the canal in hidden moments among spring's growth, the green bursting, the horse-chestnut blossoms and baby mallards, and walk, and talk, and still Tamara didn't kiss her and, for all Tamara's words, Beth would doubt anew what she had once imagined that evening in Moro so long before. Then Tamara would disappear for days into the constraints of her professional world with its boundaries before re-emerging, and in those times, the urgency of their communications was like nothing Beth had experienced. And still the sunny vista was touched with hell when Tamara didn't answer her messages and Beth, sensing impending rejection, worked hard, with little peaks of panic, at becoming a more appealing version of herself. She started to read basic psychology guides. She reshaped her eyebrows. She memorised subjects for conversation. And then Tamara would redirect the beam of her attention, and somehow Beth was the most interesting person she had ever met. Intoxication rendered everything outside its orbit dull.

And there was Sol beside her, a different breed. Cats and dogs. Earth and air.

'I'm thinking we should maybe go to Newport the moment Fern quits school?' he said.

Beth glanced at her diary, racing through possible work reasons to stay in London longer.

'You are so distracted,' said Sol again.

'No, I'm not,' said Beth, and she smiled at him and kissed him.

Lately they had lacked even the conventions of romance, subsiding instead into a routine of practicalities, debates about when to leave for the annual trip to Sol's mother in Rhode Island; questions about each other's day, well-worn resentments and predictabilities, the domestic and the transactional dipping, on very rare occasions, into nostalgia for the beginning of love. Beth went through the motions of discussing the American trip, during which they usually took turns working, Sol flying to different jobs, while Fern was at her happiest disappearing with a crowd of cousins.

Sol was his grumpy, hardworking, kind self, behind a coating of privacy, and he and Beth drifted through days, bobbing against each other with an unease that, from past experience, would develop either into a row or a period of deeper intimacy. They were not good at distance.

Sex barely occurred. For the first time, Sol would not or could not, and when she finally tried, he was limp, as he rarely ever had been.

Friction turned to blankness that allowed Beth space in which to dream, only background worries regarding Sol niggling at her in her relief that he no longer questioned her.

'Mum,' said Fern after school one day, resting her head against Beth so Beth jolted at the first communication for weeks. 'Hello.'

'Hello!' She put her arm round Fern, tentatively.

'Do you really want to go to Newport?'

'Of course—' Her voice wobbled. 'Why wouldn't I?'

'Well why haven't you booked the tickets?'

'We will! Let me discuss with Dad.'

Tamara rose up with her smile, and Beth spoke with a speeded tone that overlaid the image, Sol coming in.

'I like this,' said Sol, nodding at an unfinished painting Beth had propped on the table to study in different lights. The river was a flow of gulls, and hair floated among the birds, and she couldn't help it, couldn't help delineating each sodden strand. Was guilt edging at the darkness? A thought hit her. Tamara slotted over the top.

'Thank you.'

They prepared supper, talking of a new commission of Sol's, the sky luminous with a fading brightness that made sunshine of the kitchen, and as Beth was fetching plates with one hand and stirring salad with the other, *Tamara B* appeared on her phone. She crouched over it. She glanced at Sol, and left the room. Beneath a confusion of voices she heard a suppressed sob.

She walked out of the kitchen to the yard.

'I need to see you. Angus is a madman.'

'How?'

'He's shouting at me ... He's being cruel. Really – heartless. I don't know why. He won't even go and get my medicine.'

'You're ill?'

'I seem to have come down with something – nothing bad. Throat again. It's usually tonsillitis.' She dropped her voice, so Beth strained to hear her, a chaffinch loud from the gutter high up. 'He's *shouting* at me. I'm afraid of what he might—'

'Put him on,' said Beth.

'No! Of course I can't do that.'

'Then I'm coming straight down to you,' she said. 'Just wait there.'

She ran back into the kitchen, where Sol had laid the plates out on the table and turned the radio on to catch the headlines.

'I—' said Beth, flustered. The lying had developed a diseased smoothness. 'I need to go and see Ellie.'

'Do you? It's dinner.'

She pulled on a jacket and grabbed her bag as she talked. She had taken to keeping make-up in her bag in case of such events, as she had done in her teens.

'Have you booked the tickets now?' said Fern without looking up.

Beth paused. She glanced at Sol. He shrugged.

'We *will*! Don't worry.'

She tried to kiss Fern goodbye. Fern jerked her head away. Beth hesitated and scanned a scene frozen in awful knowledge: House of Cardigans.

'I need to go—' she said, scrabbling. 'Ellie's got a problem.'

Her spine stiffened.

Fern lifted her head and stared at Beth with the unblinking gaze she used for their Outstaring competitions, in which she habitually triumphed. It was the first time she had looked directly at her in weeks.

Beth gave an awkward smile. She turned.

Fern was emptying out her bulging pencil case.

'I love you both,' said Beth, but they were already busy.

* * *

She tumbled out of Kennington tube and squeezed along the passage, now unruly with honeysuckle and jasmine that pressed its green-white scent on her, the flowers bright in the falling light. She knocked on the door to Tamara's consulting room before remembering that this was not where she entered any more; and she retraced her steps. Beth heard Tamara's voice laughing at her, eyes among the leaves, splash of skin. She didn't look ill.

'Are you still my patient?' she said, pulling Beth into a wild hug.

'I wish I was,' said Beth without meaning to.

'Do you? No, no, too restrictive. We're past that now.'

'Yes.'

'Oh, sweetheart,' she said, then coughed as she led Beth into the hall. 'Meet Angus.'

'I want to sort out this dickhead for you.'

'Oh no, really not. I love your occasional vulgar expressions. Angus's as gentle as a sheep! No, that's not right, is it? A lamb. He always is—'

'But you said—'

'Oh, it was not very much, really,' she said, and she gave Beth a graze of a kiss on the lips. 'Sorry. I got overdramatic. Here he is.'

Beth stared, the shock of the brush of Tamara's lips still on hers, as the husband shambled into the hall, carrying a shopping basket of a feminine design that gave him the air of an old European man. He looked somewhat surprised to see her there. He was, oddly, halfway as Beth had imagined him, with his faded fairness and his glasses, his style redolent of the architect he was not.

She hesitated, then returned his handshake with a stony expression.

'This is Angus. Beth, who is a famous artist.'

Beth turned away. 'I'm not. Are you all right now?' she said to Tamara.

Tamara smiled. 'Oh yes, Angus decided he wouldn't get me my painkillers as some kind of protest. Apparently I was behaving badly.'

'I'll go and get them for you,' said Beth. 'What do you need?'

'Oh no, no, thank you, you're kind,' she said, the voice wrapping her so that again the tone came before the words. 'Angus will go for me now; there are several other things I want.'

'I have my list,' he said, peering down at a column of handwriting whose familiarity to Beth lent it a bloom of intimacy in the hall, memories of the unknowable Dr Bywater's signature on NHS letters. The husband was tall and broad but uncertain, stooping in the hall-way of a house whose proportions were too small for him, only the length of the blond-grey hair straggling down one side of a square face defying Beth's precon-ceived image. She could see the remains of moderately good looks that would have once appealed.

'What kind of an artist?' he said. 'It's Tamara who is our curator. Collector, I should say. The family expert.' He smiled at her.

'Roughly – urban landscape. Symbolic landscapes.'

'Ah! Abstract or figurative?'

'Neither, exactly.'

'Oh, silly, real artists won't categorise themselves like that,' said Tamara. 'Come and have tea, Beth.'

Angus looked at Tamara, but she had turned. She and Beth passed the rooms stuffed with paintings and quirky antiques that contained very little sign of chil-dren. He followed them down to the kitchen, stooping and turning intermittently to Tamara, as though wait-ing for her approval.

Tamara looked at him, saying nothing.

'Yes,' he said after a beat. 'I must go to the chemist.' He glanced at her between sentences.

'La Martorana ...' said Beth, examining a photo on the fridge.

'Yes, we have Palermo plans for a late-summer holiday,' he said, glancing at Tamara, who merely smiled into the distance without looking at him. 'Mar has friends there,' he said, brightening. 'But we're thinking about Edinburgh at Easter. If that's what you'd still like?'

'Darling,' she said, turning abruptly and running her nails down his sleeve, the action brushing Beth with a flare of jealousy. 'Late-night opening hours aren't forever. I need my ...'

'Yes, yes, of course. And the foundation. Is it shade One or Two?'

'Two for summer.'

'You *know* this stuff—' Beth began, dampening laughter.

'Oh, he's marvellously practical.'

'She's got a big conference coming up,' he said. 'I'm sure that's why there's been a bit of stress.'

'I went slightly diva,' said Tamara, turning to Beth, 'but Angus has yet to apologise, so I'm still sulking.'

He looked at her in tense amusement.

'If he thinks that is bad behaviour, I have more I can offer,' she said, and he kept his gaze on her, palpably animated.

She took cups from the dishwasher while he hesitated, but she kept her back to him, then he squeezed and stooped his way up the staircase with his wife's fabric-lined basket.

Tamara asked Beth a string of questions about her day, what she had done, who she had seen, how she was, what her family was doing. 'Thank you for coming to my rescue,' she said.

'It seems I didn't need to.'

'I'm always happy to be rescued.' She sighed. 'He's an amiable enough companion, but ...' She found saucers, took down a Japanese teapot, a tarnished silver strainer, small items, as delicate as those she carried around with her. She held the teapot absently. She touched her neck. 'He doesn't exactly light my fire.'

Tamara began rearranging a kitchen shelf, tea seemingly neglected.

'Maybe we've just been together too long,' she said, filled the kettle and forgot to put it on. 'The classic attrition. He's a great father. There's nothing wrong with him, exactly. I sound quite terrible, don't I? Hard. I do love him. I respect him. But ...' Her face stilled. 'Beth, I've got to this age and ... I'm stifled. Restricted, *bored.*'

Beth laughed a little, nodded. 'Marriage can be boring,' she said, betrayal shaming her. 'Bloody boring,' she said, compounding it. Bitch, she thought.

Tamara turned to her with a laugh. 'Sol's not, though, is he?' She suddenly put her hands on Beth's shoulders.

There was a silence.

'No,' said Beth, gripping her thumb and middle finger together as she spoke. She pressed the kettle switch.

Tamara's face was blank. 'What am I supposed to do?' She busied herself without looking at Beth so that Beth could watch the fall of her hair as she moved, and the caught, or possibly imagined, scent of her fed an image of kissing her that was growing in her mind.

Taxi engines grumbled on the street above the basement that contained just the two of them, silver evening light penetrating its area, youths shouting. Where were Tamara's children? Beth looked around for photos of them on the fridge or on shelves but she could find only one school portrait in which they were much younger. She stared in search of Tamara's genes.

'This isn't full *living*, is it?' said Tamara finally, and at last she turned to Beth, but she appeared, Beth thought, almost off-kilter, a fragility to her that was disquieting. And then a punch of desire, stronger than anything she had experienced for so many years, hit her.

'Poor you,' said Beth pathetically. 'But it's clear he's crazy about you.' She heard her own student-like awkwardness as she fawned through the silence.

Tamara shrugged.

Beth rammed at her creative powers, inventing new angles for entertainment, aware that she was now boring Tamara as much as her husband did, the result a kind of cheeky flattery that was connected with the youthful artistic persona with which she had somehow been invested; yet still Tamara's attention was elsewhere, unengaged by a personality that couldn't equal hers.

The imagined kiss with this woman, terrifying yet longed for, ballooned in front of Beth, until it was all she could think about, swaying towards it in her mind as though on a diving board, poised for the moment where courage propelled the undoable. She made herself think of Sol, Fern, her life at home. She gazed through the kitchen, the kiss temporarily deflated.

Beth spoke. Tamara didn't answer.

The thought of the kiss sliced through Beth's mind again. She hesitated, seeing the choreography in a series of jerky images.

There was a knock at the front door. 'Oh,' Tamara sighed.

Beth cursed audibly, Tamara raising one eyebrow, and she pressed herself against the washing machine.

'Who is it?' she said as Tamara reappeared alone.

'Oh, just Duncan. My neighbour.'

'Where is he?'

'I never made the tea, did I?' she said vaguely. 'Upstairs fixing the lights.'

'Why?' said Beth, no aspect of Tamara too small to collect. 'I mean—'

Tamara paused, mystification apparent.

'The – lengthy therapy-based biographical ban makes me inordinately curious,' said Beth in a rehearsed rush. 'I wasn't even allowed to know—'

'He does things,' said Tamara across Beth. 'He's good with fixing all sorts of things. It's very kind of him.'

'How often does he come round?'

'Oh, *I* don't know, Beth. Most weeks, after work. He seems to like to.'

Beth started to laugh. 'So you have a tame neighbour as your unpaid odd-job man, while your husband trots out to buy your make-up?'

'Oh, Beth, you are *bad*,' said Tamara, turning fully for the first time, eyes looking straight into her.

Beth breathed out too loudly, then attempted to convert her exhalation into a cough.

'I know that sound,' said Tamara.

'How?' said Beth abruptly.

'I've heard it in my time.' Tamara smiled, not looking at her, and put her hands behind Beth's neck. There was a series of hoots outside, doors slammed. 'Oh, Beth. But we can only play.'

'The dragon Ann Penrose—'

'Ann – oh. I'm not afraid of her any more.'

'Really?'

'Perhaps you'd better go. If I stay with you any longer, I fear ...' She shook her head.

'What is going on?' said Beth rapidly.

'I am not sure when Angus will get back.'

'No. Us. I feel – I feel sometimes you're – flirting.'

Tamara paused. 'Of course I am. It's very odd, isn't it? Does it really matter? You're blushing. As long as we can see each other.'

Beth was silenced. 'Yes, but – but – we're both straight, we—'

Tamara laughed. 'You old-fashioned thing. Quaint! Younger people don't see it like that. At all. They barely even know what *gender* they are.'

'Yes, yes, I know. But we've – we've both got families. Nothing can happen. Well. I mean …?'

'Nothing can happen,' said Tamara, and she gave the same smile. 'Nothing! I would be struck off, anyway. Enough talking now,' she said, taking Beth's arm. 'You're trembling! There's the whole world out there for us to explore, remember. We've agreed we can't have each other, so—'

'We can,' said Beth, clearing her throat.

Her phone went. She jolted. *Aaa Sol.*

'Oh, Jesus,' she said. She hesitated. 'It's Sol.' Her voice was too high. 'I promised to call him about when I was returning.'

'So?' said Tamara. She looked Beth straight in the eyes.

Then Tamara's arms were around Beth's waist, her mouth breathing laughter into her collarbone. Beth pressed the Reject button.

Tamara pulled away. She began sorting a pile of papers on the table with fast movements. She took a

233

sip of water. There was a thump from overhead that sounded like the front door shutting. She lifted her head, then she turned her eyes to Beth and held them for a second. Beth moved quickly towards her, and they kissed, Tamara's lips, coated in the taste of cold water, her tongue tip a suggestion of warmth revealing itself beneath.

'I don't know how to resist you any more,' murmured Tamara. She looked up at Beth as her husband's feet set off a cacophony of creaking on the stairs. 'I tried,' she said, and Beth smoothed the frown on her forehead. 'I keep trying.'

Beth held Tamara and kissed her, thrown off course by the contrast with all men: the softness, the silken smallness, Tamara's lips on hers with a shock of intimacy, a wetness, so wrong, strange, then right: a shoot of pleasure that Beth knew even then would be played back countless times, the present moment almost impossible to grasp, and all Tamara's bewildering female scents streamed into her like poison.

SEVENTEEN

When Beth had failed to recognise the house in Sefton Park, she attempted to subdue her despair, and pressed the bells of the houses situated roughly where she had crossed the road before. Silence followed, or sounds of enquiry, delays, crackling, voices at once.

She went to the nearest phone box and rang the reception in her brother's hall of residence until she located him, and as she eventually stumbled into the question about their mother's whereabouts, the foolishness of her words was immediately apparent, and he was dismissive. Had she been hallucinating?

But one day, later that week, she saw a figure from across the park.

* * *

Fern's rejection was the great sorrow of Beth's existence. To survive at all, she threw herself into both her river series and her obsession, with its drug-like properties.

'Fern,' she said one day, 'we can't carry on like this.' She faltered, and Fern froze. 'If you can just tell me honestly where I've gone wrong,' said Beth. 'Please. Fern.' But Fern turned away. 'We cannot carry on like this,' said Beth again. 'I love you. Something is very, very wrong. What?' Fern said nothing. 'I know I – revolt you, anger you, annoy you. Some of it is normal. But not this. Please. What is *going on*? Do you intend to ignore me in front of Oma in America? I love you so much. Fern, I would give everything for you,' Beth said to the back of Fern's head, a still fall of hair. Beth tried to touch her. Fern shrugged away her hand with a jerk. 'All I want to know is the cause. For this being *this* bad,' said Beth, but she could barely speak. 'Can you just tell me one thing that you think I have done?' Fern was silent. 'Just one of the things. I … I could go the other way and say that you are being unacceptably rude, obstructive, and punish you,' said Beth, and there was a twitch of Fern's shoulder. 'But I'm not going to. All I'm going to say now, if you won't, really won't speak to me, is that I love you, always, more than anyone in the world, and whatever you do, however you are to me, I always will.'

Fern stood still, her arms now folded, then, without turning, she walked away. Beth curled on the sofa until she fell into a sudden exhausted sleep.

* * *

'Ungrateful,' Lizzie Penn had called her, and worse.

'I'm her grandmother,' Lizzie had said that morning almost thirteen years before in London Fields, in a voice that expected a response, grabbing her arm so Beth shook it off and began to run in the direction of her house, back to Fern and Sol.

'Go to Bill's girls,' she called back with a pang of disloyalty.

'But—' Lizzie's face closed off.

A picture of herself returned to Beth as it often had over the years: the last time she had seen Lizzie Penn in her childhood, calling out in TJ's to a mother who was not moving towards her.

'Mum. Please. No. It's – it's much too late.' Beth spoke more softly, but she sped on. 'Please. I wish you well. You have to leave us.'

'*No*,' said Lizzie, catching up. Her gaze was so close, breath unpleasant on Beth's face. She was like some taunted bear about to hit out.

A fury that Beth had never expressed even to herself was surfacing in her throat, something vast and unstable. 'No way on this earth.'

'I think I'm entitled,' said Lizzie. Her jaw jutted out.

'Do you have no shame, Mum? No *embarrassment* about this?' said Beth.

Lizzie was momentarily silenced. 'I think we should move on,' she then said.

'So you can start again.'

'If you like. Yes,' said Lizzie, again that protrusion of chin, that wobble of determination. 'I'd like to see my granddaughter, please.'

'Oh my God.'

Beth walked faster, faster, breaking into a run, Lizzie running beside her, now gabbling nonsense, pleadings, accusations.

'... pity for ... ungrateful ... bitch,' Beth heard clearly among the stream of insults, and she picked up her pace.

She slipped into an alley, ran even faster, entering the nature reserve and then an estate as a convoluted route home to shake her mother off. It was the first time she had ever stood up to her.

* * *

Beth rose to soak her eyes with cold water before Sol and Fern saw them. There was a new text on her phone: *I want to do that again.*

She could never sleep, those nights. She spent the time from midnight with Tamara, riding glittering distortions of their real life; then in the morning she paid the price with guilt as she recalculated the stretched seconds of kissing while the husband lumbered towards them. Everything else had fallen away, the rest of life merely a distraction from desire.

She woke drained, yet with an unstoppable energy. Everything seemed washed in new colour. The discordance of bird call in the trees outside the house was a clamour of excitement.

She stared at a new text on her phone. *Tamara B. Why aren't we kissing?*

Like mercury sliding inside her.

'I think there's something you need to read,' said Sol, and his voice was not quite steady. 'David sent it again.'

'OK!' said Beth over-brightly from the window.

He tapped on a link from David Aarons and handed Beth his iPad. '"The Slippery Slope …"' she said. 'This again?'

'I think you should read it.'

'He says in his teacher voice.'

She carried on talking as she read. '"The Slippery Slope to Boundary Violation" by Dr Robert Simon.'

* * *

'Therapist's neutrality is eroded in "little" ways

Therapist and patient address each other by first names

Therapy sessions become less clinical and more social

Patient is treated as "special" or confidant

Therapist self-disclosures occur, usually about current personal problems and sexual fantasies about the patient

Therapist begins touching patient, progressing to hugs and embraces

Therapist gains control over patient, usually by manipulating the transference and by negligent prescribing of medication

Extra-therapeutic contacts occur

Therapy sessions are rescheduled for the end of
the day
Therapy sessions become extended in time
Therapist stops billing the patient (in National
Health Service settings this is not relevant)
Therapist and patient have drinks/dinner after
sessions; dating begins
Therapist–patient sex begins.'

* * *

Sol's back was turned to her. A stupid grin hit Beth's face. She looked down. *You are meant to be concerned*, a little voice told her, heard even then, and ignored.

'Interesting,' said Beth, once she could speak normally. 'Seems a bit extreme!'

Sol said nothing.

'Doesn't it?' said Beth.

Sol took a breath. 'He also says that the therapist will *always* have the power in the relationship,' he said. 'That any emotion caused by her will be magnified.'

'OK,' said Beth.

He was silent.

* * *

The warmer weather passed in a blur in which Beth lived fragments of a secret life just beneath the real one, as though disappearing down a passage to a room that was theirs alone for a limited time. The secrecy itself electrified the air. Nothing was stated – Tamara shied laughingly from the conversations, the analysis and plans Beth attempted to instigate – but the experience lay somewhere between being in love, and best friendship at school with its intensity of communication till dawn, its hysteria, the need to be in constant contact in the face of disapproval. Glances were multi-layered with meaning, and every moment was significant, a larger world beckoning. Beth felt younger, slimmer; Tamara thought her beautiful. They kissed by the canal, in the shadows, in dark.

And then, for a few hours, or whole days even, there would be nothing, and Beth suspected all over again that she was not sufficiently of interest. After all the efforts Tamara had made to see her, she couldn't match her, the writhings of inferiority intolerable.

Then a text would arrive. *I'm missing you ...*

And then she was almost perfectly happy. Tamara Bywater could create that in her. Beth had woken from her sleep to discover the world, Tamara beckoning her, a key gleaming in her hand. Sol looked at her askance.

Tamara rang at night and murmured to her, Beth answering only if she could; or they texted a time to speak and Beth wandered alone, at risk, along the towpath, and they were careful and then less careful.

* * *

In all her intensity, Tamara was frequently late. That Tuesday, Beth could no longer sit still in the gloomy Italian Tamara had suggested, presumably for its anonymity. She looked around for places where kissing could happen, weighing up the potential of each corner. Tamara was very late. There was no message of apology or explanation.

As she tried to make herself leave, Tamara arrived at the door in a flap of umbrella, lipstick, her hair wet and snaking over her cheek, her skin pale, so she looked quite different again.

Beth's phone rang. *Aaa Sol.*

Tamara kissed Beth on both cheeks; Beth pressed her thumb on the Reject button as though it had slipped, a waitress somehow instantly there from the huddle of former indifference to help.

Sol rang again. 'Oh.' Beth paused over the phone.

'Ignore it,' said Tamara, and ran her fingertip behind Beth's neck. She held her gently. 'I couldn't wait to see you,' she whispered.

'You are late,' replied Beth.

'Am I?' she said with one brow arched.

'It was really hard for me to get out,' said Beth, over-forceful in an attempt to instigate a response.

'I'm sorry.' Tamara touched Beth's shoulder. 'I ran into someone on the way and apparently we've met before, though I didn't remember. I couldn't really be rude, could I? Please forgive me.'

'Who?'

'Who? Giovanni, Giuseppe something,' she said, feeling among her bags and purses and retrieving a card. 'Here. Giovanni Lollo.'

'Who is he?'

She shrugged. 'Financier kind of thing?'

'Financier of what?'

'I'm not sure I care, but he was intriguing. Surprisingly, he said he'd read my academic work. He wants to take me to the opera next week.'

'What? Tell him where to go.'

'Straight to his very own opera box! How wonderful is that? It's the Royal Opera's *Aida*.'

'You're telling me you're going to the opera with this man you can't really remember, who is giving you a seat in his – *box* – and – could be a psycho as well as a stranger. Where else will he take you?'

'Ibiza.'

'You're serious?'

'He offered. Why not? This life is short but can be fun if you let it. Live a bit, Beth!'

'I – I – What would your husband think if you announce that this year's holiday is in *I-beetha*, with an Italian stranger?'

'Jealousy!' said Tamara. 'You—'

'Did you ever—' Beth interrupted her. 'Did you go to the opera – one day – how many months ago? Do you have a kind of shoulder thing in fur?'

'I have several! What are you saying, with your many strange questions?'

'Nothing,' said Beth. 'How on earth will Angus react?'

'Oh, he knows me,' she said with airy dismissal. 'If I only did everything with Angus, it would be the death of the soul.'

Beth tapped the table, pressing her nails into the paper cloth. Framed *Roman Holiday* stills loomed in the shadows. 'You're going to go?' she blurted before the waitress, who by now clearly imagined she was Tamara's new friend, had even left. 'I'm getting sick of this.'

'Why wouldn't I?' said Tamara.

'Er. You're married. You don't know him. Ibiza's a shithole.'

'Oh, my darling!' said Tamara, and laughed, so Beth was suddenly laughing too. Giovanni Lollo's business card sat on the table and, with a rapid gesture, she tore it in half.

Tamara gave a delighted laugh. She paused. 'I need some stimulation. Of course you're going to stay faithful to Solomon,' she said, sounding entirely unbothered.

'Am I?'

'You will stay true to your grizzled groom.'

'You haven't met him,' Beth snapped.

'I could tell a lot from our sessions,' she said, and yawned. Beth stared. Had her own mouth really met that kitten slit that curved into a flirt's smile in a Kennington kitchen?

'Oh God,' said Tamara, tapping on her phone. 'More trouble. One of the ex-patients stalks me.'

'Oh, do they? I'm getting bored with all this Whatshisname Lollo. All your fans. "I'm stalked, therefore I am"?'

'Don't be a silly! He's ill! I worry he's dangerous.'

Beth said nothing. *Fern OK?xx*, she messaged Sol under the table. The conversation stalled. Beth began to dredge up, instead, the combative yet flattering statements needed to secure Tamara's attention.

Tamara's gaze rested on her. She fingered a carnation, lifted it to her nose. 'I always loved you,' she said.

'Did you?' said Beth with an audible lack of control over her voice.

'Of course. How could I not?'

'What kind of – love?' Beth blushed.

'Love love,' she said. 'You! Defining us again! There are conformist streaks I find in you – unexpected. Sometimes you're like a Victorian bluestocking, with your quotes, your surprising strands of ... *prissiness*. This is better,' she said, and she ruffled Beth's hair to make it looser.

'But tell me—' Beth persisted.

'I would love an all-female world,' said Tamara dreamily. 'I think of it. A slender, strange, smooth-skinned kind of world. No men. Imagine that.'

'Yes,' said Beth. There was a silence. 'So have you—' she began.

'I think men can even be a bit *gross*,' said Tamara. 'The older I get, the more interesting I find – '

Beth's phone rang.

' – women. Oh, go back to your husband if he keeps summoning you. You'll be spending all summer with him in Sticksville, USA.'

Tamara gathered her bags. She started to stand, threw money down and looked at Beth with a level gaze, the tinge of melancholy visible through the radiance of her smile. Her phone then rang and she answered it, pacing towards the back of the restaurant, while Sol had merely rung to ask about some French grammar.

'Yes,' Tamara said to her caller, walking back to the table and sitting at the edge of her chair. 'Yes, that would be lovely. Perhaps in July.'

After a silence, Beth asked, 'So, are you going to go?'

'Where?'

'To wherever – he – is asking you.'

'Oh, I doubt it, I'm much too busy with work, but he does come up with tempting activities.'

'*Who? This time?*' Beth muttered, but Tamara didn't answer. 'Where is Dr Bywater?'

'What?'

'Where is that gentle person? With all her wisdom? Do you – do therapists – just lend their minds, as others offer their bodies? The – the – professionals of the public sector?'

Tamara laughed loudly. 'You're saying I'm a prostitute?'

'No!'

'The psychological equivalent of a hooker.'

'Sorry. No.' Beth grabbed Tamara's hand across the table, and Tamara ran her middle finger once over her palm.

There was another silence.

'So you're saying there are all these *men*?' Beth said, the last shred of dignity draining from her.

Tamara's eyes reflected the candles that were now lit. 'If only there were space to love all the people I want to love in this world,' she said.

Beth gaped. 'But who are *all these people*?' she almost shouted.

Tamara laughed. 'Beth, regulate yourself!'

'And what about me?'

'I can't have you.'

'But—'

Tamara shrugged. 'Rules are for fools.'

'That's what – the axiom of a consultant clinical psychologist?'

'Remember it.'

'Do – do you actually have affairs?'

Tamara's smile flashed across her face.

'I'm a little badly behaved sometimes.'

'But you can't!' Beth said.

'What? Is this the nineteenth century?'

Beth shook her head.

'Are you proposing we all stay tethered to one person, no illuminating side trips *anywhere*?'

'Yes,' barked Beth.

Tamara laughed. 'Get back to your lord and master, my darling,' she said. 'And to your century.'

'Oh, piss off,' said Beth.

Tamara gave a tilt of a smile. A flicker of pain was subdued with a shrug, and she rose and began to move away.

'*No, no*,' said Beth. She stood and pulled her arm. 'You make me feel like a fucking schoolboy,' she said.

'I'd quite like to fuck a schoolboy. Just once.'

Beth half-laughed, gritting her teeth. 'You're impossible. I think I'm going to go now.'

'Don't go,' said Tamara. 'Look,' she said, pausing. 'I'm not happy. That's the thing.'

'Why? Tamara.'

'I'm—' She cleared her throat. 'Jealous,' she said.

'You're *jealous*? About?'

'You and Sol. You being with someone else, because I want to talk to you all the time.'

'Do you?'

'Yes. That level of understanding. I don't think I have it with anyone else. Certainly not … at home. Please don't go away for the summer.' Tamara breathed slowly. 'Oh, I'm so stupid. I despair over myself sometimes, Beth.'

'Tamara! This doesn't sound like you. Don't say tha—'

'I'm trying to be honest. I push you away. I push everyone away. Because I can't bear being rejected. I just can't face that pain. You are with your husband.'

'So are you,' said Beth, as she had said before.

'I have got to go,' said Tamara.

* * *

'From tomorrow, let's see each other, go to dinner, go exploring,' Beth said to Sol later.

He looked at her, shook his head, breathed out through his nose.

'You know – Bet,' he said solemnly. 'You know we all think separations happen to other people. But what if—'

'No!' she said.

He raised his eyebrows in the mirror as he brushed his teeth. 'We have to take nothing for granted.'

She nodded, kissed his neck. In her pocket was Tamara's napkin from earlier, two overlapping impressions of her lips, a fainter one over a bloodier one, and Beth hesitated then flushed it down the loo.

She kissed him suddenly, fully and wetly on the mouth, and in stages they moved towards the bed.

Beth chased the small flame, breathing him in, tasting his neck, until she found it, wobbling semi-hidden, and made it grow. She forcibly switched her mind into the place of desire and felt the old lapping just begin to carry her. He was hot; she licked the salt from him, but there was another smell that was not there, a sweet musk that held blacker depths, and Beth began to talk to Sol to banish her thoughts. 'I love you,' she said, and, 'I need you,' without meaning to.

But as he entered her, distortions pooled into her mind again: those women she chased by the river, little glimpses in darkness, and the horror, the eternal chasing. Tamara the elusive. The shrink's hands, the make-up, the womanly slides of her voice, all came to her though she fought it, images speeding, battering, and then, as she gave in, charging through her.

She and Sol gazed at each other.

Eighteen

Beth didn't contact Tamara, and there were no messages from her.

By the weekend, Fern seemed almost bowed with scorn for her mother, as though her disgust was distorting the very set of her body.

'Who is that text from?' said Fern a week later, her sharp eyes looking across the table.

Beth jolted at the sound of her voice, and snatched her phone back. 'You speak!' she said, swallowing.

'*I need you,*' Fern quoted. Her neat little voice was an icicle. '*When are you around?*'

'What the hell are you doing?'

'Who is that? Who is "T" something?'

'No one,' said Beth.

Fern went bright red. 'Oh my God. I think I know what – what you—'

'There's nothing to worry about,' said Beth. 'You misunderstood.'

Fern was trembling. '"When women are being cruel to their children, it's usually because their minds are somewhere else",' she said in a disquieting monotone.

'What? What do you mean, Fern?'

'I hate you.'

'God. What is this, Fern? How am I "cruel"?'

'To people. Dad. You never took me back to see my friends from my first school. You never even let me meet my grandmother—'

'I've tried to explain to you about that. We—'

'No one. You care about no one, and now Dad's all quiet – and you probably don't care about that. I hate you. I really hate you. Dad's much nicer.'

Beth stepped back.

'I don't want you here.'

'Don't you?' Beth's mouth fell open.

'Nor in America. So you don't have to see me *then*, either.'

'Fern,' said Beth, 'don't be ridiculous! I want to see you above anything else!'

Fern stared at Beth. 'That's not quite true, though, is it?'

Beth drew in her breath. 'I thought I was *too* nice.'

'Yeah. And too horrible.'

'You don't want me? Anywhere? With *you*?'

'No. Why would I?'

Beth reeled. Lizzie's back through her bedroom window, the wave, the hospital later.

'Dad and I are seriously fine,' said Fern. 'I'm cool. Just leave me alone. Fuck off if you want to.'

Beth's mobile rang. *Tamara B*. She rejected the call.

Fern stormed upstairs.

The phone rang again. 'Beth,' Tamara whispered. Her voice was croaky. 'I can't do this any more.'

'What? Tamara?' she said.

'You don't contact me. It's breaking me.'

'Oh, sweetheart,' said Beth. Her legs were instantly unsteady.

'Can you talk? Sol's not there?' A sound-littered London at night backed her voice.

'He's out.'

'That's luck. Can you see me? Please.'

'Fern's here. In her room.'

Tamara was silent.

'Where are you?' said Beth.

'Near you. It took me so long to gather the strength to ring you.'

'Let me try to work this out …' said Beth, stretching and grabbing some paper. She paused, hesitated at the bottom of the stairs, then ran back and scribbled Fern a note.

FERN Popped out to get milk. Back in a few minutes. Ignore door if it rings. Ring my mobile if need. Love xxxxxx.

* * *

Sefton Park came to her, as it often did. After her first sighting, Beth had looked several times. There had been no one to ask about the possibility of Lizzie Penn being in Liverpool. Mentioning her mother's name to

253

her father would have been like pressing the tip of a knife into him.

Then, just once, she had thought she saw a figure across the park in the dusk, a slim, hurried figure who could have been her mother, and the figure disappeared behind drifts of falling dark somewhere near where she had been before, and then there was nothing: the same hostility, or silence, greeting pressed doorbells, and Beth knew she would have to give up and preserve her sanity. Or to try again.

* * *

Beth gazed at her note to Fern, put it on the table, listened to the silence upstairs, then screwed up the paper and threw it into the fireplace. She told Tamara that it was impossible to meet her, that she needed to be with Fern, and Tamara was quiet and then said that she understood.

After that, there was silence. On the fourth day, Beth turned off her phone when she was with her family, to live in a pure state liberated from the nagging of anticipation, and she loved Solomon Jacob Brierley. She worked in the mornings, and she no longer went to the Thames, added finishing touches to what she had done of her river series in her studio. It was the undertow that she found, and beneath that, another layer of terror, hinted at: uncertain depths beneath the air bubbles. Her gallerist was about to make a studio visit to see what she had done so far, and she swayed between nerves and certainty and then new doubts. She had taken risks. This was not *Ghost Walks*. But then it was not *City Lies* either. Aranxto had asked to see her latest work, but instinct stopped her, and his irritation added to the unease between them that had been growing all year.

One day, fetching some old photographs of South Liverpool she had lent Aranxto, she was passed on the stairs by a man whose blank-eyed gaze announced to her with something close to certainty that he was a rent boy, Aranxto's series of smirks confirming the supposition.

'Lovely,' she muttered to him, raising her eyebrows.

It took a moment for her meaning to sink in. 'You need a fuck yourself,' he snapped.

'Shut up, Aranxto,' said Beth. 'In fact, fuck you.' And she grabbed her photographs and started to leave.

She put her head back round the door.

'And stop messaging my daughter.'

Aranxto paused, indignant.

'No good. I know your sheepish face. Before you do the pissed-off look. *Why* would you message Fern?'

'Why in hell not? I'm her godfather.'

'Are you? The least attentive godfather on earth.'

She slammed the door.

The tension between them was a remnant from earlier times. Her worst row with Aranxto, some years before, had been so brutal that he still attempted to punish her in subtle ways once their estrangement was over, and she had never fully trusted him since. He had even apparently found housing association accommodation nearby for Jack Dorian's ex-wife, a move intended merely, Beth was certain, to irritate her and thereby entertain him.

She looked at her emails quickly. There was nothing from Tamara, increasing her resolve with a kick of pain. And yet, as time progressed, it occurred to her that in resisting the therapist who had saved her, she was demonstrating nothing but ingratitude. The echo of her own mother's accusation caught her in the throat.

'Ungrateful.'

Was there, after all, truth there? She lay in bed and the Lizzie she had been warding away came to her, the first of the scenes involving Lizzie she really didn't want to think about.

* * *

'I'm so sorry, Bet,' Sol had said, over thirteen years before, soon after Beth had refused Lizzie's request to see the baby Fern. 'I need to tell you your mother's in hospital.'

Beth felt the blood draining from her face. She paused for several seconds. 'How do you know?'

He breathed out impatiently. 'The usual circuitous. Via the douche of a half-brother. Who is sick himself. He got the hospital to call.'

'Here?' said Beth blankly.

'Your gallery. I'm sorry.'

'What is wrong?' she said at last.

'She had a stroke, honey. Sit down.'

'How?'

'We don't have all the details yet.'

'"We"?'

He shook his head. 'They. The brother.'

'She seemed quite – fit – when I saw her only what, six, seven days ago. Older, but she could still move quickly.' Beth was shaking hard and fast.

'I know, honey,' said Sol gently.

'This is what she has left? An ill half-brother in Aigburth. Which hospital's she in?'

'The Royal Liverpool.'

'Why?'

'The gallery thinks she was transferred there from London where she was briefly and where it happened. Her official address is Liverpool.'

'What?' said Beth. 'You don't mean—'

'Not your father's address. She said she has no family up there, but—'

'But she does, she does,' cried Beth.

'She doesn't,' said Sol firmly.

Beth opened her mouth. Tears were running down her face, leaving an itchy residue.

'Seems Aranxto is visiting his mother and will see her.'

'Aranxto? Oh God. I so don't want—'

'There's more,' said Sol rapidly. 'Honey, I hardly want to burden you with this. She married. Again, apparently.'

Beth drew in her breath. The past travelled by her as a sequence: a string of paper cut-outs in trousers: men, more men. Lizzie had jumped so swiftly from one to another, from her father to Colin, the man she had run off with, to any number of unknowns, the paper figures torn in Beth's mind as they were discarded in pieces on the floor.

'Who?'

'Some man she married some time ago who seems pretty useless, has an address on the city outskirts but is largely itinerant, in London. Albert Crayer. Called her brother. I'm so sorry. Bet. Come here, honey.'

He held her almost too tightly; she struggled to breathe, but it blanked the news for comforting seconds. She pulled away with a jolt.

'How ill?'

'She's— She sustained some brain damage.'

'I need to get there now.'

'On *no account* should you see her,' said Sol.

'I have to!'

'Bill can see her. His kids.'

'None of them *do*. Don't bother Dad with this,' she said in a rush. 'It would so pain him. And she doesn't deserve it.'

'I agree. She doesn't deserve you, either.'

Beth shook her head. She started the laptop and began to look up train times. Her fingers tapped. She heard her own breathing. She turned abruptly.

'Why – *why* do they think she had a stroke, now?'

Sol paused for a long time. He shook his head. Sadness travelled over his face, and he closed his eyes. He loves me, thought Beth at the sight of his expression, as though it were a new realisation. It filled her with amazement that anyone could love her as he did.

'Let's just focus on the now,' he said.

'No! Sol. Why? It's so sudden. Sol?'

He leaned over her at the computer, and wrapped her in his arms.

'It was an accident. A stupid accident.'

'What kind of accident?' said Beth very quietly and slowly.

'Christ, Bet. I so fucking wish you didn't have to hear this. She went into a pond. She—'

'Oh, Jesus, Jesus. What day?' said Beth, grabbing Sol's arm.

He pulled her harder towards him. 'The second, apparently. Last Monday.'

She lowered her head on to her computer. She tried to breathe.

* * *

Another message arrived on Beth's phone. *Tamara B. You break my heart.*

Beth threw herself into clearing the table, into ordering primer and paying bills in a switchback of remorse and desire. Tamara was overworked and vulnerable, unhappily married and gave her all to others.

'I have to meet the shrink,' she said to Sol after some time. 'Tamara.' And she felt as though she trampled over both him and their precious closer marriage in so little time. 'Soon.' She coughed. 'This evening—'

'For a dinner?' said Sol after some moments, a whiff of frost detectable. 'Or another appointment?'

Beth stiffened. Her eyes were moist. 'I won't be long.'

She watched as Sol took his phone out.

'Oh!' she said. 'Fern. I didn't hear you coming in.'

'Don't come in the summer,' Fern said. '*I do not want you to come to Oma's house.*'

Beth paled. 'But of course I—'

'I want to go only with Dad,' said Fern in a cold monotone that sounded rehearsed, and yet there was a slight crumpling of her face.

* * *

'I don't think I can stand this much longer,' Tamara said when she saw her. 'Being without you. Don't freeze me out.'

'I didn't mean—' Beth started to say. 'You too. You do that,' she said.

'I know, I'm sorry, I know, I don't mean to. Let's make a go of it,' said Tamara.

'What?' said Beth, her voice rising.

'Please. I can't hold back any more. Let's have a try. We've never even properly … There's never any chance. It's ridiculous. Let's be together.'

'What, I queue up behind … Giovanni Lollobrigida? Your stalker. Your Head of Services who clearly fancies you?'

'Oh no, please. They mean nothing to me. Beth, please. It's you I want. They're all just silly men.'

'And that bloke who rang you.'

'Who?'

'*I* don't know. Some man you spoke to on the phone. Who comes up with "delightful activities".'

'Oh, I'd forgotten about that. They – any of these men. They mean just nothing to me. I don't know what gets into me sometimes, I … mess up. I always have. I'm sorry. I'm really sorry, Beth. My love. I don't know why I do, but it torments me when I do. Please, darling. Be patient with me. I love you so much.'

Tamara gazed at her in the dark, buses, hooting, the silences of the city between.

'Oh God. Tamara,' said Beth, and she kissed her, long and hard, and Tamara kissed passionately, and Beth's knees were liquid. Tamara's hands were lightly on her breasts, nerves an electric streak.

'Darling,' said Tamara between kisses, 'I'm so sorry if I offended, hurt you. Or – put you off me.

I think I behave badly sometimes.' Her voice wobbled. Her eyes shone. 'I shouldn't have told you all that nonsense about all those men. It's not real. I don't know why I do these things. I'm – I'm so insecure underneath, really. You know I love you so much.'

'But—'

'They mean nothing to me, nothing at all, they're all because I can't have you.'

'I'm not sure if I believe you—'

'Oh, it's true. More true than you'll ever understand. Please. Please. I want you to come and be with me.'

'I must get back.'

'And anyway ...' Tamara shifted Beth's arm in the crook of hers in a warm shuffling. 'It's not nearly as bad as you think. I really don't do much of anything with anyone. Sometimes I think I'm virtually a nun. I love you.'

'I love you,' said Beth.

'Come away with me. Let's – you know –' Tamara dropped her head '– let's really be together.'

'We can't,' said Beth into her hair.

'I know, I know the practicalities. Don't, don't say anything now,' said Tamara so quietly that Beth could barely hear her. 'It will break me. Don't spoil the dream. It's what I keep thinking about and hoping for, trying to work out.'

'No,' murmured Beth, stroking her, kissing her. 'I love you,' she said again, and bit her own bottom lip hard.

'Just think about it. When you're at home, on your own. Please. Just hold me.'

NINETEEN

July heat was settling in; the river throttle of tourism and dirt rose. Tamara's arm gestured like a snake as she talked about her marriage. 'Angus's been in the spare room for a while,' she said. 'But the girls ... what would I do with Francesca? Only Angus can deal with her. The thing is,' she said, her mouth suddenly close to Beth's ear. 'If I don't do something about me and Angus, I may as well be a dead woman.'

Time was formed of a race of images through Beth's nights, the subject of summer in the States increasingly intruding. 'I'm basically done with this conversation,' Sol had said when Beth was uncertain of dates again, and he booked flights for him and Fern, Beth to follow.

'One hundred per cent stay away,' shouted Fern, and Beth cried on Tamara's shoulder.

'But just think of all the fun we could have,' Tamara said, her hand moving over Beth, 'without them.'

'Fly out after your series is finished,' said Sol, unsmiling, and a date was agreed upon.

'I'm waiting for you,' was all Tamara said, and there was nothing Beth could reply.

The night before Sol and Fern were due to fly to Rhode Island, Beth received a phone call from her gallerist about the almost-completed river series. Kevin O'Hanlon reminded her of the quieter men from Liverpool: wise men of Irish origin who had taken the vow of abstinence, or lived their religion, or those who were simply wed to family with a steady integrity, like her own dear father, his manner refreshing in the chaos of mental drama in which she seemed to exist.

'*City Lies* has problems,' he said, and together they agreed and dismissed thousands of hours of work. '*River Walk*,' he said, and he paused. Beth held her nail against her finger until it hurt. 'I'd consider this your breakthrough,' he said. Beth's mouth opened. A grin was pressing her cheek against the phone. She wanted to clutch his arm down the line.

Yes! They're bloody brilliant, they are my babies, they're the best thing I've ever done, it was Tamara Bywater, it was me, it was her, she wanted to say. 'Thank you.'

'I like them. Congratulations.'

Fern came into the room after she had finished the call, and Beth gave her a radiant smile. Seeing her mother, Fern walked straight out again.

I long for you, Tamara texted.

* * *

265

That night, Beth lay awake, excitement roaring inside her. She pretended to sleep as Sol scrolled down his iPad beside her and pottered about, adding items then putting his case and equipment by the bedroom door; and at one in the morning, he woke Fern, and Beth heard the sounds of drinks being made and his gentle murmurings.

Beth got out of bed and she and Sol hugged. 'Take care, Bet,' was all he said.

She moved towards Fern. 'No,' said Fern, her voice harder than Beth had ever heard. 'You don't need to. Don't worry. Go away.' The voice cracked.

'Of course I *need* to! You're my daughter,' said Beth, and she grabbed Fern and pulled her towards her.

'Go away,' said Fern. 'Fuck off,' she seemed to mumble, but it was swallowed as she pushed through the front door.

'Treat her with respect,' Sol snapped at her. 'She's your mother.'

'We have to sort this out. I love you,' Beth called to Fern's retreating back, but she didn't turn, and Sol turned once, with no smile. 'I love you,' called Beth again.

* * *

'Look after her' was the last thing she had said to Sol, but he had her absolute trust.

She got up, pressed a flannel against her eyes, sent a prayer for Fern and grabbed her phone as a text arrived. A small row of jubilation emojis. *Tamara B.*

Her excitement knew no end. Words stormed. *I'm waiting for you ... This is your breakthrough ... All the fun we could have.* I love you, Kevin O'Hanlon, she thought, in exultation. I love you, Sol. I love you—

Tamara. Shrinks were out of bounds, the most common fantasy largely because they were untouchable. But hers touched her. Because a part of her was brilliant. Because a good gallery wanted her again. Because she could have the world.

She spread her legs out in the bed. Tamara Bywater somehow intimated dangerous delights without a single explicit word. How could she keep away from her? She called. Tamara's voicemail switched straight on, and she listened again and she came and she came, and her river paintings appeared, one by one, on a gallery wall, and she loved them all.

She couldn't possibly sleep. She texted Tamara, didn't send it, couldn't put anything into words.

She fell into a daze. Guilt started twining through the excitement. Her heart beat a sinister tattoo. She was a shit underneath, some Scouser with aspirations, some Mummy's girl without a mother. She simply didn't deserve this. She wanted Tamara Bywater. She wanted Tamara to tell her it was all right. She needed to fuck her. She needed her. Tamara would cure her. Tamara would go to bed with her and complete what they had started. Her heart raced. Was she so brilliant? No.

It was past two in the morning. Guilt daggers stormed at her. She couldn't have a show. Kevin

O'Hanlon didn't understand. She was useless. And even if she did exhibit, the idea of critics coming and poring over her work made her want to throw up. Her mother was alone in this life. Her own cup overflowed. She turned to her pillow.

She got up. Tamara had laid her cards on the table. Beth was keeping herself from what every primitive impulse in her most needed, while the family she was with didn't want her. She wiped her armpits with a flannel, threw on a dress, took a jacket, tossed some clothes, toothbrush, phone charger and iPad in a small bag almost randomly, with handbag and some cash, and she went out into the street, the coolness on her brow a relief. She walked, turning at every sound of diesel, a night bus throttling past, two cabs full, a third lit halfway down Camden High Street. She hailed it.

'Calder Street, please. SE11,' she said.

* * *

Where would they go together? Practicalities were impossible to calibrate; nothing logistical could be approached that night. As the taxi sped across the river, she and Tamara sank on to her hall floor together, clawing at each other, kissing frantically in relief that she had finally arrived, the husband emerging useless from the spare room while they admitted what had become unstoppable.

Beth got the taxi to drop her off on the square, her mind slowing from its racing to a chill of slight fear. Angus Bywater appeared as a more solid obstacle. She could barely think. *I'm waiting for you.*

It was almost twenty to three in the morning. She made herself breathe slowly, there in the summer air damp with plant growth over petrol. Sol. Fern. Her heart pounded. Tamara's lights were on. A glare through the bars of the basement illuminated her area, and there seemed to be a blue glow emanating from the front door's fanlight. Beth hesitated. She dialled Tamara's number, but her phone rang and then switched on to voicemail.

She knocked lightly on the door and nudged her bag behind her as she became aware of music and voices. She waited. Eventually, she heard Tamara's laugh. She rang the bell.

Angus the husband loomed in the doorway, his fringe awry over an expression of residual amusement. He took a moment to register Beth, his attention still caught by the scene in the room behind him.

He looked blank, and then somewhat irritated. 'Come in,' he said after a beat. Cigarette, weed and candle smoke blurred the air, clusters of conversation above music. Beth hesitated.

After a few moments, Tamara tottered into the hall on high heels in a dress of skin-tight satin. Her eyelids were coloured a kingfisher teal with false lashes, so when she blinked it was as though they carried weights.

'You decided to attend!' she said, flinging her arms round Beth. She laughed. She gave Beth a showy kiss straight on the lips in front of her husband, who faintly stiffened. Her pupils were dilated, a chemical edge flitting over every expression.

'Attend …?' Beth said, nodding into the hall, but Tamara didn't reply. 'What?'

'Our little party!'

Beth looked blank.

'It's mostly over now.'

'You didn't invite me.'

'Of course I did. Didn't I? I did. Well, maybe I thought you wouldn't come. But you have!' The husband shambled back into the blue-glowing gloom. Tamara wobbled against Beth. 'My sweetheart. There is no one I could ever want more.'

Beth sank into the depths of Tamara's smell, and she could breathe again. Tamara held Beth's head back. 'So wonderful to see you, like an apparition,' she said, and kissed Beth, unsteadily but briefly on the mouth.

'What are you on, Tamara?'

She laughed. 'Don't ask. Am I so obvious? Too many things, I think.' She grabbed Beth's hand.

'I've come for you. I came to you,' Beth whispered beside the door but her movements were suddenly awkward. 'I couldn't keep away any more.'

'Wonderful you!' said Tamara, and pulled Beth into the back sitting room with no time for her to

270

protest. Five men and two women lay draped over sofas and on the floor. One of the men reached out from where he lay on a rug and stroked Tamara's calf as she walked into the room; a second pushed his arm around her waist as she sat down, and she snuggled against him, her hair lying across his shoulder, her eyes blank pools. She stretched her hand over to the lap of the very young woman next to her, and the woman held it. Tamara seemed to sleep, momentarily, then woke. 'Can you get Beth a drink, darling?' she said to Angus, who rose, brought Beth what appeared to be a cocktail in a clearly freshly-rinsed used glass and removed bowls while Tamara smiled blearily at Beth, and mouthed something she couldn't catch.

Beth gazed at the portrait of Tamara. It was a well-painted oil; it distorted and missed, yet it caught something of her, some essence Beth had barely seen. Again, there seemed to be no signs of children anywhere in the house. Humiliation that Beth was reluctant to examine threaded through her as her grand gesture collided with daily life. But then she caught Tamara's gaze across the room, and nothing mattered; Tamara was projecting sex at Beth through her pupils, the deepest intimacy. There was no choice left.

'Fern,' she murmured to herself, and her eyeballs ached. Fern didn't want her. Laurie?

Sol. She would work it all out later. Later.

Beth stood clumsily, went to the hall, and after a few minutes Tamara appeared. She smiled. Very lightly, she leaned against Beth.

'I can hear the dawn beginning,' Beth said, and put her arms round Tamara, her waist bird-small.

'Is it so late?' murmured Tamara.

'Let's go to bed,' said Beth blindly.

'Darling, darling, I will crash before I even get to bed.'

Beth hesitated.

'We'll find each other in the morning,' said Tamara, wrapping her arms round her. 'Won't we?'

'Find each other?'

'There's the couch in my consulting room. Sleep there tonight. Or is it this morning? I don't know, my one love. I have no idea.'

'I love you!' said Beth spontaneously.

'This is all I wanted.' Tamara gazed into her eyes. 'If I can have you, my life will be all right.'

The husband came out carrying a stack of glasses, his hair flopping over his face as he balanced the glasses with an ashtray, and Beth and Tamara pulled away.

'Angus,' said Tamara, now husky. 'It's too late for Beth to go back. She lives in—' She cleared her throat, unsuccessfully, and her words emerged as a whisper. 'North London somewhere. She can have my couch. Could you be a—'

He paused. 'Of course. You go to bed. I'll bring you up your—'

'Can you get rid of the others?' she murmured.

'Go to bed, Mar.'

She smiled at him wearily, blew him a kiss from the stairs. She climbed two steps. As though she had only just remembered Beth, she turned.

'Love,' Tamara mouthed, and Beth glanced towards Angus Bywater, who was waiting out of sight, and when she looked back, Tamara was climbing the last stairs, head bowed, spine bent.

'It's a little on the cold side over there in the winter, autumn,' said Angus in his regionally uncertain monotone. He caught Beth's eye. He had softened. 'Usable now, I think.' He was careful in his movements for all his largeness, with his enormous weekend T-shirt loose over a broad chest and the first sprouting of a pot belly, a stoop to his head in that house of low ceilings. He had a tic, blinking too emphatically. He led Beth through the little turns at the back of the house to Tamara's consulting room.

In a leap of memory, Beth reimmersed herself there, but it was different from the location of her recollections: smaller and so tidy that, unlike the rest of the house, it felt bare. The couch, latterly one of the props in her varying sex scenarios, lay in shadows. Angus showed Beth to her narrow bed, a temporary solution until she could climb into his wife's. He then re-emerged with his old-mannish movements behind a pile of pillows, sheets, quilt, and even towels, like the well-trained consort that he was, resistant yet polite.

Beth lay on Dr Tamara Bywater's therapy couch as the birds began to wake. She could only exist in the moment, on this needle end of exultation and catastrophe.

TWENTY

Beth woke with a jump on Tamara's couch at just before ten o'clock to sun glaring through the cracks in the blinds. Sol and Fern would almost have arrived in Rhode Island. She pressed her palm for their safety. Pain crashed into her forehead with a delay as she turned. Yet the simple fact that she was here, in Tamara Bywater's consulting room, was like some kind of miracle of possession. It was eerily silent, the birds thinned out, traffic a skein of sound, and the Bywater family on a Saturday apparently asleep. She listened for them through the house, hearing creaks that were real or imagined.

A moment of disbelief hammered into her. When would Sol know? He would WhatsApp, email, FaceTime. Even before he saw the background room or the inexplicable street or garden, he would know. There was nothing on her phone from the airport.

She padded barefoot to the toilet at the back of the kitchen where she washed at the tiny sink, put on some foundation, cleared her throat and called for Tamara. There was no reply. The lower ground floor was empty, the kitchen a mess of breakfast, ashtrays and wine glasses. She ventured to the upper ground floor like an intruder, detritus of the party with its smoke still evident in the sitting room, the portrait of Tamara now a shock of flesh. There was silence from the top floor. She made herself some coffee, searched for painkillers, then methodically and quite loudly cleared up the kitchen. It took some time to empty the dishwasher, fill it, wash scrambled egg and scoop away crumbs.

She stopped still at the thought of Sol and Fern. She texted a good-morning message and sent love. Words went through her mind: *I ran away to be with Tamara Bywater*. Her mind spun back on itself. The very idea of leaving Fern brought an instant prickling to her eyes, making her breathless. But practicalities had to be postponed. She sent a text to Fern: *My darling girl, I will miss you. I hope you enjoy the space that you want away from me. I hope very much that one day you can explain it all. I love you very very dearly, whatever you do. Always.* There was nothing from Sol. She crept up the stairs, observing every detail and calling softly, but doors were closed except one girl's bedroom.

Just as Beth was emptying the second dishwasher load, the front door opened upstairs. Her hand froze. 'Hi!' she called in a squeak.

There was a hesitation. 'Yes,' came a man's voice, and a creaking of floorboards. Down the stairs inched the unfavoured neighbour who fixed Tamara's lights, equipped with secateurs and a recycling bag. He gave a grunt, barely catching Beth's eye.

'Hello,' she said. They both stood there, seemingly locked in a competition not to speak.

'Pruning Tamara's jasmine,' he said eventually.

'I'm not sure she's in.'

'She said late Saturday a.m. was the best time. I have my key.'

'You can get in at the side gate to access the jasmine,' said Beth.

'I have my key,' he repeated while hugging his secateurs, and Beth suppressed amusement.

The post snaked its way through the door upstairs and she left him to his gardening tasks then went to look. A postcard lay on the mat.

Dear Dr Bywater. Thank you for your advice. I have kept the card to remind me. Thank you, thank you, thank you. Jade.

She chucked it back on top of the other post, and wandered into the yard, images of disappearing without leaving a note interleaved with a scene of Tamara waking and calling a conference in her bedroom for a joint confession to the husband. Beth paced round the Bywaters' yard while the jasmine wobbled to chopping sounds, Tamara's servant hidden from view. There was a broken mosaic on one wall, improvements to its design scrawling through Beth's mind as she paced, and she fetched her sketch pad so that she was working.

I'm waiting for you, was what Tamara had said.

Beth cursed her for delaying that moment of truth. She embellished the mosaic design with vicious baroque flourishes. The biliousness that had been swelling inside her all morning rose, and she hurried to one of the pots and threw up a pathetic trickle of saliva into a passion flower.

She picked up the tesserae that had fallen on to the ground, and when eventually she rang Tamara, she got her voicemail. She WhatsApped her.

Sol texted. *F good. Mom spoiling her. Talk later x.*

Beth stared at his name. *Hi darling. So glad. Love to Nancy, big kiss and love to F and you. Working. Will prob work quite late. Use suncream on F please please! I love you both xxx*, she wrote.

She hated herself.

There was no sign of the Bywaters. Beth eventually left Tamara a brief message on her voicemail.

She looked at her river paintings from different angles on her phone. The last one was grotesque, unsellable, and yet she had finally begun to work on it after postponing it, barely conscious of what her hand was doing. The layers were foul, stagnant, more human decomposition than water in motion.

***

And so Beth had left Lizzie that day in London Fields almost thirteen years before, when she had refused to let her see Fern, and Lizzie had then gone to the urban nature reserve nearby that Beth had wheeled Fern to so often, with its pond.

Lizzie had been found later in the water by some teenagers after her accident that was no accident, and taken to the Homerton, then transferred to the Royal Liverpool. A loss of surfactant in the lungs had caused pulmonary oedema and she had had a stroke, resulting in neurological damage.

Sol had tried every method he could devise to stop Beth going to visit, but she shook him off, bought her ticket and went straight to the station, and he followed her, protesting his way on to the train, Fern in a buggy, and stayed when she refused to get off.

Lizzie was almost unrecognisable in her hospital bed. She was wearing make-up. The combination of her stroke-slurred voice and doll demeanour was chilling, her cheeks lopsidedly plump but pulled tight in odd directions, so that Beth suspected she had had some kind of cosmetic surgery in the past, before her stroke. Her lips painted a kind of coral against too much powder lent her the puppet face of an old soap actress beaten up by her toyboy lover, or skewed by alcohol and pavement falls. Her loneliness was palpable. Where was the husband? She was so hungry for human contact that her very being was weighted with it, denture-scented and undignified.

Sol waited outside the ward with Fern. Beth placed her face next to Lizzie's to kiss her, putting her arms round tubes to hug her. 'Sorry sorry sorry,' she was saying. 'Mum, how—'

There was a sting on her cheek.

Lizzie had slapped her. Beth's scalp leaped with pain as her hair was grabbed then yanked.

'Bitch, bitch, fuck-fucking bitch,' said Lizzie. 'Bitch bitch.'

'Oh God.'

Lizzie slapped her again.

'Mum!' cried Beth.

'I ain' – not yer mum. Never.'

The voice was muffled, a new London accent overlaying the struggle to speak, mouth sunk into her face.

Beth stared.

'Bitch bitch, smelly kid you were. Did it. Dro— drove me away.'

'Mum! Lizzie.' Beth felt faint as she stood up. 'I was thirteen,' she said, trying to take deeper breaths.

'Hate you, hate you. Now you depri— depri—' She fought to say words, spat out a stream of invective, curses audible among the barely comprehensible, until a nurse heard, came over and shot a look at Beth, who backed away.

'Go,' said Lizzie.

***

By late afternoon at Tamara's house, Beth was veering between storming out and cooking the family meal.

She sat in the consulting room instead and wrote in the back of a notebook, needing to express herself to the good man she appeared to have left.

Her ear traced a sequence of door, footfall, male and female voices.

Tamara entered the room, animated and almost luminous, a creature blown in with the summer. Her clothes were quite different from anything Beth had seen on her: a gauzy waisted frock spattered with small flowers that took Beth back to girls in childhood whose mothers dressed them. There was art in the way Tamara's dress slanted in narrow folds from her ribcage to her waist. Her hair was tied back, held in a ballet dancer's bun at her neck. In a fascinating new version of herself, her arms were placed lightly around two girls: one a tall female version of the husband with a bag of the type Tamara favoured, and the other squat and darker. Beth traced aspects of Tamara's looks in the younger girl, though she wouldn't catch her eye. There was something odd about the girl's teeth, and she was squarer, with a fierce brow, as though Tamara's genes had consolidated in exaggerated form. The two seemed to spring from Tamara, loosely attached to her hips. Despite Beth's former fury, she smiled at her.

'Go up now, my darlings, so I can see to my neglected guest,' said Tamara in the softest voice to the daughters, and the elder one went, while the younger girl's squaw face went blank, then darkened into a scowl before she bumped into the doorframe and left the room.

Beth saw emotion in Tamara's eyes through the filtered light, then Tamara ran to her. 'I'm sorry, so sorry,' she said. She buried her face in Beth's neck on the couch. 'I'm so relieved you waited for me. It was awful, he dragged me out, all cross with me because I got up at nine.'

She stroked Beth's face, drawing her to her, Beth stiffening against the leap of response. 'My throat was like glass but he was in a total lather.'

Beth drew in her breath. 'You could have left me a note. Where were you?'

'There wasn't even time for that. Angus – he gets all uptight about these things – was pulling me out like a madman. It was just some stupid summer party at Miriam's school Angus spends all his money on. Oh darling?'

'Why didn't you text me?' said Beth.

'Oh,' she said, 'I didn't think of that. I think I had my phone off the whole time – speeches, endless.' She played with Beth's face, threading her hair with soft and spiky movements. 'That was stupid of me. I'm so sorry, my love. You came here in the night, and this is how I treat you. I didn't mean to. My throat's so sore. It never manages these things. I talk all week, and then I need to rest it at weekends.'

'Poor Dr Bywater,' said Beth stiffly.

Tamara lay against her, gazing down as if contemplating her for the first time, her body warmth conducted through the thin dress, and Beth kept her hands still. They kissed.

Tamara's fingertips pattered across Beth's clavicle. 'How can we be together?' she said.

Beth grazed the skin under Tamara's dress, moved on to her shoulder.

Tamara hushed her with a kiss. The backs of her nails trailed lightly over Beth's chest. 'I need to be with you all night,' said Beth.

'Let's see how we can do this,' whispered Tamara.

'You said to come to you. So I did.'

Tamara twisted Beth's hair, said playfully, 'We haven't really thought it out, have we? Practicalities. We're like two naive children, babes in the woods.'

'Yes. Well, no.'

'Angus can be a bit wary of guests. I'll come back to you later,' said Tamara, kissing Beth between each word. 'Stay here.'

Beth made a sound of protest.

'Hush. Stay here,' murmured Tamara.

There was a two-word text from Sol in response to her messages. *All fine.*

* * *

'Oh!' said Beth when Tamara next walked into the room at speed, her hips swinging. She was wearing a gleam of a dress the colour and texture of the *Wizard of Oz* shoes, her lips a similar deep red that was almost disturbing. Over it she wore a black cropped jacket.

'*Peter Grimes*,' she said, kissing Beth. 'I made a scarlet mess of your mouth. Shall I mark your cheek too? Brand you mine. Here.' She grabbed Beth's hand and rocked her lips to press a kiss mark on to it.

'What?'

'I'm late! See you when I get back. Oh, you are beautiful. Did anyone ever tell you that, Elizabeth Penn? I thought it the moment you walked into that rickety old hospital.'

She kissed Beth again and started to open the back door.

'But you're – going out? I'm here for you! What—'

'Well, I didn't know you were coming, my love. Did I? You didn't seem to be. I gave up hope a bit.'

'Who is Peter Grimes?' said Beth in a furious monotone.

'Philistine! Britten. Covent Garden,' said Tamara, and sped out, waving.

'That bloke, you mean? That box?' Beth called after her in indignation, but Tamara didn't hear, or she didn't answer. Beth thumped the couch. *Go*, she told herself. *Very obviously go.*

Her phone beeped. *Tamara B. I love you. Later. Please please wait for me.*

Beth waited.

She went out, got herself some supper, working on her iPad and attempting to get some of her admin and freelance accounts under control to ward away emotion.

You deserve better than me, but I'm not going to use that as my excuse, she wrote in her notebook, partly for herself, largely for Sol at some future time. There was no further word from him, no reply to her texts, no answers from Fern. *She doesn't even compare with you. It's not you. It's my addiction. I didn't know how to stay away.*

* * *

Beth drank wine to medicate herself to sleep, aware of the footsteps and voices of Angus and at least one daughter. In the night, she crept out and ran herself a glass of water, her scalp hot. She hadn't seen Tamara. She thought of Lizzie, spurned by her daughter, and when she began to doze, daggers tore into her: not merely raining at her, but cutting through her abdomen.

'No! Fuck, fuck,' she said quite loudly, waking herself again, and the door opened.

'Hush, shhhh,' said Tamara, pressing her forehead against Beth's. 'Strange muttering. It's OK, it's OK.' Her hand was stroking her.

'Oh, God,' said Beth, and she allowed herself to be held by Tamara in silence. Tamara breathed rhythmically beside Beth until her pulse slowed.

Tamara stroked Beth's forehead in time to the breathing, running her fingers into her scalp.

'I do that to Fern,' Beth whispered. 'Fern. God. What time is it?'

'About three. I came to get a glass of water. Hush, darling, it's all all right now. What was it?'

'But I have this, oh God, what? Terrible. Guilt.'

'Over Sol—'

'Yes, and – but – but over Lizzie. I – chose not to see her. I don't see her.'

Tamara hesitated, clearly attempting to retrieve the name in her memory. 'This is attachment to the bad object,' she said eventually, making swirls in Beth's hair '– your mother.' She kissed her ear and murmured streams of words into it. 'Attachment theory would say you feel guilt, self-loathing, to maintain your relationship in your mind with the woman who rejected you.'

Beth breathed slowly, as though in the fanned air, the peace of the consulting room, and Tamara kissed her again. 'You need to feel the pain of what you didn't have before you can lay her to rest,' she whispered, warm breath near Beth's mouth.

'How can you do this stuff at three in the morning?' said Beth. They held each other, the occasional car in the distance somehow proof, proof that all this was happening, as though pinning the intimacy to reality of time and place. 'Where were you earlier?'

'I peeped through your door when I returned, but you were asleep, sleeping so deeply.'

Beth lay still, sedated by the stroking. She began to protest, but Tamara was kissing her, her fingertips on her neck, sliding her hand over her ribs. She could smell her own desire rise like a spring of teenage hormones, in contrast with the coolness of mouths.

'You wanted me to come to you,' she said between runs of small kisses. 'To give it a go.' She stiffened slightly.

Tamara smiled, wound her hand round Beth's head, then cupped it where her neck met her skull and pulled her to her, kissing her more forcefully. 'I did,' she said. The surprising, discreet curves of Tamara pressed against Beth's body, their tongues merged.

'There is more, so much more, I can show you. Or is it you showing me?' Tamara's smile inched over Beth's lips.

'Oh, God,' moaned Beth, her breathing seemingly generated from elsewhere. Her legs moved apart.

'Hush,' said Tamara, putting her hand lightly on Beth's mouth. 'I need to take you to ... places you haven't been.'

'Fuck me.'

'We can't. We can't yet!'

'I am not going to sleep on your couch like a hitch-hiker any more after tonight,' said Beth.

Tamara laughed. 'Never one to mince words. Just give me a couple of days and we can think exactly what to do. I'm so unbelievably happy you're here. At last.'

She pulled her shoulder strap down, rapidly and unexpectedly, and Beth paused, then Tamara guided her hand.

'Yes,' said Tamara, whispering. 'Like that. Tomorrow. It's almost dawn.'

* * *

In the morning, Beth emailed Sol, stressing how busy she was.

She heard the pattern of creaks and thumps that was the Bywaters waking, the downstairs toilet flushing, voices and crockery muffled along the passage. Tamara didn't come to her. Beth thought she heard her voice, but she was uncertain. She pictured herself like a rodent in a hole, waiting to emerge and uncertain when to poke out its ferrety face. She would go home, try to make Sol suspect nothing on Skype, then return to Tamara in the evening. She left quietly by the consulting-room door, then went back to leave a note.

* * *

The emptiness of Little Canal Street took her back to Sefton Park, back to that last time there, when she was just fifteen. After that day, she had avoided it, taking a different route home and promising herself with superstitious urgency that she wouldn't ever look again, or it might turn her mad.

The lights in the flat had been on that day. And there, finally, there she was, at the window, without a single doubt. Her own mother. Lizzie Penn. All Beth wanted. All she ever, ever wanted, would ever want, illuminated by a yellow glare through drizzle, in a gap between net curtains, simply looking out at the park. An electric shock of recognition. Instant. Certain.

'Oh God,' said Beth, her throat contracting in relief. She ran up those steps. She was there. In moments they would be together. She pressed the second bell up, which she assumed belonged to the floor that housed her mother. A pause. Beth thought her heartbeat might make her ill before she could see her.

Static. Another pause. Her mother's voice. 'Hello?'

'Mum,' said Beth, and there was a catch of breath, or was it electricity, the same flap of compressed air as all those years later, when *No Caller ID* rang; and Beth spoke again into it, her voice soaring. 'It's me, Mum. Beth!'

A hesitation. The slightest sound, perhaps. A little 'mmm', and then the intercom went dead.

Beth's eyes widened. She froze. She waited for her mother to come down. She waited longer. She tried to twist the door handle.

She pressed the bell again. A mistake. The sound echoed. She pressed again and again, pushing so hard the button rocked in its cradle and she hoped she might break it. It protested, buzzing, whining. She let it shriek. No answer.

And the lights were off, the gap in the net curtains gone.

* * *

Beth looked around, tidied up. On the table, obscured by a book and a studio-lighting equipment catalogue, was the note she had written to Fern the night she had almost slipped out and left her on her own to see Tamara. Beth had torn the note, screwed it up and chucked it somewhere. Where? Probably in the nearest fireplace. Her jaw slackened, there on her own. The two torn pieces of the note were smoothed out and placed together, left there for her to find.

She didn't know what to do. Eventually, she tried to Skype Fern, who had her own log-on, but she didn't pick up. She FaceTimed her, but there was nothing. Pacing around to steel herself, she FaceTimed and Skyped Sol, who was also unavailable. She typed out a message to them both, asking them to call.

She worked for several hours. *Come back. Please* was the only communication she received from Tamara, after a quick chat with Sol, who was rushing out, on a bad connection that revealed nothing but showed the Little Canal Street house behind her.

When Beth returned to Kennington in the evening, she found the consulting-room door unlocked and the house quiet. She left her bag of washed clothes and walked into the kitchen, where there was a noise coming from above. Angus padded down the staircase in his careful stoop with his knees bent to the sides, giving Beth an uneasy nod of acknowledgement, and she realised that what she could hear above her was sobbing.

'She's not well,' Angus said gravely with a blink, but he was lit from within by a sense of purpose.

'Since when?'

'She's been saying she's in a bad way for a day or two now, but she's at the worst end of how she gets this. Throat on fire. Temperature I have to admit scares me. Hallucinations.'

'Poor Tamara.'

'Her tonsils are in a terrible state,' he said in hushed tones.

Beth's mouth twitched. 'Why can't they chop them out?' she said callously.

'Oh no, no, they are inclined not to operate now,' he said, and treated Beth to an informed medical explanation, which at length concluded that such repeated bouts of tonsillitis could reveal themselves to be glandular fever.

'I have a conference tomorrow.' He now seemed more anxious. 'My annual conference in Geneva. Over a week.' Beth watched him. He was, quite literally, wringing his hands.

She suppressed a smile. 'Don't worry,' she said in a businesslike manner. 'I can look after her. Which antibiotics are her usual? A starter dose of Amoxicillin?'

Angus folded himself like a dinosaur over the table to provide a list of tasks that ran to several pages: practical jobs; contacts for Tamara's work, which gave Beth a rush of the old regressive excitement; daughters' activities; medicines with backup antibiotics, fruit, herbs and obscure minerals.

*　*　*

So began Beth's period of incarceration in Tamara Bywater's spare room. Her cynicism was tempered by the sight of Tamara propped on a spread of hair on pillows and, once Angus had left, a kind of hectic clinging that only dipped intermittently into her old evasions. 'This is our honeymoon,' she said on various occasions in a croak, 'and I can't tell you how sorry I am for both of us that it should be like this. I'm sorry, I'm sorry.'

For all her drama, she seemed to be trying to hide the agony of her throat. Nursemaid and nanny, Beth fell quickly into a routine of soothing her; she cooked for her, contacted her doctor, talked to her, stroking her forehead as she spoke, and Tamara smiled and talked back, their conversation finally more fluent. On the first afternoon, Beth found herself collecting the younger daughter Francesca from her activities centre, armed with a note of permission from her mother.

'*Fern*,' she muttered as she accompanied the scowler back home. She FaceTimed Fern that evening, sitting with her back close to a wall, but Fern would not pick up. Neither did Sol. *Please*, she messaged him. *Let's talk.*

* * *

The centre of activity was the spare bedroom at the back of the house, which Tamara claimed was cooler than her own, and there she had stationed herself under fans in the middle of the small double bed, with no suggestion that Beth would share it after a day's ministrations. From time to time she begged for visits from her girls, yet she was distinctly less aware of them in general than Beth would have expected, hours passing with no mention of them followed by a sudden desire for their presence. Miriam floated in and out of the house at will, keeping largely to her bedroom when at home, while Francesca either hovered when back from her summer school or was glued to her mother's iPad.

'I don't think you realise,' said Tamara, looking at Beth intensely, 'Francesca is a problem child. Only Angus can handle her. I'm so hurt by her, but I worry about her all the time.'

'How awful,' said Beth, her voice insincere even to her own ears. 'What about her sister?'

Tamara ran her hand down Beth's arm, Beth's nerves rippling with a delay. 'Miriam. Oh, she's angelic. Really. Her birth mother's a raging bitch, but we've largely had custody of her, been … she and I, more like sisters. She borrows my clothes all the time; I give her jewellery. She's beautiful, isn't she?'

Beth said nothing, in loyalty to Fern. She stroked Tamara's forehead, and was asked to summon Francesca to say goodnight.

Angus repeatedly offered to fly back. 'No, no, I don't want him,' Tamara hissed. 'This is our chance to be together.' And then she and Beth would start conversations of little consequence yet seemingly of vast significance, their mutual amusement and affinity pulling them on and on into the night, Beth's curiosity about Tamara's past and present never satisfied – while the girls haunted the house. After two days, Angus intervened from Switzerland and sent the girls to his mother.

There was still no call or message from Sol. Beth emailed him, asking him when he wanted to speak, and frequently contacted Fern, who once sent back an email. Beth opened it with shaking hands. *I'm OK* was all it said.

TWENTY-ONE

Beth continued to message Fern every day, and called her mobile, but Fern cut her dead. Some of her WhatsApp messages were read while others were ignored, and she repeatedly affirmed her love, or sent her observations, pictures, jokes, emojis. Sol told her little beyond occasional reports on Fern's well-being.

Tamara's excitement about Beth's forthcoming show at the Gavron continued as a theme, her conviction of Beth's genius now apparently confirmed as she maintained that her fame would outstrip Aranxto's and refused to hear Beth's informed denials.

They had entered a period of confinement, a fevered exile in which normal life barely existed and there was no past or future but a spot of time punctuated only by contact with America; and yet when Beth crept from Tamara's bedside, she never knew who would greet her the next day. It seemed that she woke to find a different Tamara every morning. Tamara was a more changeable creature than anyone she had ever encountered, one whose fresh certainties and enthusiasms took Beth along hairpin bends that she could only attempt to negotiate, yet left her bewildered. Tamara entered people's psyches, poured peace upon them with the inner contentment that seemed to radiate from her. Then suddenly she herself would fall into despair, or agitation, or announce the need to retreat from the world. It was still intermittently impossible to stimulate her interest, and Beth found herself dancing round her as her courtier.

Despite much conjecture, the hidden meanings behind Tamara's varying behaviours were difficult to ascertain, each conclusion evaporating. 'Oh Angus calls me a free radical,' said Tamara with a shrug that discouraged further talk. Yet the rewards to such challenges were indispensable for reasons that were hard to fathom.

*   *   *

Time was passing, and Beth delayed thinking about her ticket to Newport, while no longer able to deny that Sol was avoiding her. Tamara remained where she was. 'This is always the sickness chamber,' she said. 'The traffic can't grate at my nerves here. Anyway, we can't be in my room – I must have a little sensitivity to Angus.'

'How often do you shag each other, then?' said Beth flippantly, then laughed, to protect herself.

'Oh my darling, our sex life pretty much died years ago. He's a good man, but ...'

Beth looked into the bedroom only once while Tamara slept, easing the doorknob with burglar's stealth to be greeted by traces of incense and old candle smoke, but the curtains were closed and, though she fumbled, she could find no light switch, and only the hulking outline of the Bywater bed was visible.

'What kind of a honeymoon is this?' said Tamara again with a blurry smile from her pillows, tilting Beth's chin and holding her close to her gaze. 'In a nunnery. A sanatorium. I am so sorry. When I'm better, where shall we go? Where shall we be, you and I?'

And so in conversations that nagged Beth with their more hyperbolic echoes of those with Sol in the early days, yet kept her from America and reality, they played at houses, castles, hideaways, because there was no space in that room of suffering for the intrusion of practicalities. Tamara spun tales for Beth, and Beth joined in, any obscure observation that fired through her mind returned to her in shinier form. 'You are the most brilliant creature I've ever met,' Tamara said to her. Then in the morning, there would be a force field around the room, the chill palpable as Tamara frowned at her laptop in glasses in a partial return to work.

'What are you doing?' said Beth into the frost. She frequently failed at such times to modulate her voice.

'Admin. Distressed patients. Reports. Quotes.' Tamara spoke, barely moving her mouth above the rapid typing.

'You email your patients?'

Tamara sighed. 'I don't think you understand quite how senior the job is and therefore how busy I am, Beth. Lots of people rely on me being there for them. This work never stops.'

Beth picked up Tamara's plate, leaning over her shoulder to skim her inbox. Tamara fired off replies at top speed, issuing advice, consolation, encouragement in a matter of seconds, and yet Beth knew how each sentence would be clung to for salvation. She herself had been too fearful and bound by etiquette. Yet there were hordes out there clamouring for Dr Bywater's tossed-off insights, as though she were a deity who could confer bliss on those who craved it. In her guise of wise doctor, she was oblivious to Beth.

'Where is this from?' Beth would ask, picking up an object, an item of clothing, a small antique. 'A patient gave it to me. Sweet,' Tamara would say. Or, 'A patient gave it to me, I think.'

'You think?'

'They usually give me presents at the end. The appreciative ones. It's hard to remember.'

And Beth listened with the latest confirmation that Tamara's ambivalence was all her own fault. Then, when she arrived later with breakfast, Tamara would embrace her as though she hadn't seen her for days, pulling her to her, kissing her long and cool on the mouth.

Soon after her bouts of emailing, Tamara would fall asleep and Beth would leave for some hours to go to Little Canal Street or to her studio to work and to call her family, Fern unavailable, and Sol increasingly absent. On her return, Beth sometimes found Tamara crying alone in bed with tangled hair as she sipped from a cup in an old silk garment, a glitter to her despair. 'I thought you'd left me. Don't do that again,' she said. 'You won't really leave here, will you?'

Beth paused. She opened her mouth. Tamara sat there, looking terrified.

'You helped me,' said Beth, and suddenly she wanted to cry. 'Now it's my turn to rescue you.'

The next time Beth came into the room, Tamara was rubbing some cream on her skin with such focus in a small mirror that she barely looked up, then just as Beth was leaving she flashed her the warmest smile, and she had coloured her mouth for the first time in days. It flicked on a primitive switch of desire.

Beth leaned across the bed, but Tamara would barely kiss her. There was a smallness to her mouth, a reluctance to commit herself. You could hold this creature in your lap and its eyes transfix you, and then it would just wander off, or hurt with all its sharpnesses. Tamara's power lay in the fact that she didn't essentially care. She could do without.

It became slowly apparent that the majority of conversations turned into discussions about Tamara, but Tamara confided her problems in Beth, engaging her in her dilemmas, and when Beth arrived, after circuitous rumination, at some solution, Tamara was rewardingly delighted. 'You understand me more than anyone in my life ever has,' she said.

The next time Beth approached the room, Tamara was talking in an animated fashion that softened into the tones recalled from the consulting room, and as she entered, Tamara became more businesslike.

'Who was that?'

'Oh, an ex-patient.'

'I thought that wasn't allowed?'

'He's a silly boy. He needs all the help he can get,' she said, and busied herself with the papers on her bed.

'But—'

'Perhaps you should get back to Sol,' said Tamara, bending over her computer later in the day. 'Is it fair to deprive you of him?'

'*What?*' Beth barked.

'I am thinking only of you.'

'For a start he's in America, and my flight's not yet, and secondly – and the main thing – I'm—I'm *here*, for God's sake,' she said, and slammed the door and left the house, but Tamara called her back later and she was semi-naked on the bed, with a sushi take-away on trays that she had spread all over the covers for them and five different teas for Beth to taste. Beth delivered a list of her grievances, Tamara apologised, and then they embraced, but touching her further would clearly have been an assault on her feverish state.

'You don't know what it's like to be left like this. You're here right now, in my room. If you left again, the pain would be unbearable. Beth. Darling.'

'I do,' said Beth. 'I know what it is to be left. To be so near someone, but they don't want you.'

'What do you mean?'

Beth paused. She swallowed.

'Go on.'

'One day, after my mother had left me and moved away from Liverpool, I saw her face ...'

Tamara listened, stroking, holding her.

'Why have you never told me this before?' she said at the end of the story.

'I couldn't.'

'But, darling, it doesn't make sense,' said Tamara. 'Does it? She must have had a motive for being there.' And for the first time since she had terminated therapy, Tamara was the Dr Bywater of old, her mind untangling the inexplicable and ordering it into patterns.

'But she was right there,' said Beth. 'And she didn't come to me. Didn't *want* to see me.'

'That isn't logical,' said Tamara, twisting a strand of Beth's hair. 'It seems likely that she was thwarted.'

'But—' Beth frowned.

'Where was your father?'

'At home, as usual.'

'He didn't know she was there?' said Tamara in her gentle voice, stroking Beth's forehead. 'You couldn't say anything, I suppose.'

'I really doubt it. No. Mentioning her name would be like stabbing him.'

'But, darling,' said Tamara, coughing lightly, and running her fingers through Beth's, 'she was trying to see you. It couldn't have been unintentional. She was holding you in mind, if not in body. Sometimes, simple proximity is all we have. Sometimes it's a transitional object.'

'She didn't even come down after she heard my voice. She really *didn't* want to see me.'

'You silly one. Then why would she be there? In a flat on her own? Your brother had gone; she had run away from your father. She wanted to protect her Beth. To keep an eye on you, at least, even if there was some reason she couldn't be with you.'

'Really?' Beth murmured, and hot sore tears had started to spread. 'But. She just stood there at the department store when I saw her. TJ's.'

Tamara paused. 'She could have been stronger.'

'She should have.'

'Are you sure there wasn't more?' Dr Bywater was speaking softly into her ear, skimming her breast. 'How do you know she didn't talk to your father, for instance?'

'Well, I really don't think she did.'

'Would he have told you?'

'No ...'

'Infidelity counted then, as a reason for divorce. Marital abandonment ... He'd have had rights, in the circumstances.'

'I suppose ...?'

'Beth, I doubt any mother would accept the loss of her child so easily. Especially if she put herself *there*. You were a child. You wouldn't know everything. Are you sure she didn't fight to see you? To have custody of you even? Your father would never have told you that.'

A kiss on her neck.

'You think?'

'For sure.'

Beth looked into Tamara's eyes.

'Thank you for this,' she said.

* * *

The next time Beth returned from a morning of work at her studio, Tamara was in the kitchen in her drooping antique tea gown, hair caught in a chopstick, with an adolescent perching on a stool opposite her. His hand trembled as he drank one of her perfumed teas. Beth backed out, and worked on the mosaic, knowing herself to be a fool.

'You hadn't told me about him,' she said once the eager teenager had departed.

'Oh, I didn't even think to. Mick,' said Tamara.

'Who is he?'

'I know – knew – his mother.'

'He thinks he's in love with you.'

'He's eighteen! Don't be ridiculous.'

There was a knock on the door. Beth hesitated, then rose to open it.

'By the way, darling,' said Tamara. 'You mustn't ever let a tall, blondy, red-haired man through the door. He usually wears a suit. Late thirties. Very convincing.'

'Who?'

'He was an NHS patient but he found out where I live, and he thinks I can cure him. Just say I'm not in and close the door.'

'He fancies you, you mean.'

'Oh, who knows.'

'So that's your stalker,' said Beth grimly.

'No, no, he's online. Do you want some of this nail varnish?'

Beth barely glanced at it, and with an open show of impatience she went to answer the door at a second knock, and it was the jasmine-cutting neighbour, who looked at her with undisguised hostility.

'Oh, Duncan, such a relief you're here!' said Tamara, and picked up his hand with a weak gesture to kiss it. 'You see, I'm ill. And Beth's brilliant, been helping me so much, but she's the *arty* type. I doubt she can fix a dishwasher drain or whatever the problem is.'

'Thank you, Tamara,' said Beth.

'Let me have a look,' said Duncan.

'I want to see your work on the mosaic,' Tamara murmured to Beth.

'You know – you know –' said Beth in the passage, 'I am a fucking idiot. Let's face it. I presented myself to you in a gesture of high romance, and I've ended up trotting off to summer school and clearing up *bin juice*.'

Tamara's laughter carolled through the consulting room. 'I love the way you speak sometimes!' she said.

'It's not meant to be funny.'

Tamara took her hand. 'Show me the mosaic.'

They walked to the yard quite openly entwined, and Tamara was full of praise; then she talked with tenderness to a neighbour who appeared, a young woman with a pile of washing, and Beth watched, apparently no longer there.

'Come, Beth,' said Tamara, taking her by the arm, and they kissed in the consulting room.

'You know, I actually will have to think about Newport,' said Beth. 'My ticket's Tuesday at dawn.'

Tamara paused momentarily. 'I think it's time to seduce you,' she said.

'What?'

'And why not? The time is ripe. You never caught my lurgy. Which is a wonder for us.'

'Oh,' said Beth uselessly. 'Yes.' She held the doorframe.

'Tomorrow night … I will be so much better by tomorrow night. Isn't that phrase full of promise? *Tomorrow night*,' she murmured.

'Yes.'

'So. Go out this evening, see some friends,' said Tamara, running little kisses over Beth's face. 'You need a break.'

Beth stiffened. She hesitated. 'OK,' she said. 'But would you be all right if I did?'

'I'm beginning to recover, I think.'

'Well, I could do some work then; I'm behind on the last paintings,' she said, and Tamara didn't demur. 'I need to get some more old childhood river photos Aranxto has found.'

Tamara looked up. 'I'd love to meet Aranxto again! He was adorable.'

Beth grunted. The one time she had managed to effect an apparently casual introduction a few weeks before, Tamara exquisitely dressed and entranced, Aranxto had been in a hurry.

'What do you think?' Beth had asked him the moment she could.

Aranxto shrugged. 'One of those small-time divas. High maintenance. Quite fun.'

'Oh! I somehow thought you'd be intrigued by her.'

Aranxto looked bored.

'Don't you think she's beautiful?'

'No. She thinks she is. You are more. She's not one of your nutters, is she?'

'No, she's a shrink!'

Aranxto had nodded and began to discuss his latest boyfriend.

* * *

Now, back at Little Canal Street before she began her painting, Beth picked up the landline, so rarely used, and listened to messages left there. Sol had rung. *Hi. Bet. I'd suggest you don't need to come out for the second part of the vacation.* Beth's heart slammed into a new gear. She listened to the beginning again, absorbing the date. *My thought is that you will be in agreement with that? Well.* He coughed, a Sol cough, an unapologetic bark. *Fern is good, petitioning to go to Long Island with the cousins. Uh ... it would kind of suit me in terms of work. We can both uproot there and Mom visit from Newport. Get back to me.*

He had rung the landline intentionally. Beth called him, and got only his voicemail. *Darling, can we talk? xxx*, she texted him. She gulped water, and rang again, but went straight on to his voicemail. Her voice shook.

'Sol,' she said. 'Please please call me. I want to explai— talk. Please. I love you,' she finished spontaneously.

* * *

For the first time, Beth wasn't summoned back to Tamara's, and she made herself return later than she wanted to. From a few houses away, laughter and protest were audible, floating up from the basement on the last light. She let herself in at the back through the reek of dying blossom heated by the day, and

307

though silence was unnecessary, she crept towards the passage that led on to the kitchen, where a section of the room was visible from the shadows. Tamara was out of her sickbed, and red-lipped in a tight black Holly Golightly dress with bare feet; she sat in candlelight against the dusk that pooled from the area at a table covered in napkins and wine glasses with several guests, the majority of whom were men, though Beth could only see one side of the table. The weak voice and gestures were quite gone. It was apparent that the guests were colleagues, or in the same profession, and there was some pretend competition involving the man who appeared to be Tamara's beloved Head of Services, bargaining with a psychologist from a different organisation for Tamara's future employment, each upping the stakes in goats, camels, shekels, bullion. The prize of Dr Bywater on their team was finally deemed to be beyond rubies. Beth felt sick. With the exception of an older woman who remained impassive, the guests were primarily focused on Tamara and the almost theatrical light that hovered around her, and she appeared to take it as her due, her combination of warmth and flirtation and the ability to instil confidence in others clearly keeping her Head of Services tense with hope. Then her expression altered as she turned to the older woman and began to talk very seriously to her, and without pause she was the professional psychologist, an expert in NHS and government mental health policy, frowning and nodding and changing the tenor of the room so that the others were temporarily lost, then talked quietly among themselves.

Beth tried to steady her breathing. The far end of the table was quieter, but now a voice could be heard, more measured and understated than the others, and Beth froze. The voice was known to her. David Aarons. She listened. His wife Sofia was clearly beside him.

'Jesus,' Beth muttered aloud, and still she stood there, pinned, as she strained to hear. IAPT, primary healthcare trusts, Ann Penrose and others whose names Beth didn't know, were all discussed or gossiped about, and the Head of Services made a joke about Tamara and transference that clearly delighted her. Sofia Aarons was possibly mentioning going home, but her words were drowned in other conversations. Beth shrank back into the darkness. She willed Sofia to leave.

'I need the loo. Pause the conversation! Not a word. You are all too fascinating to miss anything,' said Tamara suddenly, and Beth backed off towards the consulting room as she heard David telling Sofia he would follow her home.

Tamara turned and caught sight of Beth along the passage. 'Oh, hello, darling! I didn't hear you. How are you, my love?'

She came up, kissed Beth rapidly on the lips, then set off back to the toilet. Beth grabbed her shoulder. It felt intrusive, and she cringed.

'Sorry.'

'No, no, nice! Massage me there later?'

Beth gazed at her through the shadows. 'What in hell—?' she said.

Tamara threw her dazzling smile at Beth. 'I need to pee!'

'So you knew about this dinner party and didn't even think to invite me?'

'This is my ultimate *boss* ...' said Tamara in a hiss.

'So?'

'He would be distracted by you because you're so pretty. I need all the ammunition I have!'

Beth gaped, and Tamara slipped into the toilet and shut the door.

'You are the Belle fucking Dame sans Merci,' said Beth when Tamara reappeared. 'You truly are.'

Tamara paused. 'I'm sure you have some choice references, but—'

'You wanted me out of the way. This man clearly thinks he's about to cop off with you,' said Beth. 'You manipulated me into going. What the hell are you doing?'

'Darling, don't be silly,' said Tamara under her breath, warm against Beth's neck. 'I'm very boring really, I only sleep with Angus.'

'But I thought ...' Beth began, a familiar refrain. 'I thought you didn't,' she snapped, so much of her conversation seeming to consist of quoting what Tamara had said before or catching her out.

'Well,' she murmured calmly, 'I think we probably have more sex than most dully married couples. I must get back in.'

'But – but—'

Tamara said nothing, and leaned towards the kitchen. The sounds of Sofia Aarons leaving, calling out thanks, came through the door. 'Too soon!' Tamara called back at her, and blew her kisses.

'You said you haven't had sex with him for years,' said Beth in a mutter, trying to stop herself.

'Oh, did I? Take no notice of me. I never know what I say or have said. Angus is completely used to it – I always say to him, "Judge me on what I do, not what I say," and he knows that's right.'

'So you do have sex with him.'

'Sometimes we make love, of course. He doesn't excite me, but ...' Tamara was leaning further towards the kitchen, poised in her impatience to return. Then she looked at Beth with a radiant smile. 'In a rational world, you would all belong to me,' she said, reaching up to Beth's face. 'My darling dull husband too.' She kissed her. 'I meet far too many adorable people, and all this jealousy about it seems ridiculous to me, as long as everyone's content and thriving. What's the point of being possessive? Sweetheart, I really have to go in. Come to me later.'

'I just can't believe this,' said Beth, barely able to speak. 'You said you wanted to make a go of it with me.'

'And I do!'

'Well—'

'I do. I do. But who knows how long it'll last. You'll grow out of me eventually, darling Beth. You'll want to get back to nice hubby and offspring. Or you'll find some handsome young artist. And then where will I be? I always think, perhaps I'll grow old with Angus after all. But for now, I really don't want to tie myself down. Life is too short.'

'Jesus Christ!' Beth spat, and she stormed back to the consulting room, shouldered her bag and pushed her way through the jasmine to the street. She walked, her heart thumping, in the direction of the Tube. At that moment, all she wanted was to bump into Sofia Aarons, question upon question raging through her mind. She gazed at a night bus that passed, its passengers picked out in yellow, but David was rich, and Sofia would have taken a taxi. She slowed her pace.

She felt sickened, as though in all those months of solace, she had been taken for a ride. Did shrinks, then, switch on an identity, personality as professional tool? If so, Tamara Bywater was highly skilled, her muscles tight, her performance exemplary. Some element of Beth's precious past experience was whipped away. She could barely summon that level-headed professional in the mercurial, damaged creature she witnessed. Yet her body reacted to her as her logical mind now rebelled. Tamara's perfume was detectable somewhere near Beth's mouth, and even now – even now – it propelled a current of desire.

A car engine slowed behind her and she veered away from the kerb.

'Beth!' called a voice. 'Jump in. Lift home?'

Beth heard her own small whimper, and she clambered into the warmth, and Sofia kissed her, Beth pulling away before the second kiss and laughing awkwardly.

'What are you doing in this godforsaken area?'

'Shall we make some injections and passports jokes?' said Beth, and her voice was shaking. 'What are you doing?'

'You're agitated!' Sofia laid her hand briefly on Beth's. 'I'm escaping a dinner party. What's the matter, Bet?'

'Ha! Only Sol calls me that.'

'Sorry. David must have got it from him and it spread to me.'

'Well, Sof, so—'

'Ha. OK, Elizabeth something Penn, so what's up?'

'Am I that obvious?'

'Yes. Tell me.'

'OK then. Why,' said Beth, swallowing. 'Why— Can you tell me why, people can be so *inconsistent*?'

313

She took a breath. 'Bloody hell. Sorry. What's the root of this? Say one thing one time, entirely another thing another.' She paused again. 'Busman's holiday, sorry. I've just … been talking to someone. Blow hot, cold. They don't seem to even notice the hypocrisy, the contradiction? Or care about it—'

'Ambivalence? Avoidant personality?'

'But why on earth would people be like that? Charm, retreat—'

'Oh, that's a vast subject,' said Sofia dismissively. 'Childhood attachment issues …'

'Oh. Yes. But also, almost different *personalities*. And needing attention, focus, one way or another, shine the light on you, magical almost, confiding, inspiring, amazing, and then – oooof, whipped away … Suddenly cold, or even super-vulnerable. Jesus. OK, I'm gabbling, but someone's driving me *mad*. My – my brother's wife,' she said, blushing into the dark.

Sofia laughed, making a sound of sympathy. 'Irony of ironies, I've just left someone very like that. Dinner party as stage, limelight, very very fun and outrageous, but … You either love them or you see through them. Eventually.'

'Oh my God,' said Beth. 'Yes!' She touched Sofia's arm. 'I'd forgotten how easy you are to talk to! We just let the men grunt at each other. Why? Anyway, yes, absolutely. This – too – is a nightmare woman. So what does your friend have wrong with her?'

314

'My friend?'

'The one you've just escaped from.'

'Ah,' said Sofia. 'I'm beginning to formulate ideas about this. So is David. But it would hardly be professional to ... Anyway, one encounters people clinically along the same spectrum who make people like her look ... so, I can hardly say "mild" because they are not, but ... the need for attention as supply is at a more dangerous level. There's a diversion before Prince of Wales,' she said to the driver.

'More dangerous?'

'Oh, psychiatric issues, self-harming. My thesis was all about this. For all the glamour and show, they tend to suffer a lot of depression as well. But actually, it's the partners, family, who are really affected. There to build up the weak self essentially.'

'Tell me more!' said Beth.

'The problem is, NPD – this cluster – are always so *convincing*.' She gave an irritated sigh. 'Often some of the most vivid. Those who aren't clinically ill. Can he enter Little Canal from here?'

'No, we can stop on Bailhurst Street. Tell me? This helps!'

Sofia took a breath. 'Where to start? Well. So. Poor impulse control, preoccupation with appearance, lack of empathy, inflated self-perception, manipulation ...' she said in flat tones as though pretending to read a list. 'Control through sexual appeal, ludic relationship style ... Ringing bells?'

'Tell me more. What's NPD?'

'Ah, well, this is going to have to make us see each other, isn't it? Narcissistic Personality Disorder. But I can hardly tell you about my patients. Just as I can't tell you about my colleague – oh.' Sofia froze. A thought visibly scuttered across her face and she blinked. She attempted to disguise her expression.

'What?'

'I'd better get on. You OK to stop here?'

'Yes. Thank you. Next time.'

'Soon,' said Sofia.

'A lay tour around lunacy. Great!'

She snorted. 'I'll call.'

* * *

Beth sank her head into her hands at the table in shame over all she had done. Sol. A chill came over her. She wanted him there, waiting for her. 'I love you,' she said in her mind to him, in a moment of truth. The landline had been rung several times, with the unavailable ID of calls from abroad. She rang him, and got straight on to his voicemail. She tried Ellie, whose phone was off; she called Killian, who shouted greetings from a pub and couldn't hear her.

She texted Sol, then emailed him, and to her surprise got an almost immediate reply. *Can't talk, shooting in NYC. Where are you?*

Home, she replied. *I love you.*

You back collecting stuff?

No! Can we speak? When can you talk? Xxxx.

There was a silence.

I will come to the US tomorrow, Beth texted.

No. When are you off again?

There was a pause as Beth started several replies, then deleted them. *How do you know I wasn't here?*

Aranxto told me.

Aranxto?? Why? How?

Your lights often weren't on. I didn't need him to tell me.

The total bastard ... As soon as he can't control me, he punishes me. He's getting worse with his fucking troublemaking. Sol, please. We need to speak. I need to talk to you, xxxx.

When we can.

Darling, darling, please, I'm just mad, fucked up, stupid. Please. I love you. Please come back to me.

Talk soon.

Now! Please. Put your fucking camera down. As soon as you can? Please. I love you.

She burrowed into the back of the sofa. It smelled both of Fern's bath products and a more subtle trace of Sol. She lay her cheek against it. She semi-slept, there on the sofa. After a while, Tamara pooled, oil-like, into her memory, smiling down, sliding down, and spreading shadows that pulled Beth to her so that she was chasing her, entering her. 'Oh God,' she moaned, trampling on the picture.

317

Her phone beeped. *Come to my bed*, Tamara texted.

* * *

Once the coots called from the canal at dawn, Beth took the bus to her studio and worked on the last river painting. She couldn't stop herself, and the canvas was thick, a belching of mud, slime, translucency over the finest strands of hair, and she had no idea whether she could show it in the exhibition, or even to Sol, the only person who knew all of such horror.

Angus Bywater called early in the morning from Switzerland. 'Tamara's very upset,' he said in his nasal monotone.

Beth took a breath. 'I'm sorry to hear that.'

'She isn't well, and she needs help.'

'She's impossible.'

There was a long pause. 'She can be what I call temperamental when she's unwell. She's very ill.'

'Well that's strange, because she was fine yesterday evening.'

Angus hesitated. He cleared his throat. 'She is very upset that she offended you but the situation is worrying. I can come back, but I can't get on a flight till this evening. She is now on Flucloxacillin because her Amoxicillin didn't clear it and she has relapsed.'

Beth listened to further monologues in short sentences as she paced around the studio, nodding at Jack and Killian as they arrived. She sat at her computer. There was nothing from Sol or Fern, but an email popped up from Kevin O'Hanlon about her coming in to discuss her show. She smiled as she skimmed it.

'I am very concerned about my wife. She's very sensitive. If she gets upset, she suffers a great deal – she gives too much of herself – I think it's not safe to leave her now. She is ill, and she can become very vulnerable. If you could perhaps go over and feed her and keep her company today, I can get a flight tonight.'

'Jesus,' Beth grunted. She ran her hand through her hair. 'I'll go when I finish my work.'

'Could it be sooner? Mara needs help.'

'No,' said Beth. 'Sorry.'

She ended the call, attempted to Skype Sol and left it on in case he tried her. And suddenly, Fern was ringing. Beth swiped so fast to answer, she turned it off. She cursed aloud, tapped straight back on, but Fern didn't pick up. Beth left her a message, tried calling, WhatsApp, FaceTime. There was nothing. 'Fern,' she moaned. She tried Sol, who was unavailable.

She waited. There was nothing. It was night in the United States. Beth painted as she waited, more pond than river.

Try later, she had messaged Sol.

I will keep trying, she had written to Fern. *I love you.*

x

I love you. I need you in my arms, Tamara texted.

Please be so kind as to alert me once you are with my wife, Angus emailed.

Beth finally cleared up at her studio, and was about to turn off her laptop when the Skype icon appeared.

'Fern!' she gabbled.

Fern's face appeared, jolting between frames, but Beth could see that she was breathing quickly before she spoke.

'Lovely! How are you? I'm so pleased to—'

'What did I do wrong?' Fern asked in a blurt, her face blank with a clearly practised expression.

'Wrong?'

'To you.'

'Darling! You've done *nothing* wrong,' said Beth, but humiliation or panic flashed across Fern's face, and then she reached out and disconnected the call before they had finished. She disappeared.

Beth called straight back. She tried frequently as the day progressed.

When she arrived in Kennington, Tamara was in bed, so reduced that Beth was momentarily startled. She looked almost plain, her eyes smaller with evidence of tears, an aroma of slept-in sheets hovering over the bed so Beth threw open the window. Tamara was clearly trying not to cry, the tension vibrating in her neck, and an inability to control her voice audible. She appeared so much younger, a creature in pain, and Beth took her in her arms, and then Tamara cried, clinging to her and soaking her shoulder, unable to catch her breath.

'Please. Please please don't go. Angus won't be back till tomorrow now you're here. Please stay.'

Beth said nothing, stroking her back.

'Please.'

'Please stay on your couch like a teenage lodger while I cook for you and clear up after you and you entertain your friends,' said Beth in a low voice. 'Please be a total bloody idiot. The biggest dupe of all of them—'

'Oh, Beth,' Tamara sobbed. 'It's only because I'm so terrified of losing you. I don't know myself. I just don't seem to know myself. Sometimes I go into these phases, say these things. I don't even remember them afterwards! What did I say? I don't really know.'

Beth simply shook her head, still stroking Tamara's back.

'Whatever it is, I know it's hurtful,' said Tamara. 'I need to try to do better. I get it all wrong. Please, darling. It's only because I don't realise how I'm behaving. I'm in complete terror of losing you. I only behave like that because I want you more than anyone in the world, anyone I've ever met. I go down the wrong path.'

'I've heard all this before,' said Beth.

'I'm afraid sometimes,' said Tamara with a sob. 'I'm afraid that, after all, there's nothing to me. I'm pedalling fast on empty.'

'And all these people adore you.'

'Yes, but what does that mean? They don't know me.'

'You don't know you,' said Beth. 'Go to sleep.'

Tamara's shoulders sagged. Her eyes looked frightened. 'Yes,' she said. 'I'm so sorry.'

* * *

When Tamara came down much later, she smelled freshly bathed; she had dried her hair smooth again and was dressed in a cobwebbed clinging item Beth had never seen before. She was thinner, weary, the mania drifting in almost detectable tatters around her, even as she looked more beautiful.

'Come to me,' she said.

Beth shook her head.

Tamara perched on Beth's lap, surrounding her with her scent, embarrassing her.

'I need to hold you,' she said. She looked at Beth for a long time. 'We will plan tomorrow where to go, and we will go away together,' she said, and Beth merely listened. Tamara trailed her fingertips down Beth's neck with the lightest, most rhythmic touch. 'I knew last night with complete certainty. I can't be without you. All the others are a smokescreen. I play as a defence against not having you. I knew it when you walked into my office.'

'None of this is true,' said Beth.

'It is true,' she said, and looked Beth deep in the eyes, the strands of pigment contracting like cells of sea creature.

'I think you actually believe your own lies,' said Beth softly.

'Don't hurt me. I don't tell lies. Tonight we will be together, and after tonight, we'll decide where to go.'

Tamara's voice moved through Beth's throat. She kissed her inner wrist, her hairline, behind her ears, brushing a domino trail of nerves across her. She stroked the skin under Beth's top, fingers slipping across her chest, circling downwards, spirals and loops of touch sending shivering currents. She kept her gaze steady, and Beth was inside her mind, deep inside Tamara, her own body inching towards an arousal she tried to resist. They looked at each other, and Beth saw depths of communication and humanity, and understanding: the layers of a life lived.

'Come up.' Tamara held out her hand and Beth followed her, along the silver tunnel of the staircase to the front sitting room with its spasm of green, its spidery layers of closed curtain, pink lights. Beth was melting, weakening, all sensation pooling in a bead, no control over the rhythm of her breathing.

'We have the house to ourselves,' said Tamara. 'I have you to myself,' she said playfully, 'at last.'

Beth touched her, and still there was that feral trace of evasion even as Tamara gazed at her with her off-centre eyes.

323

'You'll have to find me, catch me,' Tamara said, and began to wander round the room, the hypnotic choreography of her movements making Beth a dumb creature, arousal like pain between her legs.

'No,' said Beth.

'No?' Tamara said, laughing. 'Then you won't have me.'

Beth shrugged. She sat back and laid her arm across the sofa. She refused to look at Tamara. She took out her phone and began to email. She could barely breathe.

'What shall I do?' said Tamara in a laughing girl-voice.

'Perhaps we won't,' said Beth.

'I'm ready.' Tamara came and leaned over Beth. 'Take me upstairs.'

Beth shook her head.

'Then I am taking you.' And Tamara linked her fingers between Beth's.

She kept the curtains of her bedroom closed, padding through its darkness, the incense stale in the silence of an unused room, then she lit a candle and pulled Beth to the high bed that threw shadows careering up the walls.

Tamara kissed Beth, almost fully, bringing the flat strange arousal of different saliva, her cat mouth more open and willing than Beth had ever known it, her scents clamouring, and she felt the roller-coaster plunge of immersing herself there, in the tug of hormones. Beth was falling into calamity. She knew with all certainty that she mustn't do this. Tamara began to unhook her bra with one hand; it felt knowing, tricksy, copied from the men who had paid homage, and Beth stopped her. Her heart was suddenly thumping with fear or premonition as a vivid image of Fern came to her, without her knowing why: Fern the name, Fern the face. She jolted. The candle flickered, shadows rearing and hollowing.

'What? What are you doing?' said Tamara, amusement coating protest.

'I – I don't know,' said Beth, standing by the bed. 'Fern. Just a moment.'

She left the room. She walked swiftly towards her bag. It would be evening for Fern, possibly dinner time, and yet instinct told her to contact her. She checked her phone, her email; there was nothing. The instinct felt urgent.

She took a breath and switched on Skype. Fern was available. Beth raced to the loo, washed her hands, splashed water on her face, dazed, a woman who had stumbled from the bed of another woman, and was about to call her daughter, but Fern was ringing.

'God,' said Beth. She hooked her mess of hair behind her ears, swiped at the screen. 'My darling.'

The connection was broken. '*Mum*,' Fern kept saying. There were words, fragments of speech, a frozen screen. Fern talked. The words were garbled, but her tone seemed to veer between anger and apology.

'Fern, are you *drunk*?' Beth kept asking. Sobs were interspersed with laughter.

The image froze again.

'The cousins,' said Fern then, giggling, swaying. 'I have to tell you.'

'They got you drunk?'

Fern gave a childish grin.

'Tell me, tell me. Anything at all. No judgement, no trouble.'

There were words Beth couldn't hear, laughter sliding into what seemed to be tones of grief. '... and when you stopped liking me ...' Fern said through staggered images '... didn't care ...'

'You don't think this? My God, Fern, I care about you, love you, more than anyone in the world!'

'People you don't love ... the ones you ...'

'What? Fern? Speak slowly. Who?'

'... Dad ... your mum, who ... you didn't want to come to America, you ...'

'Fern. Baby. The line's freezing. Say again.'

'... annoying you, I know I do ... my old Mama, I never thought ... you look out of the window ... who is T? ... you don't kiss me goodnight ... you need to stop me. Mama. Mum ...'

'Stop *what*, Fern?'

'I ... I get scared ... you don't ask me questions any more ... lonely, Dad ... grizzly-bear Dad, how can you kill him? … *my* parent … is so lovely … love my dad … get divorced?'

Truncated sentences, pixilation, buffering. Fern spoke again, through repetition, static, slow motion, comments about a boy that Beth could almost grasp, and then were impossible to fathom. Then Fern said something else. Beth couldn't hear the words, but there was a familiar rhythm that nagged her.

'Are you now telling me a *poem*?'

Fern spoke again.

'I know this, don't I? What is that line? Fern. God, you've frozen again.'

'I love you,' said Fern into the static, and burst into piteous howls.

'I'm flying straight out there,' said Beth.

'Mum.'

'I am coming to you.'

* * *

'I need to go,' Beth said to Tamara. It was past two in the morning, and Tamara had dressed herself.

'No you most certainly don't,' said Tamara, standing in the bedroom doorway, her appearance again bewilderingly different, almost hidden in the dark, and she danced about Beth, her nails on her neck, her hair, a laughing kiss pressed on to her cheek. She gave Beth her abrupt smile.

'There is not a flight till three in the afternoon anyway,' said Beth, frowning at her phone.

'You're not going.'

'I need to get there.'

'Go running back to hubby then,' said Tamara in languorous tones.

'He doesn't want me.'

'I do, though.'

TWENTY-TWO

'*Till then my windows ache*. What *is* that?' said Beth. 'I think that's what Fern was saying. I know that phrase. What is it?'

Tamara smiled, shook her head. 'You need to come back to bed,' she said. 'It's late.'

Beth scrolled down her phone. 'I wish there was an earlier flight,' she said, and emailed Sol about times.

'There isn't. Forget it. Till tomorrow. Here you are, and here am I, and it is now, this is now,' she said, her voice descending to a wisp. 'No one to stop us.'

'What is that smell?'

'Incense. Musk. Me. Expensive wax.'

'And these lights …? That's a gas lamp? And you. You've changed as well. What is all this?'

'I dressed. How did I know how long you would be in there?'

'You have … What have you done?' Beth stroked Tamara's face, closed her eyelids, touched the glitter there. She glanced down, and in the shadows and the pools of light Tamara had created, she glimpsed her corsetry, small waist, must of vintage shops, of perfume; the buttons, hidden hooks and tightness diving to curves that fitted precisely.

'Undress me, then,' said Tamara. 'You left my bed for hours. This is my challenge for you. I made you an adventure.'

She moved towards the bed in snapshots between shadows, a geisha once more, her skin now white, lips red: a mirage of limbs, tiny straps, silk seams, the body in glimpses to be unwrapped.

Tamara raised her mouth with its stained lips. Beth pushed her with her fingertip on to her back and Tamara lay there, uncurled herself and pulled Beth to her by the hair, and Beth kissed her, drawing in all she had wanted, and it was there for the tasting, that darkness, the golden-brown scents of her, Tamara's body twisting over her. A woman was making love to her. Dr Tamara Bywater in her hospital office.

Tamara's hair was on Beth's shoulder, her mouth on her nipple; she was running one hand lightly over her pubic bone while the other tugged at her top. Beth held her breath, tightened her jaw, her body sliding fast, but she smelled again that almost mildewed undertow, the sickness of her, and then she was falling, she was lying in a mental ward; they would inject her soon, and then she would be lost.

'Please,' murmured Tamara, and Beth pulled her hand away and held her wrist above her head on the pillow, making Tamara widen her eyes, a fresh flush of excitement to her as Beth pinned her down, and she was wet, and she must hold back, she knew, but any moment she would be beneath her and in her, in that dark longed-for place, and as they were entwined, Beth's head leaped above them, watching that remarkable sight, two women, and she couldn't feel it in its entirety, disbelief tangling with something almost mundane. 'Fuck me, now,' Tamara muttered, cupping Beth's groin, and Beth was maddened with a longing to be inside her and fucked by her, and it would be slippery, tight, the caves in which they were lost, and there was no way out, Beth realised: no light before or behind, just the dark exquisite smell of triumph, and defeat.

'I love you,' said Tamara into Beth's neck, and her eyes were distant, a smile hovering over her lips, and she would be off in the morning, Beth understood with a jolt of understanding. If Tamara had her, she would then evade her. Beth's heart thumped, an insistent tattoo.

'We will. We will tomorrow,' she said, hearing herself playing Tamara at her own game. 'I'm tired now.'

Tamara made a small sound of protest, then her mouth moved into a skew-whiff seductive smile, and she skimmed the back of her nails over Beth's nipples, buttocks, crotch. Beth kissed her and turned. 'In the morning,' she said.

Tamara fell asleep rapidly, her breathing deep and unselfconscious, and Beth moved away from her into a pocket of wet heat, her open legs seeming to float, and she made herself come very quickly, and slept.

**

She was woken by the first strip of sun slicing through the curtains in the bedroom. She had fallen asleep near Tamara in a crumple of damp sheets, pillow, hair, sweat. She closed her eyes several times to become accustomed to sunrise illuminating the room with its band of dust. Tamara lay beside her; she didn't move; Beth blinked and looked around the room for the first time in the daylight, her gaze travelling in stillness. On an open drawer sat a tangle of underwear in vivid colours: small bras, strips of satin, lace in ivory, bright violet, peacock, with red and black silky straps, candles and jewellery on the surface above. All around were framed pictures: a couple of sketches, and many photographs. Beth lay still, breathing softly and willing Tamara not to wake as she studied them, peering through the various light till she could ascertain the subject of each image: photograph after photograph of Tamara Bywater.

There they all were: two photos of Tamara beside a younger and more handsome Angus; a snap of her captured head back mid-laughter with the children; a dozen or so of her alone at different ages, each one almost discomfitingly flattering. There were facial portraits, full-length shots, and two naked studies in discreet lighting. There was Tamara at a nightclub, Tamara at the opera, Tamara on grass, Tamara in shadows, every last trick of light-bleaching, shade-painting artistry on show. Even old Polaroids had been pinned to a board, charming in their washed-out colours. Beth tilted her head on the pillow to find a larger framed portrait above the bed: a silver-toned solarised profile reminiscent of a Man Ray that must have been professionally commissioned. The Bywater marital bedroom was a shrine.

She heard Sol's scorn in her mind, and tried to catch her breath in the prison of egotism in which she lay, the curled-up body with its spread of hair like a selfish little animal beside her.

Tamara stirred as Beth moved her head.

She woke, saw Beth there, registered her sleepily and gave her a smile. 'Good morning, darling,' she said, and ran her hand through Beth's hair. 'How are you?'

'Good morning.'

Tamara leaned over and kissed her. 'I'm busy today. I mustn't be late back to work. But first – first … I must seduce you into staying here …' She kissed Beth's neck then lay back.

'Yes,' said Beth. 'But it's early. Get some more sleep now.'

Beth waited for Tamara to doze again. She looked down at her hair, the dead-dyed nest of it; she gathered her clothes in one hand, and walked out of the room and left.

Twenty-Three

Number 4 Little Canal Street stood in silence in the morning, the water's surface a spread of duckweed that draped detritus and slowed the moorhens. The scent of another human was all over Beth; she ran a bath and took an inhalation of Tamara Bywater's perfume and poison, then paused, absorbing that moment when she was still covered in her, then lay under the water, and washed herself.

She looked in the mirror as she emerged, her lips parting, then shook away the reverie, bought a ticket on her credit card, and began to pack.

On my way, darling xxxxx, she texted Fern. *On my way x*, she texted Sol.

We're coming back! Fern texted almost at the same moment, followed by Sol's terser *Fern wants to return*.

* * *

Beth sent a prayer. She laid her head on the back of the sofa and thanked its fabric, and God, and her life. The world woke, its water-light swaying lilac. She raced round the house, clearing the fridge, tidying Fern's room, the morning warmth creeping in.

The phone rang. Angus Bywater. Beth hesitated, then answered.

'I am back,' he said.

'Hi,' said Beth.

'But Tamara is *extremely* distressed that you left the house. Could you talk to her? Can you return?'

'No,' said Beth, and she squeezed her nail into her thumb, filling the silence with the distraction of pain, as she tended to, to prevent herself from speaking.

There was a pause. 'I don't think you understand her fragility.'

'How much more drama is there going to be about her?'

'I don't understand what you mean,' said Angus.

Beth waited.

'Mara is not safe when she's like this,' he said, his tone of urgency that of an emissary who would be in trouble if he failed. 'She is very sensitive.'

'I know.'

'No one sees the danger. And she has to work tomorrow. If you could speak to her—'

'Sorry,' said Beth. 'But no. Really no. And I thought it was today she was working.'

There was another silence. Angus seemed to be digesting the response.

'If you could reassure her?'

'Sorry. I—'

'She was—' Angus coughed. 'I should tell you ... I'm afraid Mara had a breakdown many years ago. Briefly. It was serious. I do always fear a repeat of this.'

'I'm sorry about that. But she's a survivor. Best of luck to you. I mean it.'

Beth put the phone down, and she was shaking.

She glanced at the time. There were still several hours before Sol and Fern were due to land. The house was strangely silent, the canal light mobile. There was a missed call from Sofia Aarons. She left it.

She glanced at the clock repeatedly, willing a conciliatory or hostile Fern into her arms. There were hours, still; hours to go. Tamara was smiling at her, the curve of her breast visible, the mouth that could take her in, stroking, withdrawing, and Beth lingered there for seconds, then snapped the image shut.

She rose, and she had to do it, finally: there at home, where she had transported the picture, she painted. The last of the series, the one she couldn't finish, and the mud-hair was rising, no becalmed Ophelia, but a scream into the water, death, please death, and the body was now emerging, not ambiguous as it had been before, but an arched spine, and lungs filled with mud. Beth's forehead was wet, tears were spreading over her cheeks, and yet she painted on.

When she had run from Lizzie over a decade before on London Fields, Lizzie had pursued her with entreaties that turned to insults as Beth raced back home in order to grab her little daughter, who was being minded by their friend downstairs.

Beth tried to shake Lizzie off by crossing the urban nature reserve she visited with Fern, with its much-loved pond, its bulrushes and dragonflies, its tadpoles and ducks among the lily pads. The ground was frozen tussocks. The rain had begun to slant. She heard words behind her, the burblings of the unguarded, or even mentally ill. She heard, 'Pond shit water, you little slut, at least I married my men, whose is that baby, little bastard, had a bastard child, don't deserve her. It. Where is she now? Not with your child now?'

Beth ran. Lizzie now seemed to be shouting out a poem, the words repeated but garbled. It turned into more insults: ' ... pity for ... bitch' were the last words she heard, and then she hid in the first path she came to in the estate adjoining the reserve, crouching near some bin storage sheds with a needling of cold in her lungs, and she had shaken her off, her heart pound-ing, heard nothing more but the faintest sound like a movement of water, then she dismissed it as her own anxiety-laced imagination. It bothered her as she rushed down Beck Road in the rain, but still she ran on to Fern, clinging to luck and magic, not believing her mother would do that, trusting that things would be all right; that it was her own fearful mind only.

Yet she had heard. She knew, in her truthful moments – when drunk, or stumbling between sleep and awake, or in sudden lucidity – she knew that she had indeed heard. That sudden silence, then a folding of water like a sheet over a head, a human breaking the surface, hurting her dear limbs with the freeze, her lungs, her complicated mind. And Beth had let her mother do that.

She always remembered the moment, half a minute later, when she had run to the house, taken Fern from the neighbour, and the sound and the silence began to worry her again. The anxiety with its ballooning into fear. Hastily, she put Fern into the buggy and was about to run back there, no time to attach the rain hood, but Fern cried, and as Lizzie was lying down around the corner in the mud, Beth leaned over Fern, untwisting the buggy straps and trying to comfort her, but Fern cried more, red-faced, straining, and Beth buried her face in her daughter's, and soothed her as she bawled, and stayed there in a panic of indecision, telling herself her fear was in her imagination, then taking Fern into the house, her uncertainty increasingly tinged with fury, and she decided she wouldn't go to her mother, and her mother tried to drown herself.

* * *

There was an email from Sol that he must have written from the airport. He had arranged for Fern to spend the late afternoon with Laurie, and then return for dinner. *No*, wrote Beth in protest, but Sol's brief comments about their need to talk made her delete her answer.

She watched the hours as they passed.

A text arrived. *Aaa Sol. By bus stop.* She leaped up, and ran down to find him, her legs unsteady, the sun beating down on her as she entered the shade of the canal, widening her eyes in the dark after the glare. She saw Sol appear in the distance before he saw her. He was carrying a rucksack while lugging his equipment bag, his appearance distinctly more American, with his suntan and some sports jacket she would have to hide. The greyness of jetlag was visible beneath his tan as he approached.

She kissed him in a clumsy collision with his lips, and grabbed his hand. 'Oh God, I'm so glad you're back.'

'You are?' Sol stopped beside her, lowered his equipment bag. He didn't smile. 'Uh huh.'

'Of course I bloody am. I knew you'd say "uh huh".'

He was silent.

'Sorry. For saying about "uh huh",' said Beth. 'I'm gabbling. I'm *so* glad.' She exhaled as though she had been punched. 'Darling. Darlington.'

'Honey. Oh—' He opened his mouth, then stopped.

'You didn't mean to call me "honey", did you?'

He said nothing.

'You don't realise how happy I am to see you. And I'm, I'm so sorry. I—'

'What the hell were you doing?' he said with the abruptness of delivery that she had only seen aimed at his lazier assistants, at Laurie in his early teenage years.

'Oh God,' she said, crumpling. She shook her head. 'I was … I was … Where to begin …? I don't know what to say. I—'

He waited.

'We can talk forever,' she said. She had little control over her voice. 'I will. When you want.'

'You will,' he said.

'God, you're strict.'

'I don't want this. I don't want any of it. Beth, you can fuck off right now if you're going to fuck off,' he said into the light-flared shade, he who rarely swore.

Her eyes widened.

'No way do I want this,' he said. 'As for Fern—'

'I know, of course you don't.'

The dredger started grinding down the canal in the distance, clearing the duckweed. 'Oh God,' she said, nodding at it. 'Timing. Ignore it.'

'This isn't the marriage – partnership – that I want. You have been lying.'

She gazed at the ground. She shot a look of shame at him.

'You have been unfaithful,' he said.

'I've fucked up, I've totally fucked up. Sol. I *love* you. I know it can't be like it's been.'

'It cannot.'

'I love you so much. Sol, you don't know. I love you so much. I look at you, and you have the most beloved face in the world. I've been a dickhead. I am a cunt. I have to keep away.'

Sol merely waited.

'We need to talk about – I need to tell you what I've done. The mess. Shit.' She was trembling. 'Do you want to go home?'

'No,' he said. He lowered his cameras.

The coots were squabbling in a gaggle nearby. 'Shut up,' she snapped at them. Her voice shook. She couldn't stand still. 'I'm sorry,' she said. Tamara floated above her.

'This affair is what will kill us,' said Sol.

She looked into his eyes. She tried to speak. 'It wasn't exactly ... Kind of it was. Oh, Sol. Shit.' She dropped her head. Tears wormed from the corners of her eyes, warm in the heat. 'I'm so sorry. So sorry. Sorry is only the beginning of it.'

'There is not a lot I can say,' he said.

'I know. It's up to me to – to talk.'

'Do you know what you want?' said Sol in his monotone. 'Really?'

She lowered her eyes. She tested her own certainty, gazing at the water, the dredger forcing sloppy emerald waves before it. The old irritations of Sol came to her, the lack of lust, the pull of a wilder life, and she waited for what was scented and diseased to pool over her vision and drag her with it. She kicked the picture away.

'I am not certain you know,' he said.

'I do. I've always wanted to be with you. From the moment I met you.'

He nodded, solemnly. She saw a memory pass over his face. 'I fear this side of your nature.'

'So do I.'

He raised his eyebrows. 'You do?'

'Yes.' She lowered her head again.

'So why should I – we – trust you? Why in hell's name should anyone trust you? Least of all me.'

'I know. Why should you? But you can. You can.' She gulped. She couldn't keep her voice steady.

'What about what I might need?'

Beth paused. She felt the colour drain from her face. 'Yes. You're right. Sol.' Coots shouted in the sludge, echoed by mallards. 'I'm scared.'

'While I was there, I thought I might return to the States,' said Sol. 'East Coast. Laurie can come in the college vacations, even go to grad school there, and Fern, and I'd –' he looked despairing '– travel every fortnight, to be with her. Or she can travel now. She kept saying all summer she'd like to live in America some day.'

'Oh my God,' said Beth.

'I'm not threatening you. About Fern. She needs her mother. Perhaps she needed her mother this summer.'

Beth put her head in her hands, digging her nails into her scalp.

'She – she seems to think something wrong ... about me—'

'You have been distant. From us. I—'

'Don't say "I told you so." Thank you,' she said. She rubbed her cheeks impatiently to dry them. 'Sol. This is a nightmare.'

'I don't know whether you want to be with me. You don't tell me how you're really feeling. There are situations I just won't tolerate, Bet. And therefore—'

Beth shook her head.

'I want to return to the States,' he said. 'You know, I always wanted to return. I'd be there if it wasn't for everything here.'

'No – Sol!' Beth grabbed his arm. 'Please. Please no. I need you. I want you. So does Fern.'

'This discussion is for later. Jesus. Spell out the fucking facts, Beth. Who is he? Is it that slimy asshole?'

Beth jolted. 'Who? Listen, sorry,' she said. 'My voice's weird. I'm shaking. You really want to go to America?'

'Yes.'

'*No! Please.* Sol. No! Talk to me.'

'You fucked the Jackass?' said Sol above the noise of the dredger. 'How many times?'

'What? Oh, Jesus, you're not really still thinking it was—'

Beth turned to the canal. The dredger driver winked at her and she looked down.

'It's clear you have a boyfriend. Who? Then?'

'Is *that* why you've been making notes on your phone? Every time you think I'm seeing some boyfriend?'

Sol nodded, a wave of self-consciousness passing over his face.

'Why? For some *custody* battle? Good God. We don't need that. I don't have a boyfriend.'

'I said do not *lie*,' he said.

She felt herself colouring. She put her hands over her eyes. She pressed red pools of pressure into her vision.

'Sol, I'm not,' she said. She stretched her lips against a childish, involuntary smile.

'He—'

'She—'

'I have noted every damn time you're with this jerk, whoever he is, or talking about him to that unprofessional shrink of yours.'

Beth shook her head. She kept wanting to laugh. She was afraid of crying.

'It was that unprofessional shrink.' She swallowed her words.

'What?'

'It was her, not him. No boyfriend. I was in – it was, it was the therapist. I'm sorry.'

Sol looked bemused, still frowning, so Beth reached out and smoothed the line on his forehead.

'Look, can we sit down?' she said, and he paused then nodded, and on a towpath bench, cyclists and joggers and narrowboats almost invisible shimmers in the heat that gradually trailed shadows, she gave the details he asked for, her voice unsteady through all his silences and questions as she scrupulously strained to tell the truth.

The canal danced with gnats in the shade as they talked. The day seemed static, all time arrested, merely waiting.

* * *

'Fern will be home soon,' he said eventually, and they began to walk back.

They entered the house together.

'You need to see a therapist,' said Sol as he walked up the stairs, and threw his rucksack hard at the sofa.

She gave a small laugh. 'Remember, it was your suggestion in the first place.'

He refused to smile. 'A proper therapist. A regular one. Who obeys boundaries, does not criminally abuse power,' he said in an angry monotone.

'I promise. We will find someone dependable.'

He paused. He nodded. 'To repair some of the damage of the first one.' He stood still. 'We need to get this fucking psychologist struck off,' he said.

She hesitated. 'I can't do that,' she said.

'Except you can. You should. I need to take a shower. Your girlfriend does not deserve to make a salary from exploitation.'

She caught his eye. 'You ...' she said. 'I hardly know how to say it. You care a bit less because it's a woman, don't you?'

He frowned. The tiniest hint of a smile moved his mouth; he turned to the window.

'You do! You do! It's a relief it's not the Jackass or any other man.'

Again, he said nothing. He felt his beard.

'You're so Soli-ish,' she murmured.

'I'm not sure that's a good thing. In your book.'

'It is. You can't help being pleased, can you? Can't take it as seriously. You old sexist.'

'*Pleased?* That my wife has been having some – Sapphic liaison with some corrupt supposed professional who should be debarred? Hey, yes, Bet, thrilled. That you have been stupid and unfaithful enough to—'

'Yes, but you'd still prefer it was a chick, not a – dick, wouldn't you? It's less of a challenge?'

Sol hesitated.

'Ha!' said Beth. 'Caught that tiny wrinkle of a smile. Yeah, I kind of get that, even though you're a sexist—'

'You think I am going to be amused by this? Only you, at this time, would say—'

'Please sit down with me,' said Beth.

'Fern should be back in ten minutes,' he said, taking off his shoes.

'My heart just leaped at that. I don't know whether she will talk to me.'

'I don't know either.'

Beth looked out. The trees bent over the canal were dragging light, and the water was oiling. Sol went to take a shower.

'Where is she?' she called to him after twenty minutes, but the extractor fan was still on. 'Sol. Don't hide from me.'

She rang Fern's mobile.

'She'll be here,' he said. He shook his hair, towelled his chest. 'She'll be shooting the breeze with that flake brother.'

She called Laurie, but went straight to his voicemail.

'Please,' said Beth, biting her lip. She turned to Sol, then dropped her gaze. 'Please don't take any action against her. I mean Tam— Dr Bywater.'

He shot a look of amazement at her.

'I got burnt. But it was me too,' she said. 'It was transference. That is no excuse. But—'

'It is immorally mishandled transference. It is abuse of power. It is illegal behaviour,' he spat out.

'I'm not going to not take responsibility. I wanted it.'

'I know. That's the problem. Thank you for being honest. But fuck you, Bet. Fuck you.'

She jolted. Fresh tears gathered in her eyes. 'I don't even know if I'm crying for myself, for all this shit – or as – as a last resort to get you to soften.'

'I like the new honesty,' he said with an ironic smile, feeling his beard.

'Stop feeling your beard. It annoys me.'

He laughed. 'I fucking love you, Bet. And I am stunned by you. I don't trust you. Now.'

'Of course. I don't trust me. Except I do. I know I will have to work to get your trust back.'

He came to the window and gazed at the canal, half-turning from her. Beth's heart hammered into his silence. She summoned Tamara Bywater. Her legs weakened. Sol was behind her. Cat and dog.

'I – I—' said Beth, her heart racing. 'I'm sorry.'

'You need to put in a complaint,' he said, picking up his phone.

She paused. 'God. Can we talk about this later? Where's Fern? Look … it'll be dark soon.'

He called Laurie and spoke briefly to him.

'When did she leave him?' said Beth.

'An hour and twenty ago.'

'Jesus! Sol.'

'She knows the route backwards. It was light.'

Beth looked out at the darkening towpath, mallards arrowing the water, then ran to the front of the house, opened a window and stared down at the street. She checked the clock again.

'She's really very late,' she said. She tried Fern's mobile again, and a friend's. She sent another text. The darkness seemed momentarily, blessedly, suspended, but she glanced at her own phone and saw that only two minutes had passed.

'Tell me *every*thing she said about coming back.'

'Just what I've told you.'

'And you saw Laurie. Them together?'

'Sure.'

'It's dark.'

'Right,' said Sol, and she could hear a hesitation that reminded her of the time Fern had been so late in the autumn.

The water rippled; the houseboat's candles were now lit, their shades of red crystal the weakest embers, barely penetrating the gloom that gathered and darkened almost as she watched. She had gazed at those tiny candle shades so often, and they had meant nothing; but now, surely, they were objective confirmation of darkness.

Ring me? Sofia had texted. *ASAP?* she had added later.

'You're beginning to worry now, right?' said Beth. She pressed the inside of her fingernails, removing fragments of soap that she stared at under the lamp-light. Traces of Tamara Bywater?

She felt a tensing of her throat as she looked out at the sky with its inks. She left a further message. It was possible Fern was running away from her.

The scent of Tamara came back to her and bolted straight down her body, striking her knees. And then guilt about Lizzie hit her more brutally.

She swallowed. 'Where is she?' she said.

'Don't stress yet,' said Sol, ever calm, but she could hear his anxiety beneath.

Her phone rang. She jumped. 'Oh. Sofia,' she said. She bit her lip.

'Take it,' said Sol, and walked into the kitchen.

Beth hesitated. 'Hello?' she said unsteadily.

'I'm sorry,' said Sofia. 'But I think you may be able to help.'

'Oh.'

'Dr Tamara Bywater,' she said, and there was a pause.

'Yes,' said Beth. She caught her breath. They had never said her name to each other.

'There are various concerns about her. They're just looking for the – well, excuse. The concrete reason, really … '

'For what?' said Beth, dumbly. She stared at the towpath, the dark shapes of its reinforcements and creeper like human, or monstrous, forms.

'To – they need to get her – well, stop her, terminate her contract. I'm sorry. I hope you don't mind me calling you. I knew that she was your psychol—'

'Just a minute,' said Beth. 'I mean, sorry, but I need to call you back.'

She tried Fern's number several more times. She walked through the house, pledging ideal behaviour and payments to charity as she pressed herself against walls before returning to the windows. She stared at the dark. Aranxto walked along the other bank, distinguishable by his height and gait, his clothes smudging against the walls so he was a slow blur of black on charcoal.

She stood there and gazed for some time at him. He came back to her as a boy. That funny, scrawny outcast so few had understood, who had been her friend from the age of four. Aranxto at tea at home, flattering her mother, who had found him appealing when most parents did not. Other images came to Beth. Always, Sefton Park. Was Tamara Bywater right? Had Lizzie Penn been there to watch over her? Beth had never known what her father might have said to her mother, what actions he might have threatened. Had Tamara given her that gift? Tamara Bywater. The one who had rescued her, bestowed upon her insights that turned her world around.

Sefton Park. *Till then my windows ache.* Beth's jaw slackened. Was that what her mother had said to her, calling out, in the nature reserve? She knew the shape of those words, knew them so well. There were lines she was constantly trying to remember from when her mother had followed her, shouting at her, through the nature reserve. But had she invented them? It was so hard, with Lizzie Penn, to know what was true and what had been distorted through too much thinking afterwards. Fern. Fern had quite possibly said those words when she had called her. Beth googled the line. *So I wait for you like a lonely house till you will see me again and live in me. Till then my windows ache.*

Beth crouched on a chair and put her head between her legs.

Fern as a baby in a buggy. Peach with eyelashes. A possession to pluck.

Beth stood up again. Aranxto was still there, smoking on the towpath: Aranxto the celebrated exhibitionist who lapped up his wealth but could never sit comfortably in its presence. Aranxto in his kitchen providing fry-ups to local down-and-outs, to male prostitutes, to adoring old ladies until he tired of them. Old ladies. That inexplicable text to Fern, and then more. How many texts? He turned on Beth when she attempted to resist his casual superiority and escape his influence. The quasi-brother who wanted her under his thumb. He had punished her in barely distinguishable ways for years.

'Aranxto,' she called loudly through the window, the evening chilling. He stopped, his body language uneasy even in the dark.

Half-memories floated like sketches, usually discarded; so rarely consolidating into paint layers that nudged those first thoughts into different directions. Pochades, notes, daydreams, nightmares.

'You don't speak to your own *mother*,' Fern had said. '... She might be lonely ... What if Grandad's a neglecter as well?'

'A neglecter?' Beth had said, but Fern was veering into another diatribe of non sequiturs and blame whose logic was hard to follow.

'So why don't we ever see her?' said Fern.

TWENTY-FOUR

'You shit-stirring, cunting bastard,' said Beth when Aranxto arrived at the house.

He moved his head as though he had been slapped.

'I know what you've done.'

'Uh?' he said.

'Fern's very late. I suspect you know exactly where she is likely to be.'

'You – why would I know?'

'Exactly. Your sheepish face. Your sheepish face actually looks like a *sheep*. You think I ever trust that? Ever ever.' She shook him. She lifted her hand, paused in the air, lowered it. '*Show me*,' she said, and she strode beside him, speaking to him only to urge haste.

'How do you know?' said Aranxto eventually in the falsetto that emerged when he was nervous or about to lie. He coughed.

'I have worked it out. Good God. How could you *do* that to me? This has given me almost a year of terrible anxiety about Fern. God knows what it's given her. Because that woman is not well. She is not good for anyone. She—'

'Someone needed to give the poor old lady a home,' he said, tailing off as they walked under the bridge and along decrepit cut-throughs in the direction of Fern's school. They walked past old railway structures, sidings, bridges tangled in bindweed.

'Oh Jesus. I'm right. It is that same housing co-op, right? Jack's ex? Where the manager arse-licks you. You abuse your power, Aranxto.'

'What power is that?'

'You abuse your fame. Your wealth. You know that. This ridiculous celebrity. Just because you're a snivelling little Scouser poof underneath all this who hates himself.'

'I could have you up in front of the LGBT police for that one.' He strode ahead, his breath uneven.

'I don't give a flying fuck. Why would you do this? Bring an ill and unstable pensioner down from Liverpool? Severely impacting on all our lives. The rows this has caused me and Sol. The suspicion towards Fern. Where is this godforsaken place?' Beth was shivering. 'You really think this is a safe journey for a child in the dark?'

'I felt sorry for Mrs—'

'Mrs who? I bet you don't even know her later married name, do you? Mrs who?'

Aranxto walked silently through the bridge shadows.

'You total steaming turd. *Here?*'

He stopped on Lyndhurst Place in front of a block of flats of fading red brick, satellite dishes, sooty marigolds, folded into a knot of St Pancras.

'*All* the times my daughter must have walked alone, in the dark, along here. Aged thirteen. Twelve in fact? Jesus. Being influenced. Probably filled with terrible guilt and a sense of duty, knowing Lizzie Penn. While I waited at home.'

'She wanted to see her granddaughter …' Aranxto's voice weakened.

'Just fuck off.'

Aranxto paused. 'Sorry,' he muttered.

'You wanted to play games. You wanted to play God. You wanted to fuck me over. I will never forgive you. You know that, right?'

Aranxto flicked her a glance, nodded. She walked round the corner and waited. He rang the doorbell.

* * *

That night, Beth lay on a mattress on Fern's floor to be near her, to divest Sol of the decision about where to sleep, stroking Fern's forehead for so long that she could not imagine ever absorbing enough of her scalp scent. They talked into darkness threaded with luminous ceiling stars, while Beth murmured questions, drawing out threads of conversation in only the softest tones, seemingly inconsequential. She pieced together a picture from

Fern like the most holey puzzle: shards of facts, sentences drowned in tears and slurred into the pillow, sudden clarity, questions that she could not answer, confusions about Instagram direct messages, neighbouring flats, but largely a gabbled tale of a grandmother who had made contact with her granddaughter the summer before, via a young male neighbour on Instagram. 'I love her,' said Fern as dawn approached.

'Do you?' said Beth blankly.

'I'm – Mum – I'm frightened of her.'

The Narnia street lamp near Fern's bedroom beamed lines through her blind on to the wall. The sounds of the canal were absent, the night buses a background rumbling. The descriptions of all that Beth's mother had said and done ballooned through the night, and there were details that Beth knew were likely to tap and twist at her for the rest of her life: the smell of eucalyptus, the objects on Lizzie's shelves, Fern's conviction, finally elaborated upon at dawn, that Beth herself no longer loved her own daughter.

The picture that Fern had painted of her grandmother's home in a series of hesitations and blurts was ultimately so detailed that Beth felt she almost inhabited it. Number 11 Lyndhurst Place was a small flat: 'modest', Fern said Lizzie called it. It contained dusty ballet books, piles of old theatre programmes, poetry, ancient copies of *Vogue*. What Lizzie referred to as 'curiosities' were kept in a row on her bookshelves: miniature binoculars, a tiny shoe, a lump of fool's gold with a label, hair in a locket, ornaments from a different time that she tried to give Fern. There were cakes and old-fashioned fruit drinks for her on her return from school, and displays of love that had made Fern want to cry. Her voice, said Fern, had been muffled like chocolate mousse or like fluff that came out of the dryer. She said strange things that didn't always make sense. Lizzie had veiny hands with aubergine-coloured nails, a cat called Madam Purrington, pale eyes. Her limp made her knock into furniture.

And then Fern had asked her not to burn the scented oils that left their smell on her clothes, and Lizzie Penn's displeasure was manifest, causing a panic of guilt in Fern, a sensation she increasingly experienced despite her grandmother's kindness.

'Call me Grandma Elizabeth,' Lizzie had instructed from the beginning. 'Ferny', she always called Fern, 'my little Ferny'. She sent her cards, phone messages, bought her presents.

She had blushed and smiled and changed her voice every time Aranxto visited. She told many stories: about Beth when she was little, her sweetness, her cleverness, her drawings. But these anecdotes began to be replaced by stories about a misunderstanding in which that same daughter had rejected her own mother with incomprehensible cruelty. How Lizzie had seen Fern as a baby. 'You were a little apricot,' she said. 'An apricot with big blinking eyes. I thought of that every day of my life.'

The secrecy that Lizzie had imposed on Fern had started with the fact of her own proximity, and had grown, grown in so many small stages, from hints and denials to tearful tales, until Fern barely remembered what she had known from where, who might be betrayed, or how to hide her growing anger towards her own mother. Lizzie could barely talk about that painful past without swallowing and turning away.

Fern's voice in the dawn was in tangles, duvet over words. How could Beth ever prise open a teenage mind? In fragments, in piecing together, sudden clarity, obfuscation, as they murmured to each other through hours. *You, Mum, you didn't want me any more ... I want you, it is all I've ever wanted, you are all I can think of ... You did not. You had texts ... I know. I know. I'm sorry ... You didn't want to come to America ... I know. I have done wrong ... What was it? What did I do to you? ... Nothing. Nothing, Fern. It's my fault ... You neglected me ... Oh God. I thought you didn't want me around, couldn't bear me near ... I didn't. Because you were cruel. To my grandmother. I thought. Then to my dad, to me. I hated you. You hated me ... I loved you. More than anything on this earth. You are who I love ... I think Grandma tells lies, misses things out, told stories about you that weren't the same as each other ... I'm so sorry she did any of this, so angry with her ... I'm sorry, Mum ... No, Fern, it's me ... And me.... You smelled of perfume, you didn't kiss me any more ... I thought you didn't want me to. You dreamed out of the window ... I'm sorry ... You never wanted to be in America with us ... I'm sorry. Will you ever forgive me? ... I don't know ... I will wait ... You know I will ... I hope ... You didn't want me, and Grandma did, but then ... I wanted you every day, hour, minute ... Jemma covered for me. Grandma wanted to see me coming back from school ... I know ... She sent me cards. She got a flat where she could see you coming back from school ... Oh G— ... Mum. Mum? Say something? She didn't see me, though. Mum? ...Yes... Wasn't Grandad angry with her? Complicated? Mum? Mum? ... Oh Fern....She had this love poem about windows, looked for you out of the window. Mum? Say something ... God, Fern....Then she had me instead. But she wants to see me all the time. All the time. I'm so guilty. Talk, Mum ... I know, Fern. She does that ... Mum? ... I'm going to sort this ... I don't want her to be sad! But I'm almost scared now ... I know. Don't worry. You are not going to see her ... How? ... I'm sorting this ... I'm sorry, Mum ... I'm sorry. There is absolutely nothing for you to be sorry about. Nothing. Ever. I love you. I love you. I love you.*

* * *

And later in the morning, light-headed with insomnia, Beth looked out at the canal where the weed glared in summer gloom, and she was only grateful. She had her daughter. That was all. That was all.

359

'You haven't slept, have you?' said Sol.

Beth shook her head.

'All night?'

Beth gave a small smile, and shook her head again.

She tried to speak. She cleared her throat. Clouds were pressing against the window, and she shivered. 'Go back, go back to the States with Fern and I'll follow,' she said. 'In a couple of days.'

'Really?'

She nodded slowly. 'And after that ... stay. It's your turn,' she said, trying not to cry. 'To live where you want. And given Fern's always begging to live in America—'

'And you?'

'I'll move there too. But ...'

'Say it.'

'I don't know how to. I—'

She drew in her breath. She swallowed. He waited.

'Bet. We're not going to be together, right? You don't think we're going to be together, right?'

She sank her head in her hands. 'I thought about it all night. As I talked to Fern. About everything else. This. Sorry. I'm not making sense.'

She was crying. The coots called, muffled. The post was coming through the door. All the sounds of the House of Cardigans.

She closed her eyes. She spoke a line she had rehearsed, but she couldn't finish it. 'I have to be truthful to this good man I married. I – I—'

'Please do.'

'I don't know if I can be with you. In a true way. Oh, fuck.'

'I know you don't, Bet.'

'Or anyone. I would probably mess up any relationship. I just need to be with my daughter. Show her so much love. Be there forever for her. Both of us do. Our children are all that matter.'

'I know.'

'I know you know. And part of that is keeping her from Lizzie Penn. Keeping *me* from her. Let's go and live in the States. Apart. I mean – I mean—' She stumbled. 'But not much. Together and apart. And maybe after time—'

She covered her eyes, tears running down her hands, afraid to look in case he was crying too.

'It's your turn to have what you want. All that commuting you've done.' She shook her head, stood up, approached him to hug him, but knew it was wrong. 'And – and – then you can see your mum and so can Fern, and you all deserve that. I don't care where I am as long as I have my girl.'

'Beth. Bet. Jeez.'

'I know.' Beth drew in her breath. 'I love the House of Cardigans. I love London. You ... You know I love you. Don't make me cry more. However we do it, we're a family. You and Fern. Laurie ... Lizzie Penn is not my family. Never was.'

'What about the shrink? Psychologist – supposed. Quack.'

'They are trying to strike her off. I'm not sure I can contribute to that.'

He snorted.

'I need to sort things out with my mother,' said Beth.

He nodded. 'Uh huh. You do.'

'I need to try to sort myself out.'

'Uh huh. You do—'

'I'll let you say *uh huh* now.'

* * *

Beth made her way to Lyndhurst Place, through the canal shadows where the moorhens dipped and the morning joggers stormed past. A Sainsbury's bag, slimed green, was caught in a willow. She was hollow with lack of sleep.

There was Number 11. She stood at an angle from the house, behind some railings, and steadied her breathing, all the words she had rehearsed for minutes and for decades fusing in her mind, and there, there in that cloud-dulled shade beneath the railway bridges, there was a face in a window. Her mother was looking out. She was contained there, glazed, those old milky eyes trained at the distance, at the past, her chest visibly rising in time to her breathing. The full mouth was wrinkled, the stroke-damaged features less skewed, but strange still, the familiar distorted into the unnerving. She was framed. Beth stood there. She waited. She bent her head, reaching for more air. The years she had spent running after this woman. Once, all she had wanted to do was batter down the door of the house that contained the face in a window. Now, all she wanted to do was leave. There were no words. There were no more words between them.

So I wait for you like a lonely house till you will see me again and live in me. Till then my windows ache.

* * *

She walked away, breathing the damp summer air as steadily as she could. She reached in her bag and took out a tissue. 'That's not yours, right?' Fern had said to her in her bedroom the evening before. 'You wouldn't buy that pattern.'

Beth shook her head. 'Clever girl. It belonged to someone I knew,' she said, but she put it into her bag instead of throwing it away.

'It is your relationship with yourself that matters,' Dr Bywater had once said. 'You have to be at peace with yourself, to love others.'

Beth watched the canal's flow as she tried to calm her heartbeat, and more words came back, in the swooping soft tones, over different weeks, different times, days, nights. 'You don't need others to make you whole. Not your husband, partners, mother. You need only yourself to make you whole. Your special self. Your beautiful self.'

'No one's ever called me that.'

'Your mother didn't call you that. Others will have. You won't have been able to hear it.'

Beth held the tissue. Tamara's. Tamara. And now, ahead of her, Tamara Bywater seemed to be there, gliding along the towpath, into the shadows of the bridge. Was the woman Tamara? Was she in her mind only? Or was she really there, her back to her, winding along the section of the canal where the water rippled lazily around clumps of weed; those miniature islands on which Beth had so often imagined their bodies entwined. Was that swing of hair hers? That dark sweet scent? Was it?

Beth stopped walking.

She pressed the tissue to her nose, breathing it in, and examined its peacock swirls. She hesitated, twisted it and threw it towards the canal. It seemed to float in the air, suspended by the mist before it fell, spreading as the rusty water bled into it, then folded in on itself and sank.

She walked on. She was on her own. Only herself.

ACKNOWLEDGEMENTS

Many thanks to Lucy Ash, Smita Bhide, Luigi Bonomi, Maxine Mei-Fung Chung, Philippa Cotton, Eleanor Crow, Shpresa Dogani, all at Faber Academy, Sarah-Jane Forder, Melanie Garrett, Peter Grimsdale, Helen Healy, Alison Hennessy, Caroline Kelly, Allegra Le Fanu, Teresa Lobo, Charlotte Mendelson, Clemmie Mendelson, Theodore Mendelson, Jeremy P Morgan, Tamara Pollock, Selim Raka, Kate Saunders, Louisa Saunders, Helen Simpson, Richard Skinner, Gillian Stern, Becky Swift, Sandra Turnbull, Anya Whitmarsh, Sacha Whitmarsh, and Lauren Whybrow. Most of all, thank you to Alexandra Pringle, Jonny Geller, and all at Bloomsbury and Curtis Brown.

A NOTE ON THE AUTHOR

Joanna Briscoe is the author of five previous novels, including the bestselling *Sleep With Me*, which was adapted for ITV by Andrew Davies. She has been a columnist for the *Independent* and the *Guardian*, is a literary critic for the *Guardian*, and broadcasts regularly on Radio 4. Joanna lives in London.

joannabriscoe.com
@JoannaBriscoe

A NOTE ON THE TYPE

The text of this book is set in Linotype Sabon, a typeface named after the type founder, Jacques Sabon. It was designed by Jan Tschichold and jointly developed by Linotype, Monotype and Stempel in response to a need for a typeface to be available in identical form for mechanical hot metal composition and hand composition using foundry type.

Tschichold based his design for Sabon roman on a font engraved by Garamond, and Sabon italic on a font by Granjon. It was first used in 1966 and has proved an enduring modern classic.

Seduction
08/17/2020